FOUR CORNERS OR A BOOK THAT WILL TICKLE YOUR INTELLECTUAL NIPPLE

CARY SMITH

Preserved by Greg Hawkins L.P.
(Or Just A Guy Who Has An Obession With Having A Title At The End Of His Name)

ISBN: 0991539451

ISBN 13: 9780991539451

WHAT THE CRITICS ARE SAYING ABOUT TICKLE YOUR INTELLECTUAL NIPPLE

"This Is The Best Review of *Four Corners or A Book That Will Tickle Your Intellectual Nipple* Ever, Because I Wrote It, Period Anyone Who Says Otherwise, It Will Result In A Critical Review, By Yours Truly, About Those Otherwise Sayings That Were Otherwise (unwisely) Said. And Clearly You Know Now That This Is The Best Review And That If You Say Otherwise, Be Prepared To Get The Tissues Out, Your Insecure Blankets Out, Because I'm Gonna Make You Cry Like A Baby With My Review Of Your Saying Otherwise…"

"This is like *The Catcher in the Rye* meets *Huck Finn*, like those two meeting and combining with the greatest of historical novels. It's like why do I have to compare everything to something from the past? It's like I'm trying right now to not compare it to something else, some other art, but I just can't help myself, in fact, I find I can't really write anything unless I give a shout-out, a reference to some other work. In fact, in going over all of this shout-out business in my reviews, I now realize that I don't really like this book very much."

"I have no idea what's going on, and I'm supposed to be the Literary Preservationist of this work. I should have stuck with my Domestic Engineering job."

—Greg Hawkins L.P. (Or Just A Guy Who Has An Obsession
With Having A Title At The End Of His Name)

To my mom, who may never read this, but if it gets famous enough, at least she'll hear about it.

—Cary Smith

INTRODUCTION

For what we read here is a work from one Cary Smith, for I shall narrate this about the author: for it was ye, Cary Smith, who had written over a thousand works of text, and for I say this is fortunately the final of five works which have been preserved and kept intact by the intolerable Greg Hawkins, who titles himself as a Literary Preservationist, and who also claims to be a housecleaner on the weekends, or as he calls it and titles himself, "Domestic Engineer," and I will not respect him with either title and put an "L.P." or "Domestic Engineer" after his name, for he is shit, and I shit on his business card with those two titles on them, for I also reiterate and say, "Thank god only five." For I decree that this atrocious author, in his supposed final work, wrote the story *Four Corners or A Book That Will Tickle Your Intellectual Nipple* with history in it simply to annoy a man like me, Brad Cruise, and to annoy my follow colleagues. For I say I know he did this in a facile manner, that trivial beast that is ye Cary Smith, as I quote the author now in an interview having said this, "I threw the history in there to make Brad Cruise say, "Wheeee" (and to make all the very, very and unfortunately serious young people say, "Wheeee")." For this quote says it all, as ye Cary Smith was only looking for someone dumb enough to actually preserve his other works by writing this so-called literature, and he was able to do just that with his facile incorporation of history, and ye facile Greg Hawkins.

For I elaborate more on the author at hand, for I say his other works are intolerably mentioned here, for one book in his collection (and I cannot stress enough thanks to the heavenly gods that only five of his one thousand works have been found and preserved) he writes about being a baby and how he wished he didn't have to eat soft, squishy baby food out of small glass containers, "Especially those glass containers with a baby's picture on it," I quote

Cary Smith, and, rather, how he would have preferred that his mom chew the meat for him and then proceed to feed it to him like a bird. The title of this work was condemningly entitled *Cary Smith, Dreaming of a Bird-Feeding Childhood/On Post, Post, Postmodern Philosophy.* For I say he wrote a whole two hundred pages on the topic, and one can imagine the horror of reading it. For I mention one other work on the man, for he wrote a whole three hundred–page book on which playground structures were his favorite to play on, and, most importantly, his favorite to body build on as a child bodybuilder. For in that book, Cary Smith talks about becoming a child bodybuilder of the playgrounds, as he did countless pull-ups on the play bars and, as a result, became a world renowned child bodybuilder. The first, Cary Smith claims, to body build exclusively on children's playgrounds, which was also the title of this godforsaken, alleged nonfiction work: *The Memoir of the First Child Bodybuilder to Train Exclusively on Children's Playgrounds, Cary Smith Is That Child Everyone/On Post, Post, Post, Postmodern Philosophy.*

For I mention one last thing about this dreadful author and the man who preserved his works, one Greg Hawkins, who I simply detest more than the author himself, for if it were up to me, I would preserve none of the works of Cary Smith, for he is crap and not worthy of the literary world. For if I were to encounter Cary Smith in public, I'd throw down my gage, and then I'd pluck and shake his beard, as I've already plucked the beard of ye Greg Hawkins at a cocktail party, and when I spilled wine on his shirt, I told him his shirt was not worthy of such fine wine.

—Brad Cruise on Cary Smith and Greg Hawkins L.P. (Or Just A Guy Who Has An Obsession With Having A Title At The End Of His Name) *Taken from Brad Cruise's blog, which holds the world record for most viral attempts on a blog and for using the word "for" the greatest number of times in a blog.*

Brad Cruise is a literature scholar with an emphasis in Elizabethan literature and its culture of beard plucking as an insult, and who some say can only utilize the word "for" from his scholarly endeavors in his modern language, which makes for a very awkward man. He is known as the "Golden Retriever"of Elizabethan literature scholarship. Brad Cruise also claims to be a "bardolater" on his blog, and I (I being the one who's writing these references about Brad Cruise in fancy computer font that is probably hurting your eyes right now) still don't know what that word, "bardolater," means, but maybe one day it'll be my e-mail word of the day.

Brad Cruise is also very, very, very concerned with what university institution you went to. (He is a firm believer that school libraries do not all have the same books.)

Also, Also, Brad Cruise is still bitter about the failed literature and pop-culture magazine that he and three of his friends started many years ago out of college, which they had hoped would become a modern sensation, but of course, they told everyone they didn't want this. Their initial problem seemed to be that all four believed they had a sense of humor simply because they all drank beer and had come up with the idea for the failed magazine at a bar. And the biggest problem with the four was that each had been called a genius by three pompous buffoons (those three being the other three in their group). But Brad Cruise has gotten over that failed attempt to find a wide audience, as he is now editor of the literary magazine at the university he teaches at. And so now all of his friends can publish their work and get publication credits (and so their students are impressed, although many seem to be bored out of their minds, asking themselves why they're even there), as these university publications help publish each other, especially Brad Cruise's university literary quarterly, which especially encourages everyone to write the same, to write about the same subject matter (mainly writing what only truly very, very smart people would write about) and to please, they encourage, not write an entertaining story, because they are firm believers that intellectual cannot mix with entertainment. And then for some odd reason they wonder why no one reads their university literary publications except for the university people and a few random boring, pompous people who only buy the publication because they feel it necessary to buy such things because they are rich, and buying such things justifies why they are rich, or people just looking to get published in the magazine and feel they should buy at least one copy, and then they end up not reading a single word themselves. (And then they all blame television for people not reading anymore and say most people are just stupid.) The total number of those who read Brad Cruise's publication ends up being about fifty people (which especially includes the friends and colleagues of Brad Cruise). Some people get the notion in their head from reading these horrible, lifeless publications that the literary world is not dying, it only seems to be killing itself.

*Also, Also, Also, Brad Cruise has stated numerous times that one is always conscious that he (Brad Cruise) is surely a modern-day, intellectual atheist because he never capitalizes god in his works. His works being mainly his blog and his essays for his university publication, which he is editor of. Essays that doctors and various psychologists prescribe as a sleep aid when patients struggle with the side effects of various sleeping pills and can no longer use them for fear of becoming addicted to them and developing complete insomnia.

"This quote page is as good as Cary Smith is going to get, and still it is not that good."

—Brad Cruise

"That's right, I'm quoting myself in the quote part of my own work."

—Cary Smith

"I promise there will be vampires, zombies, and robots in this book. They will just be very, very good at disguising themselves."

—Cary Smith

"You know you've become a bureaucrat when you have finally memorized how to spell bureaucrat."

—Cary Smith

"Weird, according to an idiot, is a very good weird."

—Cary Smith

"Everyone cannot teach (especially people just out of college, unless they're teaching preschool or elementary school), and teachers should be respected and paid respectfully through that ideal, "Everyone cannot teach" (although there are a lot of bad teachers out there, so how that would be sorted out is a matter beyond my quoting abilities and really ruins this entire quote. Maybe rich people should just donate money to their favorite teachers)."

—Cary Smith

"She shuns him, him shuns her, I shun she, but in the end we all shun for Ice Cream and read the I Ching."

—Cary Smith

"There's no reason to get down. The poisoned mind only knows and wants to kill when the good man/woman has already done, said, written, or shown the world what great and extraordinary things every human mind and heart is capable of."

—Cary Smith

"With every fart comes a great risk."

—Cary Smith

"Actions cannot speak louder than words as someone must write that action down for it to be remembered through time (hey, come on, give me a break... I'm kind of a writer)."

—Cary Smith

"Any human who says that you don't live in the real world or that it's time for you to get back to the real world is only talking about getting back to the way things are for them. Getting back into the world in which they live in, living in their real world. And they also watch that show on MTV way too much."

—Cary Smith

"I am smarter than you because I know I am not, but I know you think I am."

—Cary Smith, while pretending he was Socrates for a month

"Most parents and older people can't let kids be kids because most believe they can make them into everything they were not."

—Cary Smith

"Behind the layers of every cynic there is a happy, optimistic, tail-wagging, cute little doggy."

—Cary Smith

"Never trust a man or woman who says he/she only likes things that he/she can relate to."

—Cary Smith

"It is really exhausting to be a modern writer and have to write he/she or s/he all the time. My only mistake in writing this is that I should have just pretended to be sexist."

—Cary Smith

"Only the insane can figure out and cure the insane."

—Cary Smith

"All writers should never use words they themselves can't stand or have trouble pronouncing."

—Cary Smith

"We live in a time when people come from all over the world to see...an office building."

—Cary Smith

"They say nice guys finish last. Well, good, because we don't like tearing down pretty ribbons with our chests anyways. (Mainly because our chests can't break those ribbons, and yeah, I just called myself a nice guy—so what?)"

—Cary Smith

* A Literary Preservationists note on the quotes: All quotes were taken from Cary Smith's Facebook and Twitter page. *

—Greg Hawkins L.P. (Or Just A Guy Who Has An Obsession With Having A Title At The End Of His Name)

PREFACE

To the people touching me right now (it feels awkward, but I'll let it slide),

I would like to preface myself with a preface letter before you begin to read me. I wonder if I could just be read and help somebody through a troubled time or a way of being somewhere else for a while instead of helping create more troubled times and becoming a destruction of life?

Take what you want from me, and hopefully you won't want to kill a musician with me by your side. (Now that might be insane and just a little hypocritically dumb.)

I would like to ask a request of my readers. The request is to not give or take a test based upon me, and to definitely not give out a letter because of me (of course 90% of the people I'm defending by saying that will most likely never read this or any of my other book-community friends, or if they do, they probably won't give an effort to understand it, but, hey, what the heck, at least I know it annoys the great scholar Brad Cruise that I said it, and who added on to me without my permission, by the way—(see intro), so that's a plus). I am only a book, and I cannot handle that burden.^ (And I only speak for my book self. You'll have to ask the others for their take. And let me just mention there is no persuading my bad cousin, "The Textbook," so there will always be tests and letters given out because of my bad cousin.)

I would also like to request that I not be added on to by some professor who is only explaining what he got from the book and tries to explain every-thing by using real-life biographical poop, because they're really full of poop, thinking they've explained things, and they're trying to make me really, really boring with their added-on poop. That really makes me laugh as a book, but not the kind of laugh that makes me lighthearted, and that is why I request I don't be added to by those people (mainly Brad Cruise). Especially added on by those ones who write a whole other book on the one, original book, because then I will be almost impossible to find in a library, and even a book like me has a little bit of an ego and wants to be easily found in the library... but translators of me and my fellow books, feel free to write an introduction as detailed as you please. (I say this mainly because Brad Cruise knows no other language except for English, and he's always under the pretention that this makes him an inferior scholar, or an "American scholar," as he puts it, and he always blushes at the mention of translators. So, I mainly just wanted Brad Cruise to blush at my mentioning scholars and translators because I like to see, and be reminded, that he's human also. And weirdly, calling Brad Cruise human also makes him blush. And that is what he gets for adding on to me without my permission.)

Usually if all of that ^ is happening a test is being given by one of those annoying people, and usually that test will be based on, yet again, what they believe is to be gotten from the book, which may be true, but then what is truth? (Of course, all of this according to me.) So please, no reverend professors (Brad Cruise) thinking they're actually teaching by giving out some test based on what they believe should be gotten from me or adding to me with their beliefs. This is a serious request from me and some of my fellow book community (yes, we come together and talk, except for our bad cousin, "The Textbook." He does show up to our community, but he usually just sits in the back and sulks, but at least he does show up), because it is a heavy burden, as is the killing. It just wouldn't be the same if I were read for a test and a letter, or by a stupid person. They'll be forced to memorize my vocabulary words— and usually forced by people who can't explain the need for the force, as what really can the force do? (It is advised, by me, The Book, that you do not ask this question to a *Star Wars* fan.) It certainly will not change a person, because that really can only be a forceful act of one's own self, not by ones who did that something themselves and then proceeded to misunderstand themselves and followed that with trying to force this upon others. Then being able to see through that becomes a survival force. And, of course, if a stupid person reads me, then overreaction will most certainly occur, misunderstanding and false preaching is surely to follow and then, most likely, hate and violence (of course, all of this according to me).

So please respect my request because, again, the burden and stupid people validating us as an excuse for their stupidity is far too great for a book to put on whatever it is that you would call a book's shoulders.

P.S. I just wanted to say, "You're welcome." You're welcome because the publisher of me wanted to try something new. My publisher wanted to try and make me kind of like my bad cousin, "The Textbook," and publish me in new editions, usually every two years when one or two new sentences or something very small, but new, was added on to me by the crazy man they call my author. So, for example, to have gotten to these P.S. words right here, you would have had to of bought edition number 100, because this was not added on until then.

Sincerely

The Book

P.S. Plus. I forgot the comma, and I sincerely, apologize,

1

Chapter 1, or Preface #2

Before you read one word (oh, too late) of my story on my sentence served, I must first tell you I'm not a writer, but I'm having a go at this anyways 'cause I've read some (not all... some were soo dull that Sparknotes™ were my only option) high-school education books by some so-called writers, and they were some of the worst, lifeless things I've ever read, so I figured what the heck.

I'm telling my story to show that I eventually realized that I don't really believe what I had just said above^ about those so-called writers and that I eventually realized that they were only trying to get through this life, just like the rest of us (they just did it in a rich, elitist, boring way). They were only trying to tell a beautiful story, in a style that appeals to some, and doesn't appeal to others (mainly everyone). A beautiful human attribute, the story. It's a wonder how we're soo good at it.

I realized that I'm just a friggin' human too, and I was soo tired of thinking I was better than everyone (well, depending on the day. No, I'm just kidding. I think I'm better than you). Of course this took some time. The time thing is something that a lot of people in the country I grew up in just didn't like. Things had to be soo rushed and quick, and it just didn't make any sense to me, and it still doesn't. I figure the whole rushing thing in the country I grew up in is a big reason why there are soo many man/woman children (or I should say bad, sour children, because I don't want to give a bad name to children) running around in the real world, <whatever the hell that means (Hippie talk, Hippie Dogma).

People, what people would call the literary types (such as The Bard, Sir Brad Cruise), just never seem to have that realization^ in their little Grubstreet communities (nap and sleepytime communities), and that's why it took me soo long to even start writing my story. I mean, I'm writing, and those people run everything, so I figured I had no chance of people hopefully enjoying my story. Heck, I started now, though, and I feel pretty good about it.

So please continue on, but if you wanna stop now because you're telling yourself, "Well, he just kinda told us everything," then that's understandable. Hey, at least you got to here. And there will be some very long occurrences of ( ) <these, and I apologize for that. I just get soo excited when I use them. My advice would be to just enjoy them (see Intermission #3) and to look at them as a nice break in my childish (what my human computer says, "Is that of an eight-year-old, or third-grade level") writing. (And that will be the only time I quote my human computer, mainly due to the fact that he/she just doesn't talk that much unless I force it too.)

Also, I must tell you that much of my story takes place in the inner public-school system, and if you're expecting a sophisticated, intellectual story, then you've opened the wrong book. (No, I'm just kidding of course. I only wrote that for it to be maybe used and taken out of context in the future by private schools as a marketing tool for their schools.)

And, also, also, I don't know what douchey advertising people have coined my generation yet—Gen. Video Gamers, Gen. Technorati's, Gen. Damn You People Are Uninteresting—but I think we're (<insert future lame generation name here instead of the we) pretty annoyed with douchey old people, who were just as much of douches when they were my age saying, "Oh, I just don't know about the kids today. They're soo apathetic and lazy." Stick that up your butt, 'cause we're fine. We're all just hoping that our generation and the generations after us have less and less douches that start dumb at a young age and, when they get older, say, "The kids today are just not all right. I just don't know about them," and then publish an article about it

because it's their job as the modern heroes of sociology, psychology, and bad journalism. So leave us alone and let me apologize for all you people who say such douche bag things about a generation in its infancy. My apology goes like this: "We're sorry that you never lived young, or were never young at heart, that you were sadly old, and not even a wise old while in your prime. It's not our fault that you were a douche at heart at such a young age." What a sad tragedy you are. (Minus 15 points for starting a sentence with and, and also, also. Not in MLA format, also known as Teaching-YOU-How-To-Be-A-Bad-Writer-Educators-Making-YOU-Proud. Education. <You'll see this education thing a lot. This just means that I'm trying to embrace this whole format thing and this specific, certain way I'm supposed to write, to write the correct way, but I can't seem to get around its apparent robotic poop, as my human computer is always trying to control my writing and move it in its own desired format, automatically switching my spelling of "soo" to "so," which soo really pisses me off sometimes, and then I find myself psychotically screaming, "Goddmannn youuu Microsoft Word™." The whole thing really reminds me of some squirmy professor who wishes the entire world were like him and wrote like him (see Intermission #3 for example). As if that type of person had designed the software in order to make everyone like him/her (Cary Smith is Feminist™-friendly). But, I mean, don't get me wrong, I'm all for organization (this writing here is pretty organized), but I'm not for it if it makes Cary a dull boy since Cary can't play because he gets soo annoyed and tired of the red and green scribbly lines underneath his writing that he just stops altogether.

So I'll be marking down points myself against myself for going against my computer's desired format and the other formats and styles taught to me to make me a bad and dull writer, or for other reasons, so "education" means minus 15 points, which has nothing to do with you or any of your future grades, so don't worry. It just means Cary caught himself being a bad boy, caught himself trying not to be such a dull boy. I also will not be writing my entire story using texting speech and grammar, sorry to disappoint you. But if Mark Twain were alive, I'm sure he would be able to do it.) TTYL.

Special guest corrector, Brad Cruise: "Wow, your initial one of these ( ), where you started wayyy up there ^ with "Minus fifteen points" is

just ending now? What is wrong with you? And you are supposed to use brackets not parentheses within parentheses, you cuckold. And you cannot put paragraph breaks in parentheses. That just means your parenthetical information is too long. Just give me one chance to offend thee by plucking your beard, you inane fool, then you must draw your sword against me and die."

Chapter 2 or Preface #3
or The Story Shall Never Begin

My name is Cary Smith, and if you're now wondering if my name has any significance to Cary Grant™ (Trademark <just to be safe: I have a real, constant fear of actually being humanly confined, especially of being confined and being sued simultaneously while they're putting me in jail for life. I mean, who wants to come out of a life sentence remembering that you were sued and have no money), the all-American man in the movies, I will end all your current wonders and tell you my mom was a huge fan, so naturally she would name her kid in reference to a pop-culture icon. I was just thankful I wasn't an actual kid of a celebrity, and that I did not get one of those names. My last name is Smith, which, luckily for me (in terms of my Patriotism being questioned by king and queen douches, remember, I'm Feminist-friendly), is the quintessential, clichéd, all-American last name.

I used to get mad at my name, that is, until people would tell me that I'm a hater. (Which I definitely didn't feel all the time, so that always made me wonder what kind of powers those people had on my feelings.) So, with those false accusations, my name, Cary Smith, comes in handy when my Patriotism (always capitalize the P in Patriotism...it helps for respect purposes) is questioned and people call me "ahater mang," and so I no longer get angry at my name, especially after writing those thoughts down. (And that paragraph was not for crazy liberals to say, "Yeah, ha," or to feel that I'm a part of their group. And that last sentence is not for crazy conservatives to say, "Yeah, ha," and to feel I'm a part of their group. And this sentence is meant to end these sentences, and my very long one of these ().)

I'm not one of those people who was/is someone else for certain people and another for other people. That is just creepy and is really a case of schizophrenia (Dogma), unless they pay me a lot of money, then I would. It just has not been diagnosed and put into the statistics (Dogma) of modern psychology (or modern dogmatism with some fine pills, which I've heard from nobody that they don't work as well as being sprinkled with holy water by some phony priest, who I guess was around in Jesus's time and is still here today), because they say that kind of thing (being someone else for someone else) is healthy. They say it's, "sociable schizophrenia," which is sociably healthy (or so they say).

Sometimes in my story I often got too excited when I shouldn't have when using my too's <(such as that, for example). This happened many times, especially as I run on and on in sentences, and I just lose myself (and 15 fifteen points, Education), and too get rid of the habit is quite difficult. And since the too's are in this fashion, I often used the same concept with the soo's, like I would say, "That was soo douchey," but this I came to find out was not the case with the so's. (The to's and so's are just not the same.)

I would also like to tell you that I've forgotten many words in the sentences and have no idea when to break for a new paragraph, and often misspelled words that sound very similar. And usually I misspelled very short words, such has <that, but for the most part, I hope I was able to hide all of that from you.

I would also like to tell you that I like to say, "also," and, "would also like to," and that I do not believe numbers were meant to be spelled out. I believe #'s are respresented by #'s, like 4, not four. This of course goes against the educational and supposed writing way, so anytime you see a #, it is minus 15 points as there are just too many to write minus 15 points after each one. (And if you see numbers spelled out after this, I apologize, but sometimes what I prefer and what I was trained to do collide. So please just add any of those that you may find to your "Fun Time" findings...see Intermission #1. But, remember, that is only my preference.)

The time I spent in the School System was a lot like doing time (I haven't actually done time, but I've seen the outside of a prison at 70 miles per hour, and I've seen plenty of documentaries on prisons), in terms of the confinement.

Also, also, also, you might notice that I've trademarked some words, nouns, phrases and such that you might not recognize and that you're probably thinking shouldn't be trademarked. Well, you'd be right about that. I did that mainly for future business purposes and because of a big giant wad of fear. (I say this because I wanted my original title for my story to be *Four Corners or Blank, Blank, Think Outside, You Know What, Blank, Blank* and then, on the cover, have this stick figure going outside a taco and then outside a box, and the first thing he/she can think of when they're free, or outside the taco and then the box, is Blank, Blank's trademarked, signature slogan. But as I said, if I did that, I'd be in prison for life and would come out of that life sentence with *Blank, Blank* having already spent all my money that they sued me for on cheap Blanks.)

Chapter 3 or Finding Myself

Where was I in the story?

Chapter 4 or The Chapter Where I Stop Giving The Chapters Titles

I don't know why I thought that when middle school was over that high school would be a brand new place, a fresh start. Maybe it was because all my teachers in middle school were implanting their lectures about how in high school the teachers wouldn't let you get away with this and that, and that it would be a very different place. Well, as usual, the teachers of the school system lied to me because as they always say, "It's just our duty as Educators™." (I don't know if they really say that. I told you I'm not a writer, but I did unfortunately encounter the ones who were saying that in a discreet, subtle and unknowingly way in my life, so it can really be the only thing they say. I narrowed all of their talk down to that simple phrase.)

"Man, high school is going to be soo awesome. We'll be able to drive, and hopefully lose our virginity." The words from the Messiah of my middle school shrilled and pierced into my ears like a rebel teacher scratching nails against the chalkboard. (You'll also find many sentences, such as that one^, which are quite douchey and which make Cary a dull boy but are metaphorically and simile delightful. This is the case because I realized I had written them in because of people who were trying to make me, in the future say, "It's just their duty as Educators™," so once I realized this, I told myself, "I might as well leave them in and see who they attract.")

Those words about high school being awesome were spoken at the ever soo enchanting high-school orientation. At the orientation I learned soo much from my fellow upperclassman, who were only volunteering because they actually thought a college-admissions officer would care about their extracurricular activity at the orientation.

The charmingly, ambitious upperclassman taught that hall A is the first hall, and that it's labeled with an A and contains classrooms A-1 to A-10, and that the next hall is sequential and is labeled with a B and contains classrooms B-11 to B-20. As I stood there in the heat, I thought to myself that if anyone present at this orientation gets lost on the first day of school, then they should automatically be removed and put onto their own separate island, but not those islands you see that are all paradise. It would have to be an island in the northernest part of the earth, or if they're good-looking, be sent to some horny rich man/woman and be his— whoops, or /her—pretty, expensive, high-class whore guy or girl (although I'm worried some might begin to enjoy that and it would become paradisey).

If you read that statement^ as seriousness and said, "Yeah, that should fucking happen. They should be sent to an island," please stop reading immediately and do not continue. YOU SCARE ME. <That is not a joke<. Those people make life interesting (and very depressing), and without them, that very long sentence with all the commas would not have been possible. (Minus 15 points. Education.)

It was the last day of August™ (you'd be surprised at how big and powerful the calendar business is, so trademark, 'cause I'M SCARED) and I got up reluctantly. I got myself ready for a glorious day. This consisted of putting my plain white T-shirt on, my blue jeans, and, of course, my Reebok Pumps™. My Reebok Pumps™ served as my little red shoes—not in the sense that when I tapped them together they made wonders or made me into a happy-go-lucky girlie girl with some weird tin and animal friends, but in the sense, that somehow, in some odd way, I could look down at those black Reebok Pump™ shoes at times when I felt like my mind was leaving me and I was being a fraud, douche bag, and then I would just pump my shoes.

Of course at the time I was in the school system those Reebok Pump™ shoes were long out of style, and I only wore them for situations when I had a tendency to want to pump my shoes—when douches were douching around I would just make a really lame joke and pump my shoes right after the lame joke (so I wore them basically everyday). This usually annoyed them and got them to leave, because douches either do 1 of 2 things when confronted with something they don't understand: (1) they'll say, "What'da fag," and then become violent, or if they're a girl (because, yes, that's right, girl's can be douches too. Who else would want to procreate with douchey males? I told you I was Feminist-friendly) they would say, "Oh my god, he's soo weird. I don't get it." Then they'd sit back and watch they're douchey, male counterpart become violent or passive-aggressive and say, "He is soo hot. We'd have really good-looking kids together." Or, (2) they'd just leave, but not before getting in their "fag" or "weird." And all of that because they just didn't like things that they couldn't understand, and luckily my feet hadn't grown since I was a kid, so I still had my Reebok Pumps™. (Don't worry, I wasn't some spoiled, hipster asshole who went out searching for old Reebok Pumps™ on the Internet with my parents' money.)

My mom was waiting outside in the car (Do you even remember where we were in this writing after all of that poop^, because I know I didn't, and it took me several hours to remember where I was and to start writing again.) as I finished my Cap'n Crunch™. I generally liked, and still like, to start my day with cereals that feed my ego (Dogma word), such as Cap'n Crunch™ and Lucky Charms™. After feeding my ego (Dogma) and getting excited to start anew, I entered the car only to encounter a couple of birds chirping at each other. My mom and sister were going at it like a couple of Conservatives™ and Liberals™ screaming at each other and resolving nothing on some crappy, meaningless talk show on television. (Which, really, were all of them. I've seen a whole lot of television. I mean, it practically raised me, not that there's anything wrong with that. <That was not a joke.) This bird chirping would almost always occur every morning, and my brothers and I would sit back and daydream of whatever was filling our minds (usually masturbation and sex).

Arriving at school felt very awkward and out of place. I got a real feeling inside that I knew was not a good feeling. It was a feeling of admonitions saying, "hello (Minus 15 points for not capitalizing the beginning of a quote. Education), I'm a random feeling. Do not overreact because of me…so, anyways, hey, get ready to have your fresh start disintegrate to make the old road miles longer."

By the way, many of the commas and all of that stuff are just there for kicks, because my stupid human computer kept putting annoying green and red scribbly lines in if I didn't comma, even when I didn't feel like pausing in my writing. Like, take for example, if I said something like, "OK. Peace then?" According to my human computer and the bard, Sir Brad Cruise, I should have made it, "OK. Peace, then," but who the hell pauses saying "Peace then?" Or who the hell pauses saying, "Thank you, Cary?"

It also kept telling me I must comma, because apparently it's standard to pause after most and's, or so's. And I figured, when I first started this writing as a nonwriter, that it was up to me when I felt like pausing, or if I/we/you felt like pausing with a comma or not, but guess I was wrong about that too (Education). To be honest, I have no idea where to put them. It was between a comma, a dot, or the two combined, but that just made things more confusing, so most of the time I chose a ,. I think it was implanted in my brain so much that I just, feel the need, to put in commas, and pause for no goddamn pause reason, so my suggestion would be, to ignore them, 'cause I don't even understand most, (because some were necessary after all), of them. I think, some, of those so-called education writers, and, so-called, Educators™ I mentioned earlier, especially from reading their writing, take their , wwwaaaayyy too seriously. (I should've just went the Mark Twain route and wrote this entire story in cell phone–text speech and grammar.) FML.

Also, I used "you's" a lot (a big MLA crappy and boring American education essay no-no), and YOU might get the sense that I'm talking to *you* as I write this and go back and forth from the present of writing this and the past, when the story took place. Sometimes I forgot I was writing this now to you and used wording as if I were writing it then, so I apologize. It's just I get caught up in the moment sometimes…but just to let YOU know, I can only write now, because I feel I'd be one bad writer if I were only constantly thinking to write in the then (that's a lie from me. That's my competitive side coming out so you don't become a good writer. Education). I'd have to say, since I like you, that that might make me a bit of a whore for a story, or quite simply, a douche bag. (Of course that is coming from a nonwriter.) The Educators™ in my life have said that I shouldn't talk to YOU, or mention any you's (Minus

15 points. Education. No YOU's in MLA) in my writing, but I like YOU, soo too bad for those jerks. (There was a ton of green and red scribbly lines in that paragraph, and I got a Kincaid™ reading level of 3 from my human computer, and it was scaring me that my computer was judging me on a human level. And it was really pissing me off that it wouldn't let me spell douchey or doucheyness and that it just automatically erased what I had written and replaced it with douche, so I apologize for running on and on and on),

(Special guest corrector, Sir Brad Cruise: Why didn't you put this in the first chapter with all the other introductory qualms? I need to read some Shakespeare immediately to get your baseness and stupidity out of my head. You make me want to jump in front of a moving truck at any speed over thirty miles per hour.)

Chapter 5

It was hot, yet I felt no heat because anxiety filled my bloodstream like water fills your stomach. (I'm so used to creating an opening douchey sentence, and my next sentence should be my thesis statement, then a transition sentence, then paragraph number 2. So I apologize for the dullness. Education. Plus, I'll be honest, I must throw out a defense mechanism^: I'm just not that good at them^. Them being essays, dull essays that should all be shorter than they are, or shitty writing that a phony teacher teaches and encourages in a bad writing course. Another defense is that I'm trying to break free of that kind of writing. I don't want to be one of those dull boys who should really be writing 10 pages full of 1 liners (see all modern western philosophers/essayists for examples), instead of the 100 pages of dull essay paragraphs that they do write.)

I arrived at school slightly late and in my mind I really didn't care. I walked into the classroom and heard the teacher say, "OK class, on the first day I always like to play "The Name Game."

"Basically what you guys AND GIRLS" (she was very considerate) "will do is write on a piece of paper:" (<what those two dots are for I've got no idea. For some reason they're necessary, or it's minus some points for being out of order. Imagine it without it, would it really matter? Education.): < OK, never mind that imagining poop. Just look at the arrow with those two little lonely dots and it is perceived that the two dots really just want to stay and be left alone…look how sad they seem. (Sorry, that's just part of my text-only writing style and mindset. I need to remember to leave that to the next Mark Twain™, and to not notice that the two little : < are sad.) So I say never mind and will let them be, 'cause that sad-faced two dots needed a place too:

1. Your favorite movie

2. Your favorite musician

3. Your best friend

4. Number of siblings

5. What you did on your summer vacation

"Then when you've completed that you'll turn it in to me and then get out another blank piece of paper. With that blank piece of paper you'll go around the room and ask everyone questions similar to those aforementioned and their names, but do not put your name on the paper you turn in to me, and then we'll get into a circle and play "The Name Game.""

WARNING. This is a DISCLAIMER: I REPEAT, THERE IS NO ONE LISTENING. (Any time you see this DISCLAIMER and you feel pretty annoyed with opinions (like my whiny one), then please ignore the next paragraph or 2. SO THAT ALSO MEANS ANOTHER DISCLAIMER WITHIN THE DISCLAIMER: NO TESTS ON THE MATERIAL IN THE NEXT 2 PARAGRAPHS AFTER A DISCLAIMER WARNING, because a lot of annoyed people will have skipped them, and that's only fair to not have test material be on disclaimer material. I'd say 2 paragraphs just to be safe. Also, if you do decide to read the next 2 paragraphs after being warned, I remind you that the opinions are solely mine and cannot be used without the expressed written consent of the expresser. So, if you're planning on suing the company that actually liked my book, don't, 'cause you can't. They're my friend, and they've been trademarked™. You might be able to sue me, though, but I would just recommend reading the DISCLAIMER WARNING.)

"Jesus Christ™," those were the first words that came to my mind, but I did not utter them aloud when Ms. Happy-Go-Lucky teacher explained her adolescent preschool game. I wondered, as I sat there in the classroom and pretended to care what people's favorite movie was or who their best friend was, if this teacher had any idea how ridiculous the majority of the class felt about her duck-duck-goose™ game. I mean, the only people in the classroom who were actually enjoying this god-awful game were those select few who wanted to meet everyone in the world and have everyone in the world know them as if anyone honestly gave a shit. Well, these kids were sure fucking enjoying it, or at least pretending to, this prison game (future politicians), but I sure as fuckin' (what that apostrophe represents is that there are more words to follow, so REMEMBER that. Even though 90% of people speak that way, but of course they're stupid, no, really, they usually are. So REMEMBER there are more words to follow since the lifeless, soul suckers don't count them as a real word…meaning it just can't be fuckin. Education) hell was not.

So as I sat there and ruminated I had one final great sensation, almost an evil satisfaction (Which one am I? Good or evil? You opinionate, but remember: I REPEAT, THERE IS NO ONE LISTENING.) about my responses to the great personality questions presented by Ms. Happy-Go-Lucky.

Ms. I'mGoingToHateYouThisEntireSchoolYear started to read off some of the answers that people had handed in to her, and then with the majority of the class reluctantly answering, or should I say guessing, who the person was or guessing the name, and the 3 kids who were thinking about the end of the year when they'd have every signature in their yearbook were vibrantly shouting out the correct answers of who the mystery stud was, Ms. Scatterbrain, to my surprise, began to read the answers I had turned in:

> 1. My favorite movie is the future home video that me and Carla are going to make. We're going to be celebrities. You laugh now, but wait 'til you see us nude. Wait 'til the public sees us nude. It will be a modern masterpiece. Then we'll have a reality show, be totally famous, and have kids that are completely useless to society and do drugs and are just soo totally messed up but will be great for the reality show.

> 2. My favorite musicians are the ones who do drugs, make masterpieces, and then kill themselves.

3. My best friend is my hand.

4. My siblings are pimps, and my parents are male and female whores.

5. On my summer vacation I thought about what shots and angles I want to shoot mine and Carla's future home video that will hopefully make us soo glamorous and famous, so I storyboarded it.

Ms. Sugar Pie got very embarrassed, and out of nowhere got very infuriated. First I thought, "Why the hell did she read on?" then I thought she was infuriated because The Enthusiastics™ weren't showing any signs of vitality, in fact, they seemed almost traumatized and appalled by what had just come out of their favorite kindergarten/high-school teacher's mouth. They were almost bitter, they almost didn't forcefully ignore those other feelings we all have, feelings that The Enthusiastics™ love to moralize to all about how they don't have them. No one fessed up, and I never confessed...I simply walked out of that hellhole and made my way to the dean's office.

I sat in the office for over an hour and eventually Ms. Quick Witted realized why and where I had left to and made the correlation. The dean abruptly approached me some hours later and prepared the opening line of his interrogation. Dean Mulder™ (which was my nickname for him because the guy honestly took his job way too seriously, making him a clown, so naturally I gave him a television character's name. Not that I actually disliked the actual fictional character Mulder. I think Dean Mulder™ had failed the entrance test for the FBI Academy™ multiple times, and an anonymous source, who works within the school office, saw Mulder™ studying in his office for the test. <Oh my gawd, is it true?) began his practice interrogation on me.

"Mr. Smith. What is the reason you're here?" Dean Mulder™ asked.

Yeah, I knew this guy was a douche bag. He had no respect for me ('cause he thought I was stupid, since, if I was in his office, how the hell wouldn't he know why I was in there? I'm pretty sure he didn't know) and was calling me Mr. Fake Bullshit to practice for his FBI™ test.

"Um...well, I really wanted to get to know you?" I said.

"I see we might become close acquaintances," Mulder said.

"My friend, you see well. Shall I call you My Prophet Dean Mulder™?" I asked.

"So…why did you write those answers in Ms. Heller's class?"

"Well, I really wanted Carla, who is a goddess in my class, to know how I felt about her. And I wanted her to know I'm funny, as well as in love with her."

"Do you think it was appropriate for the game?"

"Sure it was appropriate. I mean it's only inappropriate to people who are self-righteous and feel offended by a little fun and humor in an inappropriate game, or to even stupider people who think they can stop the ultimate morons who take what I said in Ms. Thank-God-You-Became-a-Teacher's stupid game soo seriously and become murderous sociopaths (Dogma) or perverts or really awkward conversationalists."

Mulder™ gave me a look, as if he were studying me, trying to scare me and acting like he knew how my mind worked. (Would those thoughts be considered sociopathic)(Dogma?) But I could tell by the look on his face that he was thinking of masturbating when he got home.

"Can I ask you this Mulder™?" (I did not wait for a response.) "Were you offended by these remarks, or did you chuckle when you imagined Ms. Heller reading them off in her crazy-hippie, hypocritical class?"

"Well, I'll be the one to ask the questions."

At this point I had fully established, in my mind—no matter what (I guess I'm that closed-minded)—that this guy was a total douche bag, and I knew goddamn well that he had a big douche-bag chuckle when he read those answers and imagined Ms. AlienRUwithus reading them off and eight billion light years (easier # to just write out. Plus, I wasn't too sure how many commas were in eight billion light years) later realizing what they meant. (I would also like to say that that remark only represents a small portion of the Alien population. So any Alien organizations thinking of suing, please don't, because I am well aware you believe there are sophisticated Aliens out there, and I am also stating that here. And I highly believe, usually on a daily basis, that if there are Aliens, that they are much more sophisticated than most humans. But I would also like to state here that there is the possibly that some Aliens are stupid. Nerd Dogma.)

"Do you think that this Carla girl was embarrassed by your remarks?"

"Well, first off, she's not a girl, she's a goddess, a woman…and, no, I don't think she was embarrassed because she knows damn well that every boy in our grade is masturbating to the image of her. Trust me, you'll have many opportunities to check her out when you walk around at lunch with your walking talkie. Who do you talk to on that thing anyways?" (I saw him on it at Orientation.)

"You're gonna be in a lot more trouble if you keep talking to me like that. Why can't you say more appropriate things in your answers, like saying something about Carla being a goddess?"

There was a dead silence.

"Wouldn't that still be funny and appropriate?"

"Sure, it would probably still be funny, in fact, it might make it funnier because it's more clever, but then Carla wouldn't be turned on and be in love with me, as I now know she is. You see, with a girl like Carla, you gotta dumb it down, 'cause to her stupidity is Albert Einstein. You know, like when an unfunny person says a lame joke, like saying, 'Nice going, Einstein™.' That's what she really means, like your stupidity is a 'Nice going, Einstein™.' With true wit, ya got no chance. It's like ya gotta be a dumb jerk so she'll understand. It's just her nature, and that seems pretty much impossible to fight," I said and knew he was thinking of ways he could accomplish that with Carla. I wanted to tell him that he wouldn't even have to try, that he would simply just have to talk to her.

"Well, I can tell you otherwise, because Carla was very upset by what happened in class."

"Well, I can tell you that that was just her mask that she shows the other students, but deep in her heart she's laughing and thought what I said was charming. And now I have the hottest girl on the face of the earth in love with me. Are you jealous Dean Mulder?"

"I'll warn you one last time to not talk to me like that, and I've about had it with your attitude. I'm going to punish you by giving you a week's worth of after-school cleanup duty and two weeks of lunch cleanup duty so everyone can watch you cleaning up." (I guess he had some kind of Nazi hatred for janitors and felt the whole profession was humiliating.) "Also, I want you to read this book. I think it might help you with what you're feeling and going through right now."

"Yeah, I've read that book. I thought it was good. I liked his hat and sister, but how am I supposed to relate to some rich kid who gets kicked out of private schools and has a bunch of money from his parents to go around New York City™ and then at the end comes out all good and well? I'm beginning to think

24

the end of that book was bullshit, especially with the start of this day, and this was only the first. Plus the kid was really humorless. I don't think I laughed more than 3 times while reading it. I'm not advocating Clownism, 'cause I don't really like clowns—since they don't know when to use humor, since they're using it all the time (but how about just a little? is what I'm saying)," I said to myself. (And, yes, I do think these ( ) in my head.)

I was also curious as to why the hell Mulder™ was telling me to read that book, and I had my suspicions that it was in some guidebook he had read. I had these suspicions and suspicions that Mulder™ definitely had never read the book, because I asked him who the main character in the book was, and Mulder™ had no response, and I left the office and mumbled, "Nice interrogation. You're sure getting close to becoming top-notch." I'm pretty sure he heard me but had no idea what I meant by it. I guess he didn't watch much television.

DISCLAIMER: I REPEAT, THERE IS NO ONE LISTENING. I was expecting him to pull a Judge Judy™ moment and have a total egomaniacal (Dogma) explosion and suspend me from school after I mumbled away, but he never had his judge moment.

It was break as I left the office, and there were a lot of people around the corridors and hallways. I figured 25% of these kids would eventually and sporadically disappear throughout the year and find themselves in Continuation School. (And this was because people who ran schools like Independence tried to make those kids into something they aren't and something they never will be. They did this with force, making these kids pass some math or science class or they'd never graduate, so they figure they might as well just leave. It was really a brilliant idea, and all because the people who told the people who ran Independence wanted those formulas, those equations, because they wanted dominance of the world. And they not soo smartly thought that one can force that knowledge upon a person, especially with those types of people like a real Einstein.)

As I ventured to find the people I used to talk to in middle school, it was funny that every person I saw from my middle school was hanging out by each other, and it seemed that they had all conglomerated with their clones from the various other middle schools that had conjoined to make the wonderful high school named Independence, and that included myself.

I made my way through the DDs, the Dead (and by dead I mean their personalities were a complete recreation of something seen on TV, including movies on TV, 'cause that was still TV. I promised you there would be Zombies in this book, and so there you go. They are just really good at disguising themselves. Education) and Douches, and found my way to the tolerable Douches and the people I used to and hitherto (I sometimes like to use Shakespearean™ words out of context) hang out with.

There were 2 new faces in the crowd, both had come from Getty's, the other middle school near mine, and this was my first encounter with a man that I could finally say was real—himself—and best of all, not a Dead Douche Bag/Zombie of the system.

His name was Cyrus, and I called him Cyrus the Great™. You might say I fell in love with him. It was love at first sight. Of course one can love and say love without it meaning that I think he had a hot ass and that I love it when Cyrus holds my hand. Sure I loved the guy, but not in a guy-on-guy way. I guess if that made me a fag, or I got a, "You're gay," then I'd gladly be a fag. <Oh my gawd, is that true? I don't get it. I'm confused? WTF. Text me back.>

"Gay, he's gay. Fags," is what people said to Cyrus and myself as we walked by them. It's funny how this empty, mindless and, therefore, meaningless phrase, and supposedly hateful phrase, is always coming from guys or a group of guys and girls (Feminist-friendly. As, again, who else would marry or date these guys?) who, well, were pretty much empty and will never have a real friend their entire lives. They'll just always be using each other. Just empty, utilizing friendships here and there. "What a faggy thing to say to end a chapter," they would say.

Chapter 6

Cyrus was in the same grade as me, and he came from one of the nearby private middle school's that conjoined with my middle school to make up the fetus freshman class at Independence High. (Did I just repeat myself? Education.)

Cyrus was essentially what his name entailed: great. His dad was a bit of a history buff and named him after the Persian conqueror Cyrus™. As Cyrus always told me, in response to my asking if his name pissed him off, "No one in this school will even know the meaning of my name, and if they do try and make fun of it, I really don't give a shit. And if you really want to know the truth, my dad's an asshole, just like Cyrus of old probably was, and all conquerors like him, and any name he gave me is a piece of shit." This was who Cyrus was...he made you not hate speech anymore when you heard him talk. He was an eccentric to the extreme, he was always annoyed so it made him funny, and he always had something interesting to say, which was rare at Independence. (Well, that wasn't exactly true, because those future Islanders were pretty interesting.) I just get soo gay for Cyrus.

Cyrus was one of those few people in the group that I was genuinely friends with. Sure there was the entire group of people, but no one was truly close friends. Aside from Cyrus, I couldn't even start up a conversation past the small talk. Cyrus was very intelligent, and he was one of those few people in my life that I instantly made a connection to. He was on the basketball team, but wasn't too enthusiastic about it, and he always talked about how all his teammates were total egomaniacal (Dogma) douche bags who were all future tyrannical leaders or public-relations people or involved with the media somehow. Cyrus always said that the only reason he was on the basketball team was so his parents wouldn't give him shit for doing nothing and always being home, because then they'd think he was a suicidal teen. Also, I think he liked to take advantage of the fact that the "Bimbo Martians," as he so elaborately called them, would instinctually flock to the jocks because they knew it would make them more popular. Don't get me wrong, Cyrus was by no means a womanizer, he was all for female empowerment, but, as he put it, "If those dumb-ass girls are going to give themselves up soo easily and don't want to establish an affection, then I'm not going to complain and lecture them on morality, integrity, and choices, because it will just melt in their brain, and they'll flock to the next guy."

Cyrus was a very honest and outspoken person, and he told everyone what he thought because, as he always said, "There's no reason to go through life kissing ass and shooting around the boat. It seems to me that everyone is synthetic simulacra and afraid to speak their minds. This is why people are soo fucked up—because their heads are filled with lies and bullshit, and then abruptly they become conscious (Dogma) of the truth and seep into a deep melancholy or they make comments on YouTube™." (I had no idea what he was talking about a lot of the time, but it sure sounded pretty.) Cyrus sure didn't believe in the concept of telling a lie for the sake of goodness. He felt that all lies would end up bad anyways, even if its original intention was good, and avoiding the truth only led to something far worse, and that's why he felt truth and humor went hand in hand. Cyrus always said that all we can do to stay sane is to laugh and mock truth but to never forget that it is the truth.

The first thing Cyrus said to me was, "That was some outlandish shit you pulled in Ms. Dildo's class, Smith. The only problem with a couple of your answers is that they were too slap-your-ass-with-a-towel humor, so now you'll get a couple of collared shirt–wearing guys who have no idea what to do with themselves coming up to you saying, 'Dude, Carla is soo hot, I totally want to hit that, and your home-video joke was fuckin' classic, man, fuckin' classic.'

And if you're ever in a conflict with one of them, by the way, just talk about the film *Rudy* and they'll become at ease and like you again. Be prepared for that shit. Trust me, I play basketball with them, and they always say stupid shit like that and then they look around after they say it to see if everyone is laughing. Every time one of them looks at me, I always have a straight face, and they always say, 'Jenkins, you didn't think that was funny?' I always respond by saying, 'No, you're a fucking idiot,' but for some reason they think I'm joking with them, and they laugh as if we were connecting on a sarcastic level, but I just genuinely feel they're fucking idiots, but sometimes they are a little funny. I mean it's not like these guys are over-the-top douche bags that you'll see in every clichéd high-school movie, but for some reason they have this thought in their brain that everyone likes them."

It was weird in my high school...it wasn't like those crappy television shows I was always watching. People usually didn't form certain groups. Sure there were groups, but it wasn't a group of jocks, it was usually just a cluster of people from the same groups but from different middle schools. I usually hated those shows, and I especially hated all those crappy beachy songs about schools and jackets. And I had no idea Cyrus was even in Ms. Heller's class with me until then.

"Yeah, I'll be expecting that. The thing is is that I don't even like Carla. She's fucking gorgeous, don't get me wrong, and I know she liked what I said in my responses and felt innately boastful, even though I meant none of it literally. She's one of those girls who pretends to be stuck-up and hate it when your basketball buddies randomly say some barbaric phrase to her, like, 'Carla, ass is looking great today,' but inside she loves it and eventually will suck off all your basketball buddies," I said in response. (Maybe I was heading toward being a pastor? Of course I may have been lying to myself 'cause my pants were stickin' straight up thinking about Carla.)

"Well, that's fine with me as long as she comes to me first," said Cyrus.

"Yeah, trust me, she'll be coming around the mountain."

DISCLAIMER: I REPEAT, THERE IS NO ONE LISTENING. It was at this point that a close kinship, a bond, was subtly formed between myself and Cyrus. We somehow, through some cosmic energy forces (Hippie Dogma) or through a conversation on blow jobs, felt each other's anger for the way people were and how we were stuck at Independence High. It was at this point that I realized that—in life—anything good, anything just, anything real, anything smart, anything that makes you think and feel is only found in a few, and I sure had wished it was in a whole lot more. (And I'm not a Mall Campaigner for the Marines™. So don't worry, I don't want you to sign up for anything solider.)

Chapter 7

It was getting toward the end of my first year of imprisonment because the weather was changing, girls were wearing shorts, unfortunately guys were wearing sandals, and things outside the prison were changing immensely with the spring. (Nothing interesting happened during the other months since I met Cyrus. They slowly went by.)

DISCLAIMER: I REPEAT, THERE IS NO ONE LISTENING. The day was pretty symbolic of the people who ran high schools (I've never been to other high schools, but, hey, what the hell) and the people who worked for the people who ran the place. Throughout the entire day, unless you were in one of the few teachers' classes who were actually real, genuine, non-douchey people, who were on planet earth, unless you were in one of those classes, the day was as mundane and bland as yesterday and the next day. (Again, a lot of commas, I know, just remember my suggestion.) Unless you were in one of those few classes, you were oblivious, you weren't shaken up, and you weren't feeling down because another shitty, catastrophic event had occurred in the world of humans. For a few hours this day I was oblivious just like the majority of the students were on a day-to-day basis...for a few hours I was actually in the majority. (Hooray! I did it Mom...people love Cary.)

The day was April 20, 1999™, and it was a day in which two seniors from a Colorado high school came to school as if World War II™ had just begun, and they were fighting on the Nazi™ side and their high school was Poland™. Ironically (I have no idea what irony means) enough, the 2 douche bags did this on the birthday of the man who was the genesis of World War II™ (or I guess that was their genius master plan—how original, right?).

It was lunchtime, and Cyrus came to me and said, "You have to come to Miles's class and see this horrible shit that's on the news." So we made our way to Miles's class, who was obviously one of the few and had the news on in his class for the entire school day. I crossed the threshold to the classroom, and there was the twenty-inch screen and an overhead shot of what looked like an indoor school with kids just pouring out of the school like an exodus. The only bodies making their way into the indoor facility were SWAT teams, or men in uniforms who were covered in body armor.

I was truly (and hopefully everyone else was too) shocked.

I was speechless.

I did not look away from that little screen the entire lunch period. It was the fastest lunch that I had in my short career at Independence High so far.

All those petty and silly feelings about douche bags this and that, tools this and that, the Real Zombies this and that went bye-bye quick, and I felt bad. I felt horrible for those people. Watching them coming out, crying. I guess I was feeling what I felt because I felt myself with them, relating to them. All because of 2 dipshits who took the petty, meaningless, emptiness of everything that is American high school too seriously, and they were soo close to getting away from the void, the darkness. Instead they decided to take things very, very seriously and shoot their guns at nothing, emptiness, at a black blankness (and, of course, they killed themselves afterward to an unsympathetic void).

What they did meant nothing to their mindless cause. All it did was make people like me realize that it's a shame to be human, especially because I never expected to feel this horrible for those people running out, to feel this humane (Hippie talk, Hippie Dogma).

I was trying to gather all the information I could before I had to go back to the majority class and be lied to and pretend like everything was fucking landy goddamn dandy.

32

What I got from the half hour I was able to watch the news was that 10 students and faculty members were dead, and police were escorting everyone out of the building as best they could without panic or turmoil. Of course it took the news 30 thirty minutes to say this. Well, Jesus™, it was understandable if the students and faculty members were a little out of it at the current moment, I mean, they were just innocent victims in what looked like war footage. The news also said, "Two boys were found shot in the head with very ominous weapons at their side, but the police are not issuing or making any conclusions at this point on whether or not the two boys were the culprits and are remaining cautious and alert, as if the killers are still at large and still in the surrounding area."

I would have had to watch the news for hours to get more than 1 report, but the bell rang, and I was going to be late, and I didn't give a fuck what the teacher or Mulder™ would do or say about it. I should've just ditched class, but then Mr. Miles would have been in shit for letting me stay in his class, and I wasn't about to put someone I respected in a situation like that. I couldn't leave school either, since I didn't have a car, and even if I did, I would have to run over the five security guards that secured the perimeters just to escape the prison grounds. I could've made a run for it, but by the time I would've got home, the class would be over, and I'd be on the bus heading home anyways… so I went to class. (And can you say "and" one more time in that paragraph? Minus 15 points. Education.)

DISCLAIMER: I REPEAT, THERE IS NO ONE LISTENING. So I got to class, which was physical education. Of course there was a television inside the locker facilities, but the phys-ed lesson plan was never to be deterred nor delayed because the phys-ed instructor, whose name was Chris, was the exemplar of the ultra, quintessential teacher who goes by the book, makes the kids lives worse than they already were, and is soo Naziesque that it is almost impossible that he does not have some psychological disorder (Dogma), such as big-fat-douche-baggery.

I told myself, "Fuck it, if these fascist fucks want to practice censorship and contribute to George Orwell's *1984*™ hypothesis" (Hippie talk, Hippie Dogma), which was frighteningly manifesting itself as time went on at Independence, "then I'm not going to get dressed in my gym clohtes and participate in this bullshit phys-ed class." So I didn't dress in my gym clothes, and I sat on the bench outside the lockers. Cyrus came in late and asked me why I wasn't in my gym clothes, and I told him what I told myself^, and he joined me in my protest. Of course no one else would join us because they were all submissive puppies who always had to dress in their gym attire since it might go on their college application or were too stupid to even realize what was happening here, and how much of complete bullshit it was. (We were soo 60's man.)

So me and Cyrus lounged on the bench outside the lockers as all the other sheltered, pampered puppies lined up for PE roll call by standing on their numbers, which had been painted on the ground by Rembrandt™ Chris. That douche bag Chris knew me and Cyrus were sitting on the bench and not getting into our gym clothes, but like the stupid fuck that he was, he had to handle the situation under his discretion and with the whole class watching the confrontation so that they would become bigger wimps and more submissive to his Stalin™ ways. (Of course I made many references to World War II™, as that was when America became the greatest, and I, of course, made those references because my name is Cary Smith.)

Chris abruptly said, "Jenkins and Smith, why are you not dressing up today?"

"We're not dressing up because you're a Fascist™ pig who won't let us watch the news and actually be informed" (at least until they went back to being their news selves and interviewed an actor about his thoughts on the catastrophe. Again, I knew a lot about TV) "on the forever changing tragedy that is occurring right this fucking instant at a high school, and you incessantly go on with class and lie to us as if nothing has happened. So if you're not going to let us be informed, then I will not participate in your illogical, escapist, bullshit activities," I said. (And then I said, "Follow me, my people," and I started to scream, and then I ripped off my shirt and said, "Our revolution has begun!" End of scene, except no one was following me.)

At this point I was not worried about anything because I knew Mulder™ could do nothing because I was in the right and the administrators wouldn't discipline a student for this, given the current circumstances in the country with students. (Fear. Education.)

My jaw dropped, for Chris began to approach me and Cyrus after I said that^, and I knew at this point that something strange was going to happen, and that I must have penetrated what I thought was impervious, that being Chris' (should I have put one of these ' there? I could never tell with those S's', they always got me. Minus 15 points) Fascist™ tyrannical ego (Dogma).

"You guys are going to suit up, whether you want to or not. And Smith, you're going to suit up and head to the Administration Office after class," Chris said.

"Well, why don't I just go there now?"

"You'll suit up first because no one puts me into a situation like you just did or talks to me that way, and I won't stand for your protesting. It's not the sixties, as you can well see, since all your other classmates are lined up and not with you."

"Yeah, I'll bet you like that, don't you?"

Chris looked like there was murder in his eyes.

"A reversal from when you were growing up when all the passive-aggressive, baby-boomer classmates would be with me and Cyrus, and you were the only little brownnoser lining up, and I'll bet you had numbers in your class back then too. Not too original there, are you Chris? You're just a fraud, aren't you Chris?" (Then I thought, "Nananana.")

"Did you steal that number idea from the teacher you used to suck off for an extra gold star?" (This would be unacceptable for educational purposes. So for educational purposes, ignore it, in fact, ignore all humor. I'm sure those Columbine kids had plenty of humor, or I'm sure, being the geniuses they seemed to be, that they really thought they did, and what they did was soo darkly hilarious. Education.)

Suddenly Chris started to move his arms and went to grab for me and Cyrus (or sorry, Cyrus and I, or me mate and I. I'm always getting told to say it this way and that way by pompous douche bags), and we both instinctually (Dogma) jumped off the bench just before ChrisohmanI'mconfusedhere's hands reached our clothes.

I could not believe this douche bag was actually coming after us. I had my gym shirt in my hand because I had brought the shirt home the previous night to wash and was going to put it back in my locker. Chris continued to approach us, and we kept backing up, so I decided to take initiative and I spun my shirt to make it into a rope shape, and I thrusted (this is not a word. Why? Because "thrust" does just fine. Why? Because they say so, so I thought I'd leave it in because I prefer the word thrusted. Education) my arm back, and as Chris came near me again, I wailed the shirt as hard as I could at his face.

In this moment I was in complete and utter consciousness (Dogma) and all my surroundings were invisible. I could hear nothing. I was only concerned with this absolute moment on successfully wailing Chris in the face with my shirt.

Chris's glasses fell off, and I looked over at Cyrus. He had a look on his face as if he had just seen his future in an 8-ball shaker thing. The whole class was watching, just as Chris had wanted, and Chris said nothing, and I looked around and I just walked the fuck away from the situation. I went to Mulder's™ office, and to my surprise, an hour later he told me I could go and that if I spoke to Chris like that again I'd be suspended. I couldn't believe Chris didn't mention what had just happened (then again, would Stalin™ admit to such an embarrassment? I think not. Education), and I was pretty sure I saw his glasses shatter as they hit the ground.

I caught the bus home. I wasn't even going to attempt to get a ride from my asshole brother who was too cool to give his brother a ride home after school, and it was a 50/50 chance he even stayed the whole day because he and his girlfriend usually went home in the middle of the day, since they were a couple of horndogs, and had sex every 2 hours. DISCLAIMER: I REPEAT, THERE IS NO ONE LISTENING. Usually I would say "making love," but in most cases at Independence High that involved a penis inserting into a vagina, it was not affectionate, passionate lovemaking, it was just 2 people fucking—either because they wanted to brag about it the next day and thought they'd become more popular by doing it or it was just two random people who like a lot thata fellin' they's a get when my's a pisser is touched. (Although, as I write that, I remember the first time I was awkward or aka had sex, and that sounded pretty close to what I said to the girl. Education.)

So (never sure when I should comma after the so's and soo's. They're very tricky), after an hour bus ride I finally got home, and luckily no one was on the couch watching the tube at my house, which was a rarity, even at 3 o'clock in the afternoon. I turned on the tube, and of course some horrible show came on from MTV™ (trademark sign every time I use MTV in this chapter, because I may use it a lot, and I'm feeling lazy this chapter), so my sister must have been watching the tube last and I immediately turned it to the news.

36

As I was changing it to the news, I thought about MTV for a second and wondered why they called themselves Music Television, when no music was played, and when music was played, it was just 5 guys lip-synching some Gypsy boy-band song. MTV should genuinely consider changing their abbreviation to T. S. N. I. T. W. I. T., which would stand for Teen Soap Network in Training, and the W.I.T. would just be extra. (Just for some optimism. For the hope that it might come to them some day, but surely the people who ran that channel never wanted that and were just like my sister's friends, soon to be MALs (**Moms Against Life**). Every month they seemed to sponsor one artist and were subtly saying, "The artist of the month is your new crush—go buy this CD. It's everywhere and cute as can be, only on MTV." Education.)

DISCLAIMER: I REPEAT, THERE IS NO ONE LISTENING. (I knew Soap Operas™ would be on television longer now that a generation of T. S. N. I. T. W. I. T was going to grow up, and those operas were a very good reason to hate television (but also made it more fun to make fun of). I often watched them when I was a kid and pretended to be sick, because they were the only thing on, and even at my young age I thought they were complete shit, but they are sadly realistic for certain people^, if you could possibly imagine that?)

The day was pretty much over in Colorado, and after 8 hours the news reported, "There were now 13 confirmed deaths, both faculty and students. Two senior males were the shooters, and they had killed themselves after opening fire on the school. The two males shot themselves in the head when police had raided the building and they knew it was over. Police are still searching the proximities for any more bodies or anyone who might have found a hiding spot and are too frightened to come out. The boys' names were not released to the public, but it is said that they were two senior males, just two weeks from graduation." Then I threw the remote at the TV and went to my room as the reporter said, "Now we bring on the star of the upcoming movie *This Movie Will Make You Light-Headed and a Little Dumber, But I'm In It.* (Of course I thought, "What a long title for a movie.")

DISCLAIMER: I REPEAT, THERE IS NO ONE LISTENING. Only 2 fucking weeks from graduation? I could not believe that these 2 kids were only 2 weeks from graduation. How stupid could you be if you were only 2 weeks from getting out forever and never having to be on a high-school premise ever again?

* * *

37

As the days went by and my first year of my 4-year sentence was ending, more and more reports and stories came out of Columbine.™ The students grieved and cried, and many students said in interviews that the two boys were always "weird and really self-inflicting" (it was hard for me to forget that these were gossiping high-school kids, after all). Then there were reports that the 2 boys were chastised repeatedly by the jocks and that they couldn't take it anymore. (At that point in time I was wishing someone would've told the 2 to wait 10 years and those jocks could've given them a really good deal on life insurance. Minus 15 points. Spell out the number. Education.)

DISCLAIMER: I REPEAT, THERE IS NO ONE LISTENING. Then, of course, there were the boys' parents, who, like most parents in my day and age, blamed a musician or some artist (goddamn baby-boomer idiots), when that musician or artist probably prevented them from doing it sooner. Or they blamed some pop-culture icon but never stood up and took responsibility for their child's actions. They just made excuses and evaded the issue. It seems that a lot of parents from the so-called clichéd Baby Boomers™ generation (Step right up and make a crappy generational name, and watch those advertisers ruin all the great songs of your generation. What'll it be? An economic-related name? How about a fashion name, a little sex? What'll it be, what'll it be? What will your lifespan be referred to as? The excitement is far too great.) liked to deflect blame and make excuses rather than admitting some responsibility, or when something did happen, they liked to blame what they made our nanny, the television or music, which was odd, 'cause some of the best came from their days. (Then I thought, "Repression (Dogma), repression (Dogma), blame, blame. Music has probably saved more lives than any other art. The MAL was everywhere, and they were the ones truly putting the blame on those things. Life was nowhere with them. Moms Against Life." Man/Woman, these people had me running on and on and on. That's minus 15 points for a run-on sentence with a half circle and another half at the end that makes no sense. Education.)

The 2 males had made a video and talked about the previous school shootings that had occurred before Columbine™ but were not as nearly cata-strophic. (Sorry again to my pompous friends. **Correction**: were not nearly as catastrophic. Education.) The two males said that the previous school shoot-ings were just kids wanting to be accepted and that people would remember their masterpiece on 4-20-1999™.

DISCLAIMER: I REPEAT, THERE IS NO ONE LISTENING. It might be remembered, but it sure as hell was no masterpiece. I'm mean, I felt like I was in prison at high school, and I felt that there were many douchey people, but never would I even contemplate killing those douchey people because their (they're, there, oh, I forget which one, so I put all 3) innocent people. They've done nothing soo horrendous to me that I would want to kill them. (Maybe get back at them, like watching them step on poop which I had cleverly planted, but kill?)

DISCLAIMER: I REPEAT, THERE IS NO ONE LISTENING. All those 2 kids were were two insecure dumb shits who thought they would make a stand, when really they only wanted to be glorified for a self-proclaimed masterpiece. (See all modern-day rappers for example.) Really, these stupid, radical, ignorant murderers only fell into the category of infamy with the man whose birthday it was when the 2 boys soo arrogantly killed innocent people, who really, whether stupid or not, were just trying to get through the day as joyfully and earnestly as the human mind and body would allow them. (And boy, what an original masterpiece those crazy, mindless white kids made. Must have been all the humor they taught in the classroom. Did I just repeat myself again? I seriously can't remember, 'cause if I could remember, I most likely wouldn't repeat myself, not really, I still would. Education.)

In the end, those masterful geniuses, who self-proclaimed their killings a masterpiece, only became what they were angry about, what infested their mind soo much, what they probably deep down wanted to be soo bad…they became the mindless meatheads. They used aggression and violence as the only means because of a lack of any other capacity, or an idle jock mindlessness that forced them to not have any other capacity. Those two geniuses, in the end, became the kings they always desired to be...they became 2 meathead, murderous, rampaging jocks. (What a master plan. Guess the joke was still on them and it truly was an unknowingly master plan.)

Chapter 8

Every year, for as long as I could remember, around the end of the school year, a time came when teachers put down their handbooks for an even more important handbook. I always wondered why, for no apparent reason (at least to me) teachers would completely drop everything they were teaching and start a new lesson plan.

I mean, literally, it came out of nowhere.

Science teachers began to teach basic formulas again. English teachers began teaching verbs, nouns, and adjectives again. We would get weird, random assignments to find the adjectives and circle the nouns. In math we would get assignments of basic equations, and the teacher would always try to play it off by saying, "This is necessary for what we're currently working on." We would have to read these really silly and douchey paragraphs and then were asked to write a really douchey essay about how the butterfly got out into the sky (Hippie Dogma). Every year this would happen, and then after a couple weeks of the weirdness, a week's worth of tests followed.

It was about that time of the year, and teachers were trying to be sly and smooth about the change...they never were, but it was sure entertaining watching them try and bullshit us some more (Education).

So we had our assignments. We tried to write a sane essay about the butterfly, and then the tests came. Everyone got a huge packet full of questions and a couple sheets of ABCD-and-E-for-none, bubble-me-in paper.

Oh the questions were soo bad, soo stupid. These questions could quite possibly make a dumb man dumber just by reading them. (Of course this would never be studied or dogmatized, so I'm full of shit, but if you'd read those questions, you'd believe me true. And 1 thing I was certain about in my life is that I would never want to have dinner with the person(s) who wrote those tests.) All day we just sat in class reading questions for 5 days. At the end of the 5 days I felt like the main character at the end of Kinsey's *One Flew Over the Cuckoo's Nest*—I felt completely brain-dead. (In case you haven't read the book or seen the movie, I thought I'd ruin the ending for you. I'll admit, I've only seen the movie, but, hey, at least I knew the author.)

I didn't know a single person who tried on these horrible tests, let alone did I know anyone who even cared what the questions were after day 1. It basically became a free-for-all to bubble in the sheets of paper so our newly acquired brain-dead brains could be deadly asleep. Of course the tests did not make us completely brain-dead, there was still hope for those who still had the brains to use their question booklets as covers to sleep behind in order to avoid the teachers who had trained us soo vigorously for these tests. I think the best way these teachers could've trained us for these tests was to stick everyone in the final scene of that movie I was talking about before and then have us try and answer or even read a word out of a practice-question booklet.

During that week the person that I least expected to be taking these tests seriously seemed to be very into the tests. During that whole week, Cyrus was always the last one to finish, sometimes he'd even go on during breaks or lunch until the teacher told him to stop. Cyrus was never using his question booklet as a sleeping cover, in fact, I don't think Cyrus looked up once until the day was over or he had to go on a break.

A couple days after the testing was over and I no longer felt like I'd been hit with a baseball bat by Willie Mays or Babe Ruth™ (trademark the candy bar also, just in case that was confusing), I started to get on Cyrus's case about the tests.

"So I'm guessing you did pretty well on the tests," I said.

"What'dya mean?"

"Well, you seemed pretty deep into it. I mean, you were always the last one finished."

"So what's your point?"

"All I'm saying is that you'd be the last person I'd expect to be the last person done on tests like these. I mean, pretty much no one took these tests seriously, and for you to is very odd to me."

"Well, I'm glad they don't try, and neither do I. I took soo much time in order to make sure that I had the wrong answer. I was reading all the questions through so I'd have a better chance of getting the question wrong, knowing I was wrong, instead of guessing, where there is always the possibility of being right."

"Yeah, bullshit. It's OK, I understand if your dad will not talk to you for a couple months if you do bad on the tests."

"No, that's not it at all. He would never check the results of these state mandated tests. Do you even know why these tests are given? Think about the horrible douches who actually come up and create these tests questions. And then you're supposed to be considered smart and educated because you're able to answer some horrible douche's dull questions that relate to nothing human? Why do you think these teachers randomly stop everything to teach us material for these tests?"

"Well, I figured it's just a dumb, mindless, aka bureaucratic, way to measure our abilities and make us suffer even more."

"Well, you're right in that regard, but these tests are a way for the state to measure the school's performance, and they even base some of their funding on these stupid-ass tests. Can you believe that? On these tests, with these questions, that's what determines if your school will receive extra funding and if you're learning anything. So I was trying to get as many questions wrong as I could because I figure that the smartest schools are the ones with no funding from these tests, because any school getting funding based on these tests and feels proud and smart about that is the dumbest school of them all. And just imagine, people pay twice the amount for a house just so their kids can go to these schools that test well. They pay twice the amount to be proud to have a human robot."

For some reason I couldn't stop laughing because I just could not believe that I never made the correlation. Also, what Cyrus told me was soo crazy that it made me laugh, and I couldn't stop. Cyrus just said, "Yeah, I know."

I just kept laughing, and Cyrus started to laugh also. Of course now knowing what I knew, and having Cyrus make the correlation for me, I went into year 2 of my sentence liking Cyrus even more, and I was more capable to laugh off a little insanity. (Write out the number 2 with a two. **Correction**: I went into year two…Minus 15 points. Education.)

INTERMISSION #1

HOW MERRIAM-WEBSTER COULD REPHRASE THESE WORDS' DEFINITIONS TO BETTER HELP YOUNG PEOPLE MEMORIZE THEM FOR THEIR VOCABULARY TESTS, AND TO MAKE THEM NOT SOO BORING

Quaff (verb) - Definition Stated

To drink deeply

Rephrased Definition

Wasted man; taking big gulps like a fraternity legend bro

Tantivy (adverb) - Definition Stated

In a headlong dash:
at a gallop

Rephrased Definition

Running as fast as a motherfuckin' cheetah
Example of tantivy situation:
Run, Forrest, Run!

Expatiate (verb) - Definition Stated

1. To move about freely or at will: wander

2. To speak or write at length or in detail

Rephrased Definition

That MoFo talks for too damn long. There's already enough words in the damn English language, and now they have to have 2 different definitions for 1 word? Forget that, I'ma just choosing 1 and making that the definition.

Hyperbole (noun) - <u>Definition Stated</u>
Extravagant exaggeration

<u>Rephrased Definition</u>
That person just makes shit up, but he does make stuff up with style at least.

Nyctalopia (noun) - <u>Definition Stated</u>

Reduced visual capacity in
faint light (as at night):
night blindness

<u>Rephrased Definition</u>

Can't see shit at night
Example sentence: People suffering from nyctalopia should eat more damn carrots.

Reiterate (verb) - <u>Definition Stated</u>

To state or do over again
or repeatedly, sometimes
with wearying effect

<u>Rephrased Definition</u>

Person who has to repeat himself 'cause no one knows what the hell he's sayin' or talkin' about.
Examples of having to reiterate:
      1. What'd you say again?
      2. Can you repeat that?
      3. I didn't catch that, what again?
      4. What?
      5. Say that one more time?
      6. This is hurting my head.
      7. Are you a damn philosopher?

Ingratiate (verb) - <u>Definition Stated</u>

To gain favor or favorable
acceptance for by deliberate effort

<u>Rephrased Definition</u>
Ass-kissing MoFo

Nincompoop (noun) - <u>Definition Stated</u>

Fool, simpleton

<u>Rephrased Definition</u>

How great is it that nincompoop is actually a word in the dictionary? Brad Cruise is a **nincompoop.** Gonna get myself a damn good grade on this vocab test, finally.

FUN TIME...
FOR END OF BOOK AS WELL

See how many times you think Cary Smith will get sued. It could be from a sentence or a phrase, or paragraph, or him forgetting to trademark something.

Write your answer here (unless you plan on reselling this copy, because then you might want it to be clean, or if you have a portable reader, then enter the number here (if that's possible). Not really sure if portable readers are capable of that yet, but just in case. And if they aren't, hopefully you received your complimentary Etch A Sketch with your digital purchase of this book, and now would probably be a good time to play with the Etch A Sketch):

Answer: Hopefully 0 for Cary Smith's sake

A NONFICTION SONG RENDITION BY GREG HAWKINS'S L.P. MOM

Mama told me
when I was young

Come sit beside me
because I am drunk, one of my two sons,
but my favorite son because you're the best-looking one,

And listen closely to what I have to say,
and even if you don't, I'm gonna follow you everywhere because I am drunk,
I'm even gonna talk by your door if you hold it shut, and talk 'til I say
what I want to say.

And if you do this, well, then, I won't talk even more, trying to make you feel guilty
for not listening to me before,

Oh, you better get out there, time is a wastin',

Get on Wall Street,
go be a salesman,
get into marketing,
and we both know any real engineering is out of the question.

(Oh yah, I'm a little drunk)
You know troubles will come if you don't,

If you don't get a high-paying job, own a house pretty soon, and for Christ's sake,
will you find a girl because I'm beginning to think your gay,

And don't forget my best-looking—and because of that—favorite son

That if you don't do these things you will be a failure, a miserable son, and it'll make
you crazier than your mom.

(Chorus)
And be a Wall Street–type of man,
Oh, be something that I'll love and understand,
Baby, be a moneymaking man,
Oh, won't you get into marketing for me, my best-looking son?
You better do this.

Forget your weirdo thoughts,
All you need is to be a Wall Street–man, a salesman, a marketing man,
Or be my Brad Pitt, my best-looking son,
All you need is to listen to me
And you will be satisfied…come out here and dance with me, you faggot.

(Chorus)
Boy, you better worry,
Because to not do these things is to not be satisfied,
And tomorrow when I wake up and you mess with me sarcastically,
Oh, my best-looking son,
I will not understand,

But just remember,
That I'm still thinking those thoughts,
I'm just not gonna say them because I am not drunk.

(Chorus)

Oh baby, I know I'm laughing like Charlie Manson's trained pet parrot right now,

But baby, just be a six-figure type of man,

One that I'll love and understand…don't be some kind of weirdo, my son,

(Laughs) (Fading out)

Whoooo, are you gay?

2

Chapter 1

As another first day of school rolled by I had begun to have the veteran's mentality of not giving a shit and coming to the realization that this was only day 1 of a 182.

As I was not yet old enough to drive, and my brothers were assholes, I was riding bitch seat with my mom and 2-years-younger sister and my sister's friends. The ride was always grueling, since my sister was a royal bitch to my mom, and my mom a royal bitch to my sister. Any excuse she had to yell, be condescending, argue, and have a bitchy attitude toward my mom, she'd take full advantage of the opportunity. I had to give my sister credit, though, she was very consistent in being a royal bitch, but while she was consistent, she was also a douche bag who I could not stand, and this was made even more apparent in her friends.

DISCLAIMER: I REPEAT, THERE IS NO ONE LISTENING. I generally avoided those types of girls that were my sister's friends because they were the type of girls that brought women power back a hundred years but could bring it forward a hundred with their beauty. (**Correction:** with their superficial, disingenuous, excessive makeup beauty. They were interesting, but depressing, and future Islanders. What am I talking about? I have no idea.) (Hippie talk. Hippie Dogma.)

Those girls weren't over-the-top, as one would see in a horrible teenage movie, but they were pretty damn close to imitating the over-the-topness. Every morning they would come in the car, and the first thing they would do, especially if it was a windy day, was, almost as if they had rehearsed it, grab their mirrors from their purses and made sure their shields were in order. (I had a lot of stoppages of breath during that sentence, sorry. Too many commas. Minus 15 points. Education.) Those girls were the exact, quintessential consumers advertisers and marketers glorified on...they fuckin' relished those girls, from their hair, to their designer clothes, to the way they acted. Then there was my sister, who every time I teased her about her friends, would always respond by saying, "I only act like that around my friends. It's not, like, that I like them, it's just, like, they're fun to hang out with."

"So then you're a douche bag?" I would respond.

"Well, no, I mean, I, like, only act like that around them. It's, like, they make me act like that."

My sister was 2 years younger than me, so at that point I would just smile and ignore her words and end the conversation. Maybe I gave her too much slack. Maybe I should've continued to call her out and tried to make her realize that what she had just said made me lose 20 brain cells, but she was my little sister, and even if I had, she wouldn't change, because she was who she was. And maybe I couldn't have a conversation with her, but she was still my little sister, so I usually always ended conversations with her at those points because, quite honestly, she'd only repeat what she had previously heard from some extraneous source on television, and an angry high-school kid can only hear the word "like" soo many times before he sticks his head out the car window and hopes for a truck to wail it off. (Example: it would be like a person hating commas and reading that sentence. Minus 15 points for running on. **Correction:** should try and make it one short sentence. Simple, not complicated. Be more like Hemingway™. Education.)

So I'm sitting bitch in my mom's car (it took me 5 hours to remember what I was initially writing about before all of that stuff up there^ and to start writing again here), and as expected, my sister is provoking and instigating my mom, and her 3 bimbo friends vainly, and not even consciously, look and mend (I read too many British books while studying on my own at the bookstore, so I say "mend" a lot and spell favourite with a U, and sometimes

I forget to add an O or substitute an S for a Z) their shields that covers their real selves.

I suddenly got a burst of energy (Hippie talk, Hippie Dogma) and in the mood to mess around (and by mess around, I mean messing around, not messing our faces and tongues together) with one of my sister's friends, who my sister claimed had a huge crush on me, and I counterclaimed (lawyer Dogma) that I was only her August™ crush. In five days she'd have a September™ crush, and then another, and another, and so on. So, (Comma after so, so, who soo knows. Education.) I asked Shelia, my sister's friend, a question, "So Shelia, what designer are you wearing today?"

"Gawd, I can't, like, believe you couldn't tell. Of course, it's the first day of school, I'm wearing Abercrombie™."

"Oh, wow, yeah, I should've known. Tell me how in God's name am I supposed to tell the difference between your outfit and an outfit I could get at an outlet store?"

"Ewaa, an outlet store, like the 2 even compare. That is soo gross to even think of an outlet store."

"Exactly, that's what I thought the difference was too. Isn't Abercrombie™ the store of rich white people who won't hire minorities because they don't look like the Photoshopped pretty boy plastered on a poster on the wall of the store, because they want the people working there to be a Photoshopped pretty boy of their own ethnicity who are all secretly Nazis? Although I heard they're letting Asians in these days."

"You're weird, and I have no idea, and I don't really care, like, because their clothes are absolutely fabulous, and it's, like, not their fault if those people applying are ugly."

"Yes, exactly, who cares. I hate ugly people, don't you? It's like what the fuck do they contribute to society? Like, just their ugliness."

"Yes."

We got to school and my sister and her friends, who were starting their first day of high school, immediately made their way over to the girls just like them, only three years older, and the two cliques must have communicated beforehand on instant messenger and told each other they had to stick together.

DISCLAIMER: I REPEAT, THERE IS NO ONE LISTENING. I stood there in astonishment and in an utter what-the-fuck, or WTF, moment on how

Darwin's™ (Dogmatist) theory of natural selection™ worked with those girls. Then I realized that they were the ultimate survivors because they didn't ask questions, they didn't think why, and they went how the people with power went or wanted them to go: they went with the flow (Hippie talk, Hippie Dogma), therefore, enabling them to be the ultimate modern Survivors of the Fittest™ (Dogma).

My first class of the day was Spanish 2, or Español 2. (I learned the true language in that class. Just like in my English class. The languages were soo true to the people of the countries. Minus 15 points for being a smart-ass. Education.) I entered the classroom, and the teacher seemed sane, some-what down-to-earth, but you can't really get an impression of a teacher from roll call.

After roll call, the teacher began talking: "Hola la clase. Mi nombre es Señor McDonald y hoy nosotros estaremos repasando lo que se requiere en la clase y en lo que espero que usted aprenderá y obtendrá de la clase. Permítanos primero el comienzo introduciendome uno al otro, así que llegaremos a ser más cómodos uno con el otro. Permítanos el comienzo con Sr. McDonald." The only 2 words I was able to comprehend from his lightning introduction were "hola" and "Señor McDonald." I think the whole class was dumbfounded and asking themselves, "Is this teacher serious?" All I was thinking about was how bad it was at that current moment to be Señor McDonald. (Oh, and I used a free translation website for that Español writing above.↑ So if it's incorrect, don't blame me. I'm just giving credit where credit is due.)

The only kids who comprehended and even remotely understood what that maniac said were the 2 Mexican kids in the class. That poor son of a bitch McDonald just sat there with the look a crazy-ass person gives a sane person.

Luckily it was the first day of class, as Zach, a kid who was always around where Cyrus and I hung out, and I say luckily it was the beginning of the school year because this meant Zach was still in school, saved poor McDonald from his misery. Zach abruptly spoke and said, "It seems McDonald is having trouble getting started, so let me get things rolling."

"No. No. No, in Español, Señor Zach," said my new insane Spanish teacher.

I didn't know Zach well, but I knew that he was one of those kids who was talking a lot, and usually when someone was doing that, a lot of bullshit was coming out. Zach seemed like a decent guy but a pathological liar (Dogma), although some of his stories were very good, and he could be a very good actor and storyteller in his own right.

Zach was a kid who would be at school for 2 months and then randomly and without explanation disappear for the rest of the year. Cyrus always told me that the school sent him off to continuation school, but that he disappeared from there too, and then he tried to start fresh every year, and he'd been in his second year for 5 years.

Zach was a bullshitter, especially when it came to doing drugs, dealing drugs, and having sex. He would make up the craziest stories, as if he were a mega rock star. No one ever believed him, but no ever called him out either because it was fun and interesting to listen to his bullshit since everyone knew he'd be gone in two months. (Minus 15 points for a bad transition sentence that was about 10 sentences. Short, simple. Where's your thesis statement? Bad writing. Didn't your human computer underline all of that with red and green scribbly lines to help you out? Education.)

At this point Zach seemed to get very annoyed with our new Spanish teacher, and he responded to his speak-in-Español request very angrily: "How the hell do you expect me or anyone in this class, except for Juan and Jorge, to speak fluent Spanish when we've only taken an introductory course that wasn't even true language? I think you're a crazy man, a bad teacher, and a horrible mentor if you expect anyone to learn Spanish just by speaking it and giving us nothing to relate it to. That would be like suddenly speaking whatever language was spoken in the surrounding culture to someone who has been isolated from the world since birth and expecting them to have a knowledge of the language in no time when they were freed from that isolation."

McDonald responded by saying, "A mí esto es la mejor manera de aprender el idioma. ¿Si vamos por su lógica Señor Zach, entonces cómo hace a personas ignorantes aprenden a hablar un idioma ellos no pueden leer y poder entender? (Freetranslation.com™, copyright. Please respect the humor, whichever way, just don't sue me.)

"Well, I have no idea what you just said. Hey, Jose, what'd the crazy ass say?" asked Zach.

"He said that this is the best way to learn the language and that if we go by your logic, Zach, then how do ignorant people speak a language they can't read or understand?" responded Jose.

"You've got to be kidding me, right? Do you even have teaching credentials?" Zach asked. "Because with a question like that, I highly doubt that you're qualified and adequate to teach us anything. The ignorant people were born and ingrained with the language, the true language of the culture, at a young age when our auditory (Dogma) and language systems (Dogma) are much more readily adaptable and capable to store language memories (Dogma). And we're all around the age of 16 in this class, and it's much harder for us to learn any language than it is in early development (Dogma)," said Zach.

I don't know if he was full of shit or not, but he actually sounded as if he knew what he was talking about that time. All he was missing were the text-book names of the brain systems (Dogma) he was talking about. (Well, come to think of it, he kinda sounded like a textbook.) They must teach you actual stuff in continuation school that is interesting enough to remember.

Our crazy Spanish teacher just evaded the confrontation and told the class, in Spanish (my human computer was feeling pissed off and didn't feel like being sociable on the Internet™ for a free translation), that this was the way he teaches his class, and that's the way it was going to be, and no more discussion was going to occur on the subject.

DISCLAIMER: I REPEAT, THERE IS NO ONE LITENING. This teacher, right then and there, set himself up for what would be an array of cheating in his class. There would be a lot of disrespect, and most of all, two pissed-off teenagers who would make his job seem as if he were in purgatory, them being me and Zach, at least for two months there would be two of us. And of course all the other kids would try their best to go along with Mr. Español but, to my delight, would cheat in his class because it would be impossible for them to earn a good mark for college in his class without cheating, and he rightfully deserved all of it. (Was there one period in that paragraph? Minus 15 points. Education.)

After going through the motions of the school day, the lunch period came upon me, and as usual I went to where I and Cyrus hung out. (Dammit, Cyrus and I. Minus 15 points. Education.) Cyrus was in a pissed-off mood because he'd just had Mr. Español's class before lunch and could not believe that he was a teacher, but then I reminded him that we were students of Independence, and his disbelief quickly disseminated.

As I stood in the hallway listening to Zach talk about the girls he wooed over the summer, I began to think about the mundane, bland routine and undertone that the school day had to it.

DISCLAIMER: I REPEAT, THERE IS NO ONE LISTENING. I started to wonder why it was like this. Why was everything the same, Monday through Thursday? And then I started to comparatively think about Cyrus's dad's job and the school day. I came to the conclusion that the system is essentially a training ground for the shitty, mundane life that awaits all except for the 1% after school, and some will be able to delay this process by going to a more sophisticated training ground after high school that costs a lot of money (Education).

I thought about how those people who ran the school basically had no hope nor faith that more than 1% would avoid a job that required a long day of mundaneness and that, in order to better prepare the mass for this, they make the school day a half day of what is coming in the future. They figured that the masses' minds would be pliant and be used to the lack of change and will keep the economy and country strong. (My name is Cary Smith. Hippie talk, Hippie Dogma.)

I was already thinking this on the first day of my second year of a 4-year sentence, and I knew it was too early for such thoughts and that I was never going to adapt or become submissive to the time I had to serve, and I knew I was in trouble. (Also, I already forgot what the word pliant^ means, so I'm sorry for using it, and just ignore it.) (Also, also, I think I should capitalize Douche Bag because it's a noun. I used to have to underline Douche Bag if it was not capitalized in my elementary grammar lessons. So I guess from here on out I'll actually make an effort to capitalize Douche Bag for educational purposes, but most likely I'll forget. Education.)

59

Chapter 2

In my high school, which consisted of mainly lower- to middle-class Americans, and a few uppers, there was a group of 8, and that group of 8 was the black kids. 7 of the 8 hung out with each other and formed a pack. The lone outsider, who seemed forlorn by his comrades, walked the halls of school, speaking to no one in particular and often giving commands to an imaginary army, and, quite frankly, scared the BaJesus (short for "Black Jesus") out of most of the students.

The kid's name was Gail, and commando was his game, speaking to himself was his forte, and showing signs of Tourette's and schizophrenia (Dogma) was his alibi (I just couldn't rhyme that last one).

He was the outcast of outcasts.

He went to a school dominated by whites™, Asians™, and Mexicans™, and the few that he could so-called relate to because they were of the same color was not the case because this deceivingly diabolical kid was really just an innocuous lonely human with lonely human thoughts. (But of course, who wasn't? He just thought about it, and that's what made him an outcast. Minus 15 points. Never begin a sentence with a word like "but," even if it is in () <these. Education.)

It must have been March the day I first befriended Gail, because the days were slower than normal, as March was a month with no days off. It was a month that consisted of 5 days a week for 4 weeks, and only 1 other month could share that claim with March, as being the slowest month of the year, and that month was October.

I remember it was a lunch period, and I was just sitting on the brick-layered seat near where our clichéd group hung out (I lied. It was soo more like an over-the-top TV group), but to me, it was more just individuals hanging out in one place.

Cyrus was talking about the previous night's basketball game. He was mentioning how the team they had played was a private school (now you know, MAL, that we were not part of the private world, so please send your special kid where I was not. <MAL. Education), and that the team stood absolutely no chance, so Cyrus devised a plan to foul out on purpose so that he could witness the slaughter secondhand on the bench. He talked about how he got 2 fouls in the first quarter, but then laid low, so as not to be obvious, until the final seconds of the second quarter, when he picked up his third foul. Cyrus then mentioned that he picked up a quick foul in the third quarter and had to sit out until the final minutes of the third, when he picked up his fifth and final foul. Cyrus was certainly right about the onslaught, because the final score ended up being 70-35. (And I had no idea what he was talking about with fouls and final minutes. Minus 15 points. Start another sentence with a word like "and," and you'll rewrite your whole paper. Education.) Cyrus then went on to mention how much bullshit it was that a public school was playing a private school, because private schools recruited their players, and he always mentioned how every time he would go to their school to play, he would get an eerie old feeling of being surrounded by an ultra-competitive, pretentious, superiority, out-of-touch energy—or as Cyrus called them, Young but Old.

DISCLAIMER: I REPEAT, THERE IS NO ONE LISTENING. What was funny about Cyrus was that he was actually a very good basketball player, but he hated the way the people on his team played the game, and another funny thing is that Cyrus came from a private school before spending his last year before Independence at a public middle school. I think he only played the game so his parents wouldn't make him work some asshole job making some rich old guy/girl richer by doing all the dirty work and getting paid only what the state forced the rich old guy/girl to pay. He said the only time he had a good time was when he would purposely entice the other players and get them riled up, which he didn't fail to mention was not a very difficult thing to do.

As Cyrus was telling his ironic (Still don't know what that means. Ironic?) story, Gail was walking my way, and it looked as if he were speaking into his hand, imitating a walkie-talkie. I had previously seen Gail doing this a couple of months ago and thought nothing of it, but for some unexplainable reason, this time was different, and as Gail came face-to-face with me I boldly uttered, "Hey Gail, who you talking to?" At this precise moment I didn't care that this kid talked to himself. I didn't care that he played commando and talked into his hand to give a reconnaissance or to engage in a liaison. At that moment I was just striking up a conversation with a guy who seemed like he needed a conversation with someone. (And I knew if a war was actually coming that Gail would know what to do since he had soo much experience, and I could look to him for guidance.)

Gail did not respond to my question, and he hurriedly walked in the other direction. I didn't follow him because I knew he heard me, and I knew he could sense the genuineness in my tone when I asked the question. (My thinking at the time, that I was being soo genuine, probably made me seem very disingenuous to Gail.) I wondered what he was thinking at that very moment when he heard a human actually trying to talk to him, one who was not giving him shit or asking him questions in a condescending tone, such as:

"Hey Gail. When's the war starting?" Or saying, "Hey Gail, they're bombing us, run." (That one actually made me giggle a little bit though.)

I knew Gail would come back around before the lunch period ended, because he generally came by twice in a lunch period, always by himself, not always playing commando but always talking to himself.

The lunch period was ending, and Cyrus had just finished talking about how his parents thought the refs had it out for him when Gail came walking by again, still talking into his hand as if it were a walkie-talkie. (Don't be repetitive. **Correction:** you already mentioned Gail talks into his hand like it's a walkie-talkie. What're you, an idiot? Minus 15 points. Education.)

This time I approached Gail right away. He seemed to tense up immensely, and I could feel his awkwardness. I asked Gail who he was talking to into his hand. DISCLAIMER FOR GAIL: I REPEAT, THERE IS NO ONE

LISTENING. I asked him if he knew of some kind of secret communication wave that our hands enabled us to achieve if only we'd believe. Gail did not respond, but this time he did not walk away hastily. So, (it's 50/50 for a comma after so, depending who you ask) I continued to talk to Gail.

Gail seemed very uneasy when it came to being around people. As I was speaking I could see and feel Gail trying to get a feel of me, to see if I was fucking with him or not. Gail actually responded to my asking who he was talking to. He said, "I'm talking to imaginary people because, when they converse with me or when I'm conversing with myself, these people don't think I rap or play sports because I'm Black™. These people don't care what people call them because they don't allow words to manipulate their emotions and become hostile, because they know that words are only a communication device that is not that serious, and if one let's people see that their words have effected them, then they know they have lost. These people wonder why it is that many Black People™ bring something to people's lives once a week on a field, and yet after that one day they forget how much they cherished it, how their whole week was based upon it, how thinking about that one day got them through the workday, at least for one day, and then they're back to hating. These people wonder why it is that soo many so-called ghettos are the way they are. Why it is that these people rely on a government that has never been there and will never be there. They wonder why it is that these people make these communities soo bad when they could bond, stop making excuses, share with each other, and never allow someone who could care less (the someone being most people in the high-up positions who could care less) to be the ultimate subject of a tragic excuse. These people are impervious and dissimilate the offender and make his words meaningless, for words are merely a communication tool that enables humans to get their point through to other humans and something that is definitely not as serious as it may seem, especially when stupidity and wickedness are involved." (For some reason I remember when he said that I started to imagine a very Douchey, egomaniac (Dogma) Dolphin getting really red and in kill mode 'cause he heard some offensive sonar about himself. I must've been on marijuana.) "These people that I converse with are the people missing from my life, people who are obsolete around these halls, so I created them myself. I've created the people I wish were real in these halls to replace the idiots and two-faces who do roam these halls." (Gail Hippie talk, Gail Hippie speak. Or some may say, Gail psycho talk, Gail psycho speak, depending on who you ask.)

"Sounds like sticks and stones may break my bones type of thing," I jokingly said. I don't think he got it, and I wasn't surprised. (I always figured when I was younger that my mom's phrases came from a very, very crazy white lady. MAL.)

As I sat in my class that followed the lunch break, I sat and thought about the what-if situation of what if I had never approached Gail or continued to talk to him despite his muteness. When Gail finished, I realized and understood what he was saying ('cause we were both crazy, and crazy understands crazy), but I could never have felt what he felt. I could never feel what it was like to be Gail and to truly be that alone and yet still be a man who philosophized and be the man that he was in a place such as Independence. To me, Gail was never some crazy ass (maybe on some days) who talked to himself and played commando, to me Gail was an eccentric, something original, someone interesting with something interesting to say, and one of the few good days in my high-school life was the day I approached and spoke with Gail.

The next lunch period was much the same, except Gail was no longer walking around talking to himself, in fact, this was the first day I did not see Gail at the beginning and end of lunch walking by. A week passed by and Gail was nowhere to be found. I told Cyrus what happened and the amazing words that had come out of his mouth, as if he were some surreal being, and Cyrus said he hadn't noticed Gail for a while, and he jokingly said, "Sounds like you're ready to join his revolution. You were probably the first person to actually strike up a real conversation with him in his history of schooling. Maybe, from what you told me he said, he felt that his life was complete and he went back to some divine place where he first came from. BaJesus™ Smith, I think you're in love with him."

A month went by, and the days went by, and still there was no sign of Gail anywhere, and Cyrus had jokingly mentioned to me, "You're Malcolm X™ has not been in English for a while, so he's probably looking down on you from his divine avant sanctuary."

Chapter 3

It was getting near the summertime, and the 1-year mark had passed on the calendar for the Columbine™ massacre. I was in McDonald's class as he said something in Spanish that no one could understand, except 1 person, Jose, since Jorge was MIA for quite some time. Apparently what the crazy (this crazy man no other crazy could understand) man was telling us was that the fire drill we had as kids was changed forever as we knew it and replaced by a new drill.

Apparently the school had been planning this new drill for quite some time, and my class was the only one without a warning because our warning was given to us by a crazy white man who wished he were Spanish. (Education.)

Suddenly we heard this fear bell ring, and McDonald, who finally spoke English (told you I was Patriotic. I like 'em all to speaka that English), told us, "Get all the desks and pile them against the door, and then make your way to the corner of the room, away from the door."

This new drill was obviously generated in light of Columbine™ and made the old earthquake and fire drill seem very old and obsolete. The drill lasted for quite some time, over 2 hours, as the whole class sat in the corner of the classroom and waited for a police officer to give the call of all clear on the intercom. During the 2 hours, which were very long and grueling, the class was not allowed to talk, but everyone whispered because I told the class, "It's not like McDonald can send us to the office, because were not allowed to leave the room." So people whispered until McDonald threatened to deduct points from our grade for whoever he caught talking, and the class was confused, for no one even knew that McDonald used a point system. So the whole class sat there in complete silence, and every 20 minutes or so, someone (the school Sheriff) would come to the door and try to open it, and bang on it violently and scream, "Let me in, I'm trying to get into safe passage." Of course McDonald was preconditioned not to open the door under any circumstances. (Education.) I asked McDonald, "What if this was really happening and that kid was scared to death and really needed to get into this room, and then boom, shots were fired, and later on when you opened your door, there he was, dead?" He told me to be quiet and told me I just lost 5 points, but it was a worthwhile loss of 5 points to ask him that question. And as expected, as if programmed to, just as his "If You Wanna Be Spanish" teacher handbook had told him to do, he evaded the issue and changed the subject (Hippie talk, Hippie Dogma).

DISCLAIMER: I REPEAT, THERE IS NO ONE LISTENING. As I sat in the classroom in silence I began to imagine that if this situation we were having a drill on did actually happen, I would just make a run for it. (I'm no idiot. I'm not gonna try and be the hero of high school by trying to stop a bunch of mindless, murdering teenagers. Hey, you can't call me a coward, because Independence inspired those kind of thoughts. Who the hell wants to be the high-school hero?) Most schools that I had been in were outdoors, and Columbine™ was an indoor school, so the kids were stuck inside, which is exactly what the school was now drilling us to do, to keep indoors. I figured if the situation did occur that I'd just make a run for it across the street and not stop running until I got home. I'd rather take my chances running across the street, which most of the classrooms were close to, than sit in a room full of students, protected by only a half-ass constructed door, a pile of weightless desks, and a crazy white man who badly desired to be of either Spanish or Mexican descent.

Finally, after two and a half hours of sitting in my worst class of the day and being stuck with Lucifer's shit (McDonald), I was ready to get the hell out of hell, but then a Sheriff came into the room and started to lecture about school safety, the perils of intruders on campus, and to always report it if you hear any talk about guns, knives, or any kind of violent act. Then he slipped a great reenactment of what we just went through and what we should do if we find ourselves trapped near the confines of the intruders into the VCR. (Which meant try not to get shot, but the video basically showed you ways that would definitely get you shot. Education.) The reenactment was made courtesy of our school's fine drama department, the reenactment (I'm tired of saying reenactment) made the whole situation seem comical, which was very hard to find in the given scenario, but those damn drama kids found a way.

DISCLAIMER: I REPEAT, THERE IS NO ONE LISTENING. The day ended, and with it, so did the drills of my childhood of hiding underneath the desks, waiting for an earthquake to collapse the wall in and smash the desks and then smash the class. Or standing in an orderly fashion and walking out, as a fire burned right at our feet, to the parking lot and listening to the teacher call roll as the class watched the school burning down in the background. Now the drill was to lock yourself into a room and pile desks on the door and wait to see if the intruders, who could bust down the door if they really wanted to, would choose your room and shoot you dead or not. (Education.)

That was the new drill of school, and it makes you really miss the old silly but charming drills where you practiced for a natural disaster to smash the desk you were hiding under and then subsequently you are to neatly and orderly file out of a burning building and then take roll call while the building burned to a crisp behind you, not an unnatural psycho who was shooting up your school... or for a bomb to wipe us all out, or some psycho with a bomb strapped to him (MAL Dogma, fear Dogma).

This was the drill of today, and hooray, hooray for today.

Chapter 4

Generally when school would end, the people who didn't work some shit job, like me, flocked to someone's house and essentially would do what we did at school. Most of the time (non-basketball season time) I found myself at Cyrus's house because no one was ever home there, he always had a ton of food and drinks, and any place was better than my place after school, where either my sister would be watching some reality teen glamour show or a show about today's new fashion and how you could be fashionable and in today (but not tomorrow, unless you watched and tuned in tomorrow, of course) or my brother would be watching the three o'clock SportsCenter™, trying to multitask making out with his skank girlfriend and watching four ex-jocks talk about their depth charts for a season that was six months away. (This made me often wonder why I watched soo much television.)

Usually I would take the bus to Cyrus's house, and fortunately his stop was always the first, although it was quite a walk from the stop, and I got a sense from that walk as to why Cyrus was soo skinny.

When I arrived at the house, Cyrus usually accompanied me, and the first thing we'd both do was grab a bite to eat. After eating for 20 minutes and screaming for release from the school day (we would literally scream for a minute. I'm not kidding, and it felt great. No, I'm just kidding, we didn't do that kinda crap, we weren't that insane or that dorky), we'd usually head over to the video games, where we would fry our brains for an hour until more people came knocking on the door.

As more people came over nothing really changed, the only thing that really changed was that more people were watching the video game currently being played, and more people wanted to play next. Often there were people outside smoking weed, because the first time the Potheads™ (it was, like, soo TV high school. Bimbo Dogma, soon-to-be MAL Dogma) came over they tried to hotbox Cyrus's bathroom, and Cyrus then proceeded to become very angry and pulled the kids by their hair and threw them out. Eventually Cyrus let the Potheads™ back in because, except for that one incident, they were usually calm and didn't speak much. (Since they thought they were being enlightened. It is a known Pothead™ proverb, at least when they're not high, that all Potheads™ believe they are Buddha under the tree while high, and let's face it, if they smoke enough weed, they start to think this even when they're not high. And have fun trying to talk to these so-called wise, Pothead folks.) They would just laugh out of the blue every now and then, and Cyrus loved to talk to them because he thought that they listened soo well.

Every now and then Cyrus would have some random, hot slutty girl with him, and the two would disappear for quite some time. It was always funny because Cyrus would pretty much ignore the girls that were often with him, as if they were nonexistent. Cyrus, when he was usually done or had lost in a video game, would charm the girl and goof around with her, then he would look straight into their eyes, and they always forgot how he had treated them just 10 minutes ago and would disappear with him, and then he would come back, and it always appeared that the girl had left. **(Correction:** good god, man, could you run on any more in a sentence and say "and" any more? Take a breather every now and then. Education.)

I think there was only one time that Cyrus brought back a girl a second time, and he said, "It was because she was the only girl to ever not forget that I treated her as nonexistent and called me out for it, but the second time is always a charm, and charm her I did, and soon she forgot." The girls that Cyrus had with him, usually a new one each week, were the girls my sister hung out with and the next-in-line inferior girls who wanted to be hanging out with the girls my sister hung out with. Cyrus often joked that he would never touch my sister, but he never failed to mention that she did hang with these girls and seemed to follow them and that he is not the only guy they flock to, as he so assholely put it, "I'm just the guy this week, and next week I'll be the guy of the week for another Bimbo."

I knew that my sister did, in fact, hang out with these girls, but I really played dumb as to whether or not she was in the weekly pool. I had to do this for my sanity's sake, for all that keeps me together. Well, she generally does follow them and always has her little monthly phrase, such as last month, when she was saying, "Gotta love it." Every time I saw her around the house or in the morning when I first got into my mom's car, she would just annoyingly say, "Gotta love it," and she thought she was soo funny. At first I thought she might be trying to reach out to me in some subtle, discreet way, but then the next day, Shelia came to Cyrus's house, and I heard her saying, "Gotta love it," every time she initially saw someone she knew, and immediately the reaching-out theory became as vague as I had first thought it to be. It was just her monkey-hear-monkey-say phrase that her little dildo friends were saying that month. (Of course, I want to stay away from these thoughts of my sister being a follower with such a group of people for my sanity's sake, of course.)

This was about all I would do after school was (I think that was a fragment or an error, 'cause my human computer put a green line underneath it, so ignore it for educational purposes) first have Cyrus tell me, "You're coming to my place to do something today." Then me trekking to his house to sit around and feel my brain fry and disintegrate (it was going to happen naturally anyways, MAL, so keep quiet) as I played and watched video games.

DISCLAIMER: I REPEAT, THERE IS NO ONE LISTENING. And don't get me wrong, video games were a great means of mind rape and time killing, but only when used in moderation. I was doing this every day after school, adding to the mundaneness of the day, which I thought was only possible at school, but every day at Cyrus's house that was proven wrong. Any time I would suggest going somewhere else, such as the movies or…well, that's about the only other legal activity a teenager could do, unless you were into sports or illegal things like Marijuana™ and Alcohol™. (Which I was on occasion and in moderation, just to zip things up a bit.) My suggestions were very scarce, and no one ever wanted to leave their seats, which were imprinted with giant ass marks. I was all for sitting around and doing nothing while thinking I was doing something, but once again, only in moderation. It seemed that everyone had to do everything to excess, moderation was a word floating in the obscurities of space, far and distant from the earth. (And by moderation, I mean not doing the same things a lot and just switching the couple of same things every other day, so technically, it wouldn't be excessive with the whole every-other-day theory, but there wasn't much for your average teenager to do. And it was always funny to hear people's parents during this time in my life talk about video games, yet they didn't cause us to get into any trouble.)

So this is what I did every day after school, and every day my brain felt as if it were shrinking more and more into the abyss, and eventually I was not even going to realize that I had become dull, that I had stopped asking questions, that I had become submissive because the technology, the luxuries, and commodities that surrounded me made it soo easy to become submissive and lazy, and it was the thought that this was exactly what they (whoever they was) wanted you to do (Hippie talk, Hippie Dogma). To be warped into their technology, lavish in it, and enjoy the easiness and continue to enjoy their glorious products for the rest of your existence, which seeped into my brain all the time, and that kept me from actually falling into the abyss. (Although, never mind, I played all their games, could name all their characters, they got me and I loved them. I was in the abyss, but what's soo wrong with a little easiness in this mad world? Better them as my friend than a dog who would shit and pee everywhere.)

DISCLAIMER: I REPEAT, THERE IS NO ONE LISTENING. What angered me most, though, were the old Douche-Bag tools who would always say that video games should be banned because they made slovenly, indulgent people, especially since those types of people would be that way no matter what, no matter what they partook in, and have been around since the dawn of the human mind.

Most of us played video games to pass the time, and oh my god, so we passed the time with video games instead of baseball. (And don't worry, we gamers will still support baseball, because we're not as stupid as those old douches believe us to be. 'Cause we know if we don't support baseball, then we're not going to be able to play the baseball video games anymore.) Things pass, and it just pissed me off that there were always these people trying to make our thing that will eventually pass be banned because of a few lazy, indulgent, mindless monsters who play all day every day as they're high as a kite all day and every day, and eat all day and every day. (Not surprisingly, these were usually the kids of these douches who wanted such things banned.) Those old fools. I just didn't get how people could become that dumb and annoying with age.

Often, when I chose not to go to Cyrus's house after school, which became a lot, I would walk endlessly around my house's neighborhood. I had no intention of going anywhere...I had no mission. I just simply did not want to be in Cyrus's house playing video games, sitting around and letting my brain fry every single day. I couldn't do things to excess, it never was something I ever liked to do because it seemed to me that people who did things in excess—whether it be drinking, working, studying, exercise, or an array of things—simply scared the shit out of me.

DISCLAIMER: I REPEAT, THERE IS NO ONE LISTENING. It seemed to me that those people did those things excessively because they were scared to be alone with their minds (Hippie Dogma, Hippie talk this whole comma-filled paragraph). They were afraid of what it might say. They were afraid they would not be able to control it. They were afraid of themselves, so moderation was out of the question, and excessiveness allowed their minds to be constantly occupied so that they didn't have to be alone with themselves, to know themselves. I would think about those people, not in a condescending way, but compassionately and empathically (so basically in a condescending way, which made me feel good about myself and soo I didn't feel soo mean) because they were scared of themselves, and I was scared of them too. And those people truly and not faultily (is that a word? Minus 15 points. Don't ask a question in a sentence that you cannot answer. It is a word now. Education) failed to slow down and actually be alone with themselves and get to know that once one spends some time with themselves the knowing then manifests itself in everything. (Whether good or bad. Hopefully good, but possibly not, but that's not really up for me to decide, I just call them douches...and masturbation occurred often in that alone time for most people. After that very long sentence, could you now tell that people who did things in excess made me nervous?)

I would contemplate this regularly, and always I would think of Gail and what could have possibly happened to him. Cyrus had mentioned to me that one of his Bimbos, who worked as an office aide, told him that Gail had to move to New York™, but she didn't know why, all she knew was that he moved to New York City™ because his aunt came into the office one day to check Gail out and got all the records of his grades.

I would often wonder if I would even think about Gail had I never talked to him. I thought about how amazing the words were that Gail spoke to me. I thought about how everyone thought he was just a very crazy kid who talked to himself and played commando, but those people didn't hear Gail speak the way I had heard him speak (suckas).

I kept replaying in my head (insanity) what Gail had said to me about who he talked to. This was all I knew about Gail, and as the words kept repeating in my head, I became more amazed and fascinated with Gail (and a little more insane) and began to understand why he was always by himself because no one would understand him, and if someone did understand him, they wouldn't want to. I began to understand why he was the one out of eight, why he was the missing member to the other seven black kids at Independence, who essentially transformed themselves into MTV™ characters in order to fit in with people who just did not care to understand them outside someone they had seen on TV. (I sure was glad all my TV watching didn't make me this way.)

I began to understand that Gail had experienced things in his life that I could barely begin to imagine. That he perceived things differently than myself, yet with all these differences, I felt a lot like Gail, maybe not from the outside, but certainly where it genuinely and earnestly mattered, on the inside. (Hippie talk, Hippie Dogma. Minus 15 points. **Correction:** why do you have to ruin a nice little paragraph by saying, "Hippie talk, Hippie Dogma," at the end? Education.)

Chapter 5 or Cary Tries To Remember Where He Was in the Story But Forgets That He Was Not Going To Title The Chapters Anymore

What chapter is this? Am I still writing about year 2? Intermission will come shortly. And remember, I don't say this in a demeaning way. As a reader, I get the same things, and as a writer, I honestly forget where I am.

Chapter 6

The second year of my sentence was coming to an end, and I was turning 16, which was supposed to be a big birthday because you could finally drive. All anyone ever talked about at Cyrus's house was how, when they turned 16 and got their licenses, things were going to change, and their video game, sitting-around days were going to be over. Well, many of the people at Cyrus's house turned 16 before I did, and the only thing that changed was, instead of them walking or taking the bus to Cyrus's house, they drove to his house.

I woke up on the day of my license test and, surprisingly, I felt a bit anxious and nervous, mainly because I knew if I failed, it was another year of riding bitch next to the Bimbos, hearing my sister condescend my mom and my mom condescend my sister (or me condescend both of them at the same time and equally), and riding the bus home or to Cyrus's house.

I drove my mom's car to the DMV™. My mom was in the passenger seat nagging me about doing this and not doing that and giving me advice for the test. We got to the DMV™, and 2 hours later, my testing supervisor came up to me and asked me, "Are you ready?" Jesus™, am I ready? Sure I'm ready, now after watching 50 people take an eye test and 20 of them failing. Sure I'm ready after watching an extremely barbaric biker-bar man scream and almost go into a rampage because his motorcycle was towed on the premises for being parked in an employee's spot. "Sure I'm ready," I said to the lady.

As I walked to the car and got ready for the test, I thought that while the DMV™ makes you wait a beard-growth amount of time (it takes me a long, long time to grow a beard), they did provide you with very interesting and exciting entertainment.

"So back up, and turn left at the DMV™ sign," said the testing supervisor. The lady kept telling me to "turn right here, turn left here, keep going straight," and the whole time this was going on I did not move a muscle in my body. My 2 arms were tightly gripped to the steering wheel, and those were the only signs of life in me, and they only moved when told to "turn right here and turn left here."

We were approaching the DMV™ office and the lady said, "You did a great job, but I sure hope you don't drive like Frankenstein™ every time you get behind the wheel."

I laughed pretty hard (I probably even snorted) because I was tense, and I certainly wasn't expecting her to crack a joke. I didn't even know why I was tense, because I knew nothing would really change with me having a license, maybe subconsciously (whatever that means. Dogma) I really, with my life on the line, did not want to ride bitch any more with my sister and her Bimbo trio of friends.

I passed the test, and the lady told me to wait in the line to get my photo taken. I waited about 20 minutes, which seemed slower than the previous 2-hour wait because the entertainment value in this line was lacking. I got to the podium and the lady told me to stand on the sticker feet imprinted on the ground, so I put my 2 feet on the 2 sticker feet and looked up, and abruptly the lady took my picture. She didn't say anything—no warning, no nothing, she just took my damn picture.

DISCLAIMER: I REPEAT, THERE IS NO ONE LISTENING. A couple weeks later I got my official license with my photo on it, and I looked like I had just been sent to prison and I was already being raped as my picture was taken.

The first month I had my license actually felt like a change. I somehow felt more grown up (however that feels), but then, like every machine, I grew tired of it as the newness became sameness. (I think I just wanted to not grow up and be a Toys"R"Us™ kid (too much TV, but I liked it.)

I think a good majority of the disconnect with my newfound driving privileges was the crazy road rage–induced maniacs who cut me off and tailgated me, even though I was already speeding (I never knew people wanted to get to a red light soo fast until that first day I started driving and people wanted to push my car off a cliff in order to sit at a red light), and most of all, the disconnect was paying for insurance, gas, and general maintenance on the car. And because of my newly found costs, I was forced to work an asshole job.

Chapter 7

I started my new, glorious summer job as a Busboy/Host™ at a local restaurant near my house so I could walk so I wouldn't have to work extra hours to pay for extra gas.

DISCLAIMER: I REPEAT, THERE IS NO ONE LISTENING. The job was horrible. I was essentially the slave worker of the place. I had to clean up after all the fat, disgusting people who came in, and I don't even know what they ate because it seemed that I had to clean off most of the food from their table. I had to greet people as they came into the restaurant, pretending to be cheerful, as if I loved my job and the establishment. I felt dirty all the time and was highly underpaid because minimum wage was soo low, and people like my bosses were always making sure that the minimum wage increase legislation never passed so that they'd earn $200,000 instead of the $180,000 a year they'd get if they had to pay their workers $1.25 more an hour.

I felt no loyalty to the restaurant or to my bosses in a place that was all about teamwork and loyalty, but like most group endeavors, few actually did the work, while others remained out of sight and let the others do the work (The Bosses™).

The only perk of the job was that I befriended the chef, and he would always make me a meal on the side every now and then, and there was also a smoothie bar which I took full advantage of. I didn't feel bad for getting my free nutrition, because I was underpaid for the work I was doing in the place, and that's what happens when you treat people with a superior attitude, as if they aren't humans just trying to live in the world: you get disloyal people and rebellion that is justifiable. (I was no Anarchist™, I just did not like Fascist™ owners and their tool managers who preached loyalty when they could care less about you. Corporate Dogma.)

The worst part of the job was not all that, it was the other employees who made me soo depressed. It was as if I was surrounded by the people who did every activity, joined every club at school, and didn't even know why. There was no one to talk to or relate to, except the chef (but that was only for meals 'cause he was too busy most of the time). These kids and so-called adults I was working with made me feel soo sad. I knew that all the robot movies about the future were completely off because there would be no need for robots if this was how most people were at my age. These fellow workers of mine were sure disappointing. Cyrus said they were all probably Young Conservatives. (I always keep my promises, and as I said, I promised there would be zombies, vampires, and robots in this book, they'd just be really good at disguising themselves as human.)

DISCLAIMER: I REPEAT, THERE IS NO ONE LISTENING. After a month of working that asshole job, I started to become more comfortable and deceivingly earned the trust of my bosses, so I started to do things honestly and not always have a fake smile on my face and tell people that the wait would probably be 50 minutes instead of the 10-to-20 bullshit and then as a result have a bunch of people coming up to me, asking, "How much longer? It's been 20 minutes already. I see a table open right there. Why can't we have that table?" So instead of repeatedly telling people that they couldn't have the table because they're not next on the list, I'd just tell them a true estimate of the wait, and generally they'd leave, but I didn't give a shit because I was underpaid, and if my boss wanted me to bullshit the wait time, then he could come and deal with the annoying pampered fucks that were constantly whining in my ear like a gnat on a late hot summer day. (My name is Cary Smith.)

84

DISCLAIMER: I REPEAT, THERE IS NO ONE LISTENING. Most of the people who came into the place were old, middle-aged white, Asian, and Indian people™, and they were always the ones whining and complaining about the service. It was horrible to have to cater to pretentious, pampered people who thought they were superior to the world and they deserved to be catered to specially because they had played their society cards right and had a nice, advanced degree and a cozy job. Those people were all alike in the way they talked and beat around the bush all the time. Often the employees of the place thought of tainting their food, especially the ones who whined and came off as pompous tight asses, but everyone felt that if they did that then they'd just be like them. They felt they would become Douches just like them, so most felt like it was meaningless (at least the chef and I felt this way).

One night at the restaurant I was busing tables. (**Correction:** obviously you were busing tables, you already established that was your job. Don't be repetitive. Education.) The restaurant was very slow that night. It was very desolate, but 1 old lady came in and almost made it my last. (Very nice. Simple, short sentences. Plus 15 points. Education.)

As I was cleaning the table of some fat slob who had just left, I saw an elderly lady come in, and she looked innocuous from the outside, like your clichéd sweet grandma. The service was very slow that night because the lone waiter who was on the shift was new and not a fast learner. Our manager was nowhere in sight, he usually disappeared for a while, probably went to the movies or his dirty Fascist™ how-to-be-a-good-modern-day-corporate-tool meetings.

What was funny about a guy like my manager was that he thought people would become submissive if he was a dick and always correcting people, but what he failed to realize was that people would only be submissive when he was around, which wasn't very much, because when he was not watching the floor, or going on one of his disappearances acts, the employees that he thought he had supreme control over were doing whatever they could to fuck him over, and I was beginning to like my coworkers. (Back to your not-simple, not-short sentences. What'd I tell you? You think your paper is the only one I grade? Hemingway. Remember Hemingway. Minus 15 points. Education.)

So the innocuous sweet grandma was now the only customer in the place, and she had been there for about half an hour, and she still had not gotten her food. Understandably and justifiably she had every right to be impatient and annoyed. (I would be too if I were old and hungry, because I imagine being old and hungry is scary business since, if you get too hungry, you never know if you might die. Cary Smith is not an ageist.) I was standing at the cashier counter, having my third smoothie of my shift, when suddenly I see Hitler's™ widow come storming toward me. I knew she was going to complain. I knew she was going to lecture me as if I had any control over the situation. I knew she would be condescending toward me, but I just, at that moment, did not give a flying shit what she had to say. (Of course I would not turn into Hitler's™ widow if I were annoyed, old, and hungry, I'd probably turn into his little nephew.)

She approached my counter and shrilled (she even got me talking and using words like her) at me, "I've been here for over an hour, and I have not even received my drink yet. This is completely uncalled for."

"Well madam, I'm only the busboy. There's not much I can do for you. I can get your drink for you. What was your drink?"

She was now violently yelling, "Where is your manager? This is unacceptable service and no way to run a business."

"First off, madam, you need to calm down, because I can't talk to emotional people without becoming a bit emotional myself. In regards to my manager, that is a very good question. I often wonder the same thing: where is he?"

She then interrupted me and was bright red, and if I had poked her with a needle right then and there, she definitely would have burst. (I thought maybe I might have been able to collect the tomato slices from her bursting and made a very tasty tomato sandwich to go along with my smoothie.) "Who do you think you are talking to me like that, and telling me to calm down? I want to speak to your manager right now."

"Well, my name is Cary Smith, that's who I think I am, but if you're into Eastern philosophy, which it doesn't sound like you are, then I think I'm nobody, I'm empty. I'm one of those 2 words that make me something/nothing." (Oh man, I was even confusing myself.) "Do you really think Buddha had a revelation under a tree by himself?"

She said nothing.

"Yeah, neither do I. I think one would have to be around other people, don't you?"

She looked at me like it was time for her next meal (me).

"I'd love for you to talk with my manager too. If you do get a hold of him, can you ask him what movie he saw tonight?"

"You little smart ass.

"You little shit.

"Grow up.

"I will not stand for this, and I'll let it be known to the owners of this place how impolitely you spoke to me."

"Well, then you should've sat down before you started our little talk here, and I bid you a good night my dear, sweet lady."

After I said those words Hitler's™ widow left the building, and an hour later my manager showed up, but I didn't care to speak to him because my shift had just ended, so I left without giving him an explanation regarding the 20 messages that were left on the phone. Quite frankly, the friggin' Douche Bag didn't deserve an explanation, he deserved to be worried, and as I left, I did have a great urge to ask him what movie he saw, but I resisted the urge and left.

DISCLAIMER: I REPEAT, THERE IS NO ONE LISTENING. (Also, when Hitler's™ widow told me to grow up I started to wonder what that even meant, especially since insane, uptight people were always saying it to me. Those people who seemed to be saying this seemed to be those people who could never get out of the whole normal-phase stage. That's why these people were always alike and telling people not like them to grow up. They'd have their college phase, their 30's phase, their middle aged phase, and their old phase. They'd always be trying to change their personality for their next phase and telling people like me to grow up and pissing people like me off.)

The next day I went into work I knew I would immediately be confronted by the owners because their cars were in the parking lot, and those 2 Douches only showed up when something like what happened the previous night happened, or if someone important was coming into the place, like the local food critic™. Other than that, it seemed as if they just collected their salary and went their own way (sounded like a pretty good gig to me).

As I made my first step into the place, there were the two owners standing with my disappearing manager.

"Smith, can you follow us? We have a situation to discuss," said one of the owners.

"Yeah, sure."

"Well, as I'm sure you're well aware of what situation we're talking about, since you were there, I'll start by saying I'm not making any assumptions, and I'm asking for you to explain the situation," one of the owners said in the back office.

"Yeah fucking right. You're not making any assumptions," I said to myself. Who is this guy going to believe, some rich old lady, who gets her Hitler™ widow money each month, or some little shit like me? So I began to explain the situation, and I told him exactly what happened and how the only thing I ever said back to her was to calm down.

"Well, you were a little bit sarcastic with her, and she said that you wouldn't get the manager. She said you kept telling her, 'That you would love for her to speak with him and that all the employees wonder where he is.' Why didn't you get Fred?"

"Well, first off, I was only being sarcastic after she called me a little shit. I would say that's a little obnoxious." At this point, there was no way I was going to cover for a Douche Bag like Fred, who was on some power trip (Dogma) and treated his employees like dirt and disappeared for hours on end. So I told them that I looked for Fred everywhere, which I hadn't, because I knew he wasn't there. I told them that no one could find him.

The two owners told me OK and to go punch in and get to work.

DISCLAIMER: I REPEAT, THERE IS NO ONE LISTENING. The only thing that saved my Casper ass from getting fired was that Douche Bag Fred. Fred was not there. The owners asked all the employees, and they confirmed my statement that he was nowhere to be found. No one was going to stick up or be loyal for a person like Fred, who felt he was better than his employees and thought he could be constantly stern and earn people's respect. Fred found out the hard way that, in the end, if you go about things alone, you'll find yourself in a desolate and very isolated place. (I think Fred and Hitler's™ widow, who was available, would've made a splendid couple. Oh man, she still had me talking like her, saying splendid. I need to get her propaganda™ out of my mind. I LOVE JEWISH™ PEOPLE.)

Fred thought he could win people's approval by being domineering and overbearing nonstop, but that never worked out in any situation because people would become angry eventually, and once a group of people become angry and come together, then the power lies in their hands. (And I should know since

I have never been a part of one. **Correction:** repetitive. This whole sentence, after I love Jewish people, is unnecessary. Minus 15 points. Education.)

All the employees and myself wanted was to be treated like humans and to be talked to like humans. It's a very simple thing, the problem was that Fred was not on Earth, he was in Douche Bag Tyrannical Egoland (Dogma), and he was the type of kid who used to write in his journal about ruling the world (Creepy Creeper Dogma).

DISCLAIMER: I REPEAT, THERE IS NO ONE LISTENING. I really didn't care if I was fired, but I wasn't, so I remained at the restaurant another day. I needed to pay for my stupid car, which unfortunately was a necessity where I lived because the public-transportation system was designed by complete morons (or it was designed by the Nazi™ car manufacturers who wanted you to get soo angry that you would just say, "FUCK IT," and buy a car) and was completely inadequate, or I could just suffer with the Bimbo trio and Queen Condescending in my mom's car, so I chose the stupid car. (Or I could say "or" again. **Correction:** the handbook says to use better transition words in your 5-paragraph essay. Minus 15 points. Education.)

That night, Fred was in the office my whole shift, and unfortunately it was my turn to close. As I cleaned the place up I tried to feel some sympathy for Fred, because empathy was out of the question, but I could not conjure any feelings of hate or love for Fred. I felt nothing.

Fred walked out to his car, and I started walking home, and the owner, who had to be the manager for the night for the first time since he and his partner bought the place, stayed back and locked the place up.

I was walking down the street and could not hear a thing because I had my Discman™ with me (hey, come on, at the time I was wearing my Reebok Pumps™, so that's why I didn't own an iPod™, and they were super expensive when they first came out. Plus Reebok Pumps™ and a Discman™ just go together. Don't worry, once again I wasn't some hipster™ going around searching for Reebok Pumps™ and a Discman™ with my parents' money. They were just items I had from when I was a kid. I also really don't have a problem with hipsters™, I'm just kidding around, you loonies) and was listening to music (soon to be MAL'ed away, the music that is) when I saw lights go by me, and then suddenly those lights seemed to veer violently back toward me. I could not make out who was in the car, or what kind of car it was, for whoever it was in the car had to of had their brights on, because I could not see a goddamn thing.

Then I saw 2 guys come toward me, and then the next thing I knew, I was on the ground, and my face hurt like Gandhi™ did for his people. The 2 started kicking me as the backup singer on my Discman™ sang, "Oh yeahhhh, yeaaahhh." I had no chance to fight back, as I was ambushed and cowardly attacked. (I had no time to run for the hills, which is my main attack strategy.) I got a last kick in my face, and I waited a few seconds, and then I felt no outside forces damaging my body, so I opened my eyes, and there was the coward, there was the Douche Bag Fred. (I'm sure you're tired of me saying Douche Bag at this point, 'cause I kinda am. But Fred was 15 years older than me, so I think this situation definitely warranted a big ol' fat Douche-Bag stamp for Fred. **Correction:** spell out 15, fifteen, and may I see this Douche-Bag stamp? I would like one to decorate my hand. Education.)

Apparently he had to go get his sidekick to help him kick my ass (to help give him some cowardly courage). As he got into his car, he looked at me, and I wouldn't give him the satisfaction of words, just as Gail had said, "These people don't let the offender get satisfaction by giving him an angry and hostile response, they do by not doing because the offender will not get his satisfaction then, for he will not understand doing by not doing, as he is always so inclined to do the opposite." (That may have been lame, and "do" may have been said often, but it felt pretty good to do not do.) Not word for word of what Gail said, but it was what he meant in his words—at least that's what I got from them. (Or was that Gandhi™ who said that? Who knows? Not me.)

So as Fred got into his car I just looked at him and smiled and waved good-bye. I knew this upset Fred, because he got a weird look on his face, and I knew that he was expecting words and some pissed-off response from me, but I didn't give him that, and honestly I didn't even have one inside me. I knew that Fred was going to get his (or at least my mom always told me that people like Fred would get theirs, but I was beginning to think my mom was crazy).

DISCLAIMER: I REPEAT, THERE IS NO ONE LISTENING. Fred was a coward and had to get help from his Douche-Bag friend who would come to wail on a person he hadn't even met, or seen for that matter. (Whata guy. He

90

probably graduated from Independence a while back and was going on his 8th year at the local junior college, and so he had a lot of idle time on his hands to go and do things like that.)

Fred had to use means that are the only means Fred knew, which was being an overbearing barbarian and using the only force he knew, which was violence. Fred needed someone to blame for his firing, for his ego (Dogma) and pride's (ego in a different word. Dogma) sake, and he chose me, which it was partly my fault, along with Hitler's™ widow, but still, Fred got what was coming to him (thanks Mom). He was fired, and that's why he came after me with his outstanding and honorable friend. (You already told us he was fired, why repeat it? Education.)

I made my way home and immediately hit the shower because I knew my mom would ask me a million (I would rather spell that number for laziness purposes, although writing this has taken, probably, more time, so I apologize for that. Education) questions about what happened to me and would call the cops™. Maybe Fred deserved to be arrested, but I highly doubt that would have changed him. I got out of the shower, put some bandages on my face and stomach and went to sleep. I went to sleep not discombobulated (discombobu-lated was a big word that was easy to say, so I decided to use it there, and I truly hope you don't have trouble pronouncing it, because I like to try and stick to my word (see quote page at beginning)), not vengeful, not angry, and not even thinking about Fred. I went to bed thinking to myself, "I sure am going to be sore as a motherfucker tomorrow."

INTERMISSION #2

A GUIDE TO SHAKESPEARE'S PLAYS IN 30 SECONDS OR A 5 CENT REFUND

*For five-cent refund: all entities whose time exceeds thirty seconds must rip this page out in anger for stated thirty seconds being a lie (all entities must genuinely feel the anger; bad-actor, Soap-Opera anger is prohibited) and mail the page in to the address provided on secret website, which must be discovered through hard, laborious, never ending detective work. We will give you one secret to the main secret. We have provided the knowledge of the website to one very chatty sixteen-year-old girl, who is standing somewhere in the world waiting to gossip the website knowledge she recently received. She's especially eager to gossip this information because, when we told her the website, we also told her we trust her very much with this information to not tell anyone and that she seems like a trustworthy person to share such personal information with, and that also the information she was about to receive was very, very, very true. Also, if you have started your timing, sorry, void it, The Guide To Shakespeare has not started yet. No Shakespeare has even been mentioned until now (NO, still can't start the timing), and we are legally covered to reject your five-cent refund should you have started the timing back at the beginning of this long, very smart, very engaging, very getting legally protected, very informative, very coherent paragraph.

This makes the guide very sad and depressed to even have to mention, but as a guide, it feels it must.

Also, do not start your timers yet. If you have started your timers, set them back to zero. This does not count in the thirty-second timing for the five-cent refund.

So back to the thing that makes this guide sad and depressed to have to mention, or is forced to mention. Just because this guide makes a little joke about Shakespeare does not mean it does not enjoy Shakespeare's works very much.

Also, a note on the five-cent refund. If your time in reading this thirty-second guide to Shakespeare's plays does exceed thirty seconds and you do decide to rip the page out in anger and mail the page in for your five-cent refund, remember that it could take up to twenty years to process the refund, as we have a tedious procedure to adhere to and many people working at the refund headquarters. Here's a tiny example of what the process is like just to receive the mail (receiving it, meaning, just getting the mail inside the Five-cent Refund Headquarters):

First, a lady goes out to the mailbox. That's it. She just goes out to the mailbox to make sure the mailbox is still there.

Second, an intern boy/girl goes out to the mailbox to see if there is mail. If there is not mail, then another one comes out to check three hours later, and if he/she doesn't see mail in the mailbox, then no one checks until the next day.

If the intern boy/girl discovers that there is, in fact, mail in the mailbox (which usually consists of 90% five-cent refund requests and 10 percent death threats), then he/she goes back inside to the five-cent refund headquarters and records it in the log. A lady, once she gets off her lunch break, which could be a week later, processes the log and sends in a request for one of the mail agents to grab the mail out the mailbox. Once the man who receives the mail agent request gets off his lunch break, a lawyer comes in to decide who is best suited, or who rightly and justly deserves, to go on a mail run for this particular turn (usually by this time, the mailbox is filled to the brim with two weeks' worth of mail).

Then, finally, the chosen mail agent (chosen by the justly and rightly lawyer) goes out to the mailbox to grab all the mail, only to find out that the mailbox is empty because the mail carrier had thought all mail was sent to the wrong address, as the mailbox had been filled for two weeks straight. (This only occurs 99% of the time, so maybe you'll get lucky and be part of the 1%, although, I hate myself for saying that, because I just made up that 1% to make myself sound like a better person. It really occurs 100% of the time.) The mail agent is usually unaware of this, and so he/she usually files a report against the intern boy/girl for falsifying that there was, in fact, mail in the mailbox. Then they usually fire the intern boy/girl, and the intern boy/girl usually responds by saying, "Why would you fire, basically, a volunteer? I don't even get paid you morons." (The others who don't respond this way could really care less and, in fact, seem very happy and proud of the fact that they were fired from the five-cent refund headquarters.)

Once the mail agent's boss finds out the free working intern was wrongly fired by the justly and rightly lawyer's investigation (which usually happens 99% of the time), and that, in fact, the mail carrier had stamped all mail, "Return to sender. Wrong address," then a request is put in to the department that deals with the postal service company to get all mail back, as the address was not wrong.

Meanwhile, as all of that is going on, more mail is coming in, and a new intern boy/girl, who is unknowingly soon to be fired, is logging in a request to have a mail agent come pick up the new mail out of the mailbox. And all of that is just to receive the mail, so now you can see that a twenty-20 year waiting period for your five-cent refund check is no ridiculous estimation.

*Also, we at the refund headquarters hope this is not too late. It is recommended that you not break your e-reading devices in anger since you could not rip the pages out and send them in to us. We honestly don't care if you have already broken them, because now, by stating this, we are legally protected, and we have one of the best lawyers.

START TIMERS NOW

STOP TIMERS. WAIT! The guide must legally throw one last thing in in very small print now: The guide will not accept five-cent refunds for people who purposely read slowly when the timers start. We have a team at headquarters that investigates such matters rightly and justly. Also, no five-cent refund can be issued via e-readers. We have nothing against such devices or technology. In fact, we like them very much. It would just be nearly impossible, and we do not want you to break your e-reader and send them in to us.

START TIMERS NOW.

- Characters introduced.

- Characters wronged, other characters are the one's doing the wrong, whether consciously or not. One or two characters do all the deceiving.

- Some wrongly accused characters go in disguise.

- It's such a shame to be human.

- Some really profound lines.

- Deceiving characters' plans are thickened, and characters that were wronged are wronged even more.

- Some really more deep and profound lines.

- Characters in disguise are revealed.

- Wrong people die, usually the best-hearted people. People die or revenge is consummated, usually resulting in people dying (unless a comedy).

- Really, really, really, really, really profound lines.

- Being human is a tragedy...or really funny.

STOP TIMERS. NO CHEATING. PUT THEM DOWN. RIP PAGE OUT IF NECESSARY.

A NONFICTION STORY BELIEVE ... AND IT JUST MAY COME TRUE

By

Greg Hawkins L.P. (Or Just A Guy Who Has An Obsession With Having A Title At
The End Of His Name)

It was a cold spring morning,
And all across the high school people were saying, "Another morning.
I wonder what bullshit I'm going to have to ignore today."
And in the corner of the school stood the locker rooms,
And in the boys' locker room stood a group of boys getting ready for PE.

The boys got together,
And these 14 year-old boys had hit puberty quite soon,
And all the boys were saying, "Look at my pubes."
"Oh yeah, look at my pubes."
Then way off in his own corner, little 14 year-old Greg Hawkins stood,
And he knew he had no pubes.

Then the boys noticed little 14 year-old Greg over to the side, and they screamed,
"Hey fag, why don't you show us your pubes? Everyone else has 'em. I'll bet you
don't got 'em, 'cause you're a fag, and fags don't have pubes."
And little Greg said, "Fag? Huh? Didn't you guys all just show each other your

penises for fun, and I'm the homosexual?"
This made the boys really mad
And so they huffed and puffed, and said, "Pull your pants down,"
And so little Greg had no choice,
And his pubeless groin was revealed.
And all the anti-homosexual, huffing and puffing hyenas, who had
just all showed their penises to each other, had a big laugh all together.

And so at the end of that day little Greg ran home, as he wasn't that much of a baby
as to run home immediately after the anti-homosexual hyenas laughter.
And when little Greg got home, he went into the bathroom,
pulled his pants down,
looked at his clean, babyish groin,
And little Greg began to pray.
Little Greg prayed to God,
And little Greg's prayer went like this,
"Oh God, if you give me pubes, I'll believe in you.
Oh God, just give me pubes,
and if you do, I'll do anything for you."

And so 1 year later,
Around puberty time for little Greg,
he saw one little lone ranger pube sitting right above his wee-wee area,
And little Greg said,
"Oh God, thank you.
It's a start, I know, but just a little more would be good."

And so, 1 year later, the now 16 year-old little Greg pulled his pants
down one morning very quickly,
As he had eaten fast food the night before (and for the slow person,
a courtesy: he had diarrhea), and little Greg noticed,
while giving birth out of his ass, that he had a full set of pubes,
Curly and everything.

And little Greg said, "Oh God, thank you. Thank you so much. It took you a couple years, but thank you."

And so this was the day little Greg believed in God,
And little Greg turned out to be a very hairy Greg man…at least until he met a very vain and very superficial girl at a club and she demanded Big Greg shave all his hairy hair.
But that, my friends, is for another horrifying and very itchy story.

3

"He goes from the first day to March in a matter of ten pages. Cary Smith is poop. What about October, November, December, etc, etc?"

—Brad Cruise

"Well, nothing really happened during those months."

—Cary Smith

Chapter 1

DISCLAIMER: I REPEAT, THERE IS NO ONE LISTENING. Year 3 of my term is beginning, and at this point, I'm feeling like a Zoo™ animal that has lost all ambition for the future and realizes that being free will never be and that the purpose of my life was to entertain kids so parents didn't have to do any parenting for a little bit.

Once again I was making my way to the first day of school, but in year 3 of a 4-year sentence, the first day felt like day 63. (You already said it was the beginning of school again. Repetitive. Is it necessary to state that again? Education.)

People said the third year of my sentence was going to be easier on my mind, I mean, I would have my own car, therefore, allowing me to be free of my sister being a bitch to my mom (my mom a bitch to my sister) and the three friends who made me hate school and gave me the feeling that I was in Purgatory.™

I put on my Reebok Pumps™, which had been there all the way through the sentence with me, ate some sugar cereal (the MAL had threatened to fear my sugar cereal, and it was soon to be sugarless and taste like paper because parents let their kids be obese), and made my way to the meditation that would be my car.

As I made my way out the door, it was then that I saw 4 mirrors, lip gloss, and every single fashion accessory in last week's issue of *Not This Week's In Fashion Magazine*™.

My first reaction was to scream violently, "Godammitttttttt," then a melancholia swept in and overtook my body, and finally I just began to laugh hysterically as the first two reactions mixed and crossed insanity within me.

I made my way toward the car and asked my sister what she was doing in my car. She responded, saying, "Oh, Mom said you have to carpool for her, and she'll pay for your gas and insurance." It was understandable why my mom wanted to rid her day (which was already tough enough) of my sister, but this newly found duty of mine was not worth a lifetime supply of sugar cereal (Why did the MAL want to take away the good things in life? MAL.), let alone gas and insurance.

I really had no choice in the situation, as it was my mom, so I made my way to year three of my four-year sentence, which was now seemingly like my deep, deep nightmare in which I was not riding bitch anymore but playing the role of chauffeur.

"Gawd...this summer...was, like, soo awesome. Shelia you, like, were soo lucky that hot banker guy hit on you," said my sister.

"Yeahhhh...I know...he was soo hot. I wish I would have got his name," said Shelia.

"Oh, like it matters. He was so hot," said one of the other girls.

An uproarious laughter came upon my car after those words were uttered, and the Zombie™, self-conscious (Dogma) laughter made me want to drive the car straight into the tree, and if I were to survive the crash, I would climb the tree and make my home atop of it for the rest of my life (Hippie talk, Hippie Dogma).

At this point, the 2 reactions (anger and melancholia, as you can tell) were swimming around in my body, and I said to Sheila, "So, Shelia, what week was the banker?"

"Uh," responded Shelia.

At this point, the girls got their cell phones out, and two of them started talking at the same time, while the two others were typing words into their phones (and I wishing I had written this all in text lingo so they could understand it). It was at this moment when I told myself that this would be the first and only day

I would do this. I didn't need a car if these 4 were my repercussions. I knew Cyrus had a car, which was nicer than mine anyways, and that he'd give me rides every day, so I told my mom I wasn't doing the perilous deed.

"Then you're going to have to pay all the expenses and work every day at the restaurant after school," said my mom.

"No, I'm not, because I don't even want the car, because having it only makes the day worse. I hate working at that hellhole restaurant, and I can't take driving with Martians (I'd hate to give Martians such a bad name, not ever meeting one and everything, so let me correct that)...The Real Zombies any longer."

After this conversation with my mom I confirmed with Cyrus that he'd give me rides, and I went to work and said, "I'm done for good. Thanks for the opportunity. It's been a joy, and have a nice life."

The only problem with getting rides from Cyrus every day was that it meant I had to go to his house after school, at least until basketball season, but frying my mind in excess was better than losing my mind—I mean at least it was a gradual process instead of an instantaneous one.

At school, Zach had made his glorious return and ambitious go at sophomore year. As I listened to Zach feed us his bullshit, I began to wonder if this guy was just afraid to leave Independence. I wondered if he really believed that people believed his horseshit stories or if he was just a dumb shit with really good textbook answers for insane, white, male Spanish teachers. (I've got a fascination with shit. See^ bullshit, horseshit, dumb shit^. Those of you who were confused about me before, there you go. Education.)

Zach was talking about how he and his friends were doing Ecstasy™ at some festival, and they miraculously found 2 gorgeous girls, who happened to be sisters, to make out with. Zach kept talking because he loved to hear his echo as he spoke, and I began to think that this guy was no longer entertaining, not even for the 2 months I knew he would be here. Once you become a veteran in anything, people like Zach were just sad and made the day seem much, much longer.

I made my way to my last class of the day, and I noticed on my schedule it said, "English: O'Hara." The instructor was well known, mainly because she actually made you do some type of work, or so they said. Mainly she wasn't like 98% of the other instructors, where you could get by with never reading anything, failing every test, and still somehow come out with a C. (I'd hate to ruin the secret, sorry.)

O'Hara was not that kind of teacher, and everyone hated her, especially because she not only made you read actual words, she mainly lectured and had class discussions, which usually meant her speaking and the class mindlessly listening.

I wasn't worried about her class, though, because I figured what's one class of actual semi-work going to hurt? I had gotten by to this point with doing absolutely nothing at all and earning straight Cs down my transcript. And I figured if the teacher was going to make me do some work, I might as well earn a B, but then I thought that I didn't want to break the successive Cs that I had worked soo hard to get on my transcript, so I thought I'd do very little work, instead of no work, and earn a C. (Of course I wouldn't be able to use these run-on sentences in O'Hara's class, 'cause then I'd see "run-on, run-on" all over my paper, and I probably would not get a C, but when I'm on a roll, I just wanna keep running on some more, with some more, commas. Education.)

Chapter 2

When I entered O'Hara's class my first impression of O'Hara was that she was one hefty woman. Cyrus was in my class, so I sat next to him, and O'Hara began talking.

"There are four general rules in my class:

"1. No calling me fat.

"2. No using the phrase, "Well, it's always been done that way."

"3. No saying, "It's all been done before, so what's the point?"

"4. No mentioning fast food, because then I'll become hungry, and when I'm hungry, I'm moody.

"Violations of any of these two rules will result in writing the word fat one thousand times or writing the phrase, "People who want tradition destroyed are only people who are recreating that tradition in their name and want it to be destroyed to make it seem like they're actually doing something different, and so no one will know they're really a tyrant and stupid. Tradition should be respected and remembered, but we should not always do what has been done before, as then we only re-create and try to fix history, and the times then become devoid of any life whatsoever. Sometimes, though, a better value comes along, and tradition needs to be pushed aside but not devoured, as death gives rise to birth," five hundred times, depending on your violation.

"Failure to conform to these rules will result in a referral and your grade will be docked, and as I'm sure you've heard, getting your grade docked in my class is a serious consequence, because unlike the other teachers, I do not give out extra credit of any kind that allows you to earn all your missed points back. This classroom is not a Democracy™, it is a Dictatorship™."

Cyrus yelled something incomprehensible in a German™ (poor Germans just have a bad history with the whole Nazi thing. It's really hard to forget about it) accent and then gave the salute that the Nazis™ gave to Hitler™ during World War II™. (Hitler would've been a trademark moneymaking machine if he didn't blow his brains out, and I have a feeling he would've sued to get complete control of the Hitler trademark.)

O'Hara gave the class the book *Nectar in a Sieve* and told us to read the first hundred pages by next week.

This was a surprise, both to be given a book on the first day and to be given an assignment on the first day, since assignments generally weren't seen until about week 3, because that's what the teacher handbook and teacher-preparation program said (Education). Obviously O'Hara did not have a handbook or completely ignored it.

O'Hara and her overbearing, fat-cat ways didn't intimidate me. I just thought that, in my third year at this joint, I got O'Hara, and that was the luck of the draw, and all that was necessary was a little work, at least in order to keep the successive Cs alive.

As I sat in class and listened to O'Hara talk about her past and how America™ was a country built to live in discordance with nature while most of the other countries she had been to were built in accordance with nature, I happened to look over at Cyrus, and he did not look too happy to be in O'Hara's class.

Cyrus generally did not like teachers, whom he felt were mostly scared, college graduates afraid to work a shitty job for a bit because they were too good for it and because they had the inclination to become teachers when they weren't even ready to teach, and the other, older teachers were often just people who forgot that they once were in our position. As Cyrus always said, "The teachers who do remember that they were once in our situation, yet still are Douches,™ were those kids in class that always ruin the curve because they spend all their time kissing ass and studying the nothingness and end up the dumbest people of all. Those damn lifeless, scared robots."

"I HATE STUPID PEOPLE WHO ARE NOT WITH US RIGHT NOW AS THEY READ THIS SIGN."

This was a sign that O'Hara had plastered on the top of her wall right above her head. The sign was very transparent, considering it took up half the wall behind O'Hara (I would have to write "fat" 100 times for that).

O'Hara was still rambling on about America's™ stupidity to think that nature would elude them and about how all humans have in their power was to put up barriers, but when nature took its natural course, nothing could barricade it. After O'Hara had said that, some kid in the left corner said jokingly, "What if we create a dome inside a dome, where everything would be synthetic, yet it would consist of all the natural elements and gases that humans need to live? Then when nature takes its course, it wouldn't matter because we'd be inside our dome within a dome."

I saw the look on O'Hara's face when this kid was speaking, and it looked as if she wanted to scream, and when the kid was done speaking, O'Hara aimlessly stared at the kid for a good minute and said, also jokingly, "I hate stupid people."

I liked that kid.

When O'Hara said to the kid, "I hate stupid people," something in Cyrus seemed to jolt and turn on, because he was now attentively listening, which was something Cyrus rarely did, unless it was a recorded playback of him talking. (I think what Cyrus hated most about teachers was that the majority never brought or understood dark humor in the classroom, proving to himself that most were scared, uptight Douches afraid to do other things until they were actually ready to teach. Education.)

O'Hara went on speaking, and it seemed like this was going to be what the class was all about: O'Hara speaking, people playing along by responding, and O'Hara saying, "Thanks for playing."

Through the whole class, Cyrus sat straight up and attentive, so either he was meditating or he was listening to what O'Hara had to say. He probably couldn't believe that this rare of a moment was actually happening, where a teacher was real, smart, and had her own thoughts and knowledge, which gave her something to say, other than what a teacher handbook had said, and that this teacher seemed to care less what the state mandates were. (Of course those handbook writers were soo good and were soo concise and wrote in short, simple sentences. Minus 15 points, short and simple. Like Hemingway™. Education.)

Apparently this was the case with Cyrus, because as O'Hara was talking about so-called bad words and how they're just a means for stupid people to make up for their lack of vocabulary and make themselves feel smart and good about themselves, Cyrus jumped in the discussion, which I had never seen him do. Generally he just sat back and never said anything. Usually he daydreamed and would rag on the teacher at lunch, but for some reason only known to Cyrus, he partook in this discussion.

"Who makes and claims these bullshit words to be bad? Pompous intellectuals like you? As of right now I'm claiming a couple of words you used just a minute ago as bad: bon ton and imbroglio.

"Anyone who uses these two words in conversation or in a lecture are pompous, self-indulgent people, saying, 'Look at me. I'm soo well read, and now I can actually use words like imbroglio and bon ton because I don't want to feel like my reading with those words in the text was for nothing.' So anyone who uses these words is the bad kind of intellectual, so, therefore, I'm claiming these words as bad. So now fuck, shit, bitch, ass, bon ton, and imbroglio are bad," said Cyrus.

"You see my point exactly. Thank you, Mr. Jenkins, for providing a perfect example to go along with my statement," said O'Hara.

"Thank you for proving my point that you are a self-righteous, grandiloquent—you like that word?—Nazi™," said Cyrus.

The bell had rang, and I knew if it hadn't, Cyrus would've argued with her for the rest of the day, and he'd probably come out the victor because he seemed to have a remark for anything anyone said (and because even if he had lost, he would still tell himself he had won).

As Cyrus and I were leaving class, O'Hara asked Cyrus to stay after class, and Cyrus just smiled and kept on walking. For O'Hara to get Cyrus to stay for a let's-talk-about-it-after-class-tea party, she would have had to get an army of men to hold Cyrus down and sedate him, because even if the men held him down, he would find a way to not listen, so an ambush and sedation would be O'Hara's only answer. What was funny about the conversing between Cyrus and O'Hara was not the actual conversation, it was the fact that 95% of the class had no idea what was going on or what was being said, and generally could care less. (Of course they'd pass the test. Education.)

At lunch Cyrus did not talk about O'Hara and what had happened. Cyrus had nothing to say. Maybe it was the fact that he had participated in class, so he had to continue his un-Cyrus likeness and not comment about O'Hara. All he said to me as the lunch period was expiring was, "I can't believe we have a teacher that can actually teach and talk about relevant things without notes."

Chapter 3

The next week in class O'Hara gave us our test on the 100 pages she had assigned, and I prepared myself with just enough effort and reading to get myself a C.

O'Hara was one for embarrassing people, and after the test, which was graded by the class because trying to cheat in her class was nearly impossible, O'Hara would look through the tests and say, "Helen, maybe next time. Smith scores in the middle. Francis, big thumbs down. Jenkins, very nice."

"Jenkins, very nice." These words had meant that Cyrus actually gave his full effort and did very well on the test. It wasn't that I was jealous, it was that I knew Cyrus, and Cyrus was worse than me in terms of actually doing work. Something had happened to Cyrus. It was as if O'Hara had planned it. O'Hara had got to him on a level that I and everyone who knew Cyrus felt was level 13, and the elevator only went to level 12.

I didn't mention anything to Cyrus or ask him how the book was so far, because I knew he didn't want to talk about it, and apparently whatever O'Hara sedated him with got to him and was making him, at least for 50 minutes of the day, seem as if it were the first time I was meeting him. (Yeah, we got it. It got to him. Something was changing. You said that twice in the paragraph. Be more like Hemingway.™ Repetitive. Minus 15 points. Education.)

That day in class, O'Hara's assignment, in addition to reading the next 75 pages of *Nectar in a Sieve*, was to write a poem about anything. She said it was to be a poem of free, creative flow and that there were no rules. She said she just wanted to use it as the first stepping stone in what would hopefully enable us students to reach the pinnacle as progress is made throughout the year. (I think she was big on negativity helping fuel progress, as most poems were soo dull they only made one negative.)

As always I wasn't going to give much effort, and quite frankly, I would consciously (Dogma) make all my writing the same and mundane the entire year so O'Hara would think I was a dummy that had made absolutely no progress, but still good enough from beginning to end to earn a C.

The class day had arrived when the poem assignment was due, and not being a veteran of O'Hara's class yet, I had failed to even think that she would read them aloud, and that was exactly what she did. (Luckily for her she didn't have the writers read them 'cause I was ready to give a jolly (again, I read a lot of British books) performance. **Correction**: how can you put one of these ( ) inside one of these ( )? Education.)

The first poem she read was absolutely horrible, and it was obvious who had written it, because there was only one kid in the class who thought he could play the guitar better than Jimi Hendrix™.

> *Jimi and me riding down the street*
> *Battling for release*
> *I had release*
> *of my guitar skills that is*
> *but Jimi was intimidated*
> *so his skills weren't released.*

(The kid in my class might have been able to play the guitar well, but someone at that moment desperately needed to tell that kid that Hendrix™ could write a song with the best of them, and that's exactly what O'Hara did say to him.)

I knew when she got to mine, and I tried not to smile and giggle (I was soo young and soo silly, so please excuse me) as she read it:

4 hours a day
x 7

_____

=28 hours a week
+ an extra 5, give or take

_____

=33 hours a week of television
168 hours in a week
-6 hours of sleep a day because school starts too early
-42 hours of sleep a week

_____

=120 hours of consciousness (Dogma) a week
-33 hours of TV

_____

=87 hours a week doing what?
Eureka! I have found the answer.
This is the equation,
get out of my way you fools.

Luckily O'Hara did not read the names of authorship, so no one knew who had written that. The only obvious authors were kids, such as the kid who thought he was better than Hendrix,™ or the kid who wrote about being in the NBA™ (even though he was 5'5, white, and couldn't shoot), or the girl who wrote about being a movie star, and Cyrus. It was as if Cyrus had known where his poem was in O'Hara's stack. Before O'Hara said one word, Cyrus got up and walked out of the classroom. O'Hara read on:

If you punch him in the face
he will not be scared and weak any longer,
as you always say he is.
And you better watch out,
'cause you're about to find out
that you're, in fact, the weakest of them all,
and why he was so damn gentle before…
but still you never see,
and this is why I must go.

My first reaction was to run after Cyrus, because, as she read those words, I felt a deep sting, and my body became weak because I thought Cyrus had just written a suicide note (I didn't understand poetry very well. Who does, really?), and hopefully it wasn't too late ('cause the note wasn't very good). A few minutes after Cyrus had left the room, O'Hara was reading another poem:

Abercrombie™ for me.

Abercrombie™ for you.

If you don't wear Abercrombie™

Then I don't like you.

During the middle of this torturous poem, Cyrus had walked in and sat back down at his desk. "Where the hell did you go?" I asked.

"I just went to the bathroom," said Cyrus.

"What the hell are you doing walking out after writing a poem like that?"

"What'd you mean? O'Hara already read my poem about Hendrix™. Do you really think I would turn something good in?" asked Cyrus.

"Yeah, you might. How do I know? You seem to take an interest in this class," I said.

"Well, O'Hara already read my poem, and I just went to the bathroom, OK, Mom?"

I left it at that because I knew Cyrus was a stubborn bastard, so there was no point in continuing with the conversation, and I also knew Cyrus was lying about the poem, but I also knew that he was never going to tell me since he had never lied up to this point (Want to know what I also knew some more? Education.), as Cyrus always said, "Lies are what make people dumb and make people crazy. If everyone told the truth, then things could be talked about, and people wouldn't feel alone. The truth liberates, and lies exterminate, and there is no such thing as a good lie, a lie for the betterment of things." I thought Cyrus was full of shit when he said that. (I think if I followed his philosophy of truth, someone would've shot me a long time ago.)

I knew if he was lying to me for the first time, then he was never going to tell me, and so I left it at that. I wanted to tell Cyrus that I understood and it didn't bother me. (Of course things like that never really happen. Sorry, I just wanted to say hello to all the real realists really reading this right now, really, seriously, I wanted to tell him that, but we know it never could've happened.)

O'Hara had to have put Cyrus on some sort of drugs, because that was the first time I had ever truly felt that Cyrus was deliberately lying to me, and it kind of sucked, especially when a person is soo honest until a certain point. It makes you really appreciate true honesty.

The whole rest of the day, Cyrus did not speak very much. On the ride to his house after school, he just turned the music on louder, and when we got to his house, he immediately went to his room and said he was going to take a nap.

I went home that night and read the entire book that O'Hara had assigned to see if maybe there was something soo profound in it that had transformed Cyrus. The book was certainly profound, but nothing that Cyrus wasn't already aware of or that would transform him. O'Hara had triggered something in Cyrus that was lying in the abyss and somehow miraculously made its way back to land (as if it were dragged back, with Cyrus pulling for it to stay put), and it was definitely something I had no idea about and was way beyond me.

Chapter 4

Like any mundane and usual morning, I awoke to no delight, got out of bed reluctantly, thought to myself, "School starts way too goddamn early," put clothes on, laced my Pumps, pumped my Pumps, and headed down for some soon-to-be sugarless cereal. (I figured since the MAL was soo annoying and generally got what they wanted, I'd better get ahead and start eating paper from now on...to get used to my future breakfast.)

As usual, I waited for Cyrus, who was generally late. It was a typical fall morning, foggy, little chilly, but with the feel that the day would soon heat up. (As I wrote that, I just could not understand why people liked to write like that. It was soo bad and dull to me, but that writing was usually found in the mandated reading, and sometimes it just pops out of nowhere in me and out of my fingertips. So I apologize. Education.)

I sat at the table since it was too cold outside, and suddenly I saw Cyrus running to my door, and he banged the door as violently as his nature would allow. I let Cyrus in, and I knew something was weird because Cyrus never came to my door. He always just waited outside my house and honked his horn relentlessly. He would even honk his horn as I was opening the car door and was beginning to sit down.

"Turn on the TV. New York City™ was attacked," said Cyrus.

I immediately turned on the television, and just as I turned it on, the headline on the news read, "Pentagon™ just attacked. A plane crashes into Pentagon™. America™ is under attack."

"No goddamn way are we going to school when our country is being attacked. You know goddamn well that those morons at the school will censor us from the news and pretend as if the day were a normal one," said Cyrus.

"Yeah, I know, but we won't be able to stay here and watch it because my mom will become tomato faced if we're here when she leaves for work in an hour. We can stay here until then, but after that we'll have to go to your place," I said.

"That'll be fine. My parents should be gone by then, and even if they aren't, we'll just have to drive around until they leave. This is some frightening stuff. I wasn't sure if I should come over here or not because I couldn't take my eyes off the TV. This could be it, you know. We could start nuking whoever did this, because we're sure to retaliate, no question about that. And now more attacks are happening. When I had left my house the news just said that the World Trade Center™ had been attacked. Both towers were struck by planes, and they had footage of the second plane because it hit the second tower about thirty minutes after the first," Cyrus said.

As Cyrus was speaking I had an eerie feeling throughout my body that simply could not be described. (Also, I was feeling a little lazy and didn't want to write anything extra, like describing that feeling.)

I was at a loss for words, and the news was reporting that some fifty thousand people were estimated to be dead (but to me, the news generally had a Douchey, bad Hollywood™ action-movie quality to their estimates). The feeling I had in my body was not a vindictive feeling, it was not a feeling of indignation. The feeling I had while watching the news was a feeling I got when Cyrus and I were freshman (I lied, I just decided to describe the feeling anyways^).

We had ventured to the park because Cyrus wanted to play a pickup basketball game with some guys from our school (this is the story of when we were freshmen. Don't worry, you're not dumb if you weren't following. I would've had trouble too, plus sometimes my writing isn't enough like Hemingway's), who had earlier that day made a wager to Cyrus that he could not refuse (again, I've seen a lot of things on a screen).

After Cyrus had won his money, he played a couple more games, and on the last game, out of nowhere, this enormous, red-haired man with no shirt on picked up another man and literally body slammed the man (and it wasn't like American wrestling on TV, this guy really did body slam the other guy). The other man stood no chance because the red-haired man attacked abruptly and out of nowhere, and he was far stronger naturally. As the other man attempted to get up, the red-haired man threw a multitude of vicious punches, and blood went flailing every which way. The red-haired man and his friends then fled the scene and left the man lying there. Cyrus and I got the hell out of that park immediately after and never returned. To this day I have no idea why the red-haired man became so vicious and suddenly attacked that man, and the feeling I got watching that incident up close and personal was a feeling I thought could never be felt again, until September 11, 2001™. (**Special Guest Corrector**: "That analogy to the devastation of September 11th was an insult to America™. Horrible. No one even died in your analogy, and it was far too long." —Brad Cruise. Minus 15 points. Education.)

"We better get out of here, because I'm certainly not in the mood to deal with my mom," I said.

"Yeah, let's go right after they confirm where this other plane crashed," said Cyrus.

As we sat there on my couch, neither of us said a word. 4 eyes were stuck to the TV, as I'm sure was the rest of the country, except in places were fascists and censorship reined, such as Independence High (or where Conspiracy Theorists™ were around). A few minutes went by, and some official came on the news and talked about a fourth plane crashing in a field outside Pennsylvania and that there was believed to be no survivors.

"All right, let's get out of here. I can't fucking believe this is happening. Do you have that same, indescribable feeling as the day at the park when that guy started attacking that other guy out of nowhere, but as if that feeling has just taken over your body and is a million times stronger than at the park?" Cyrus asked.

"That's exactly what I feel. I don't know what to feel. I think the feeling is because I can't stop imagining those people in the plane, those people in the tower, those people in the Pentagon™, those people jumping out of the towers, those people running from the debris, and those who are running into the chaos as everyone else runs out." (Cary Smith, the Patriot, said.)

As we approached Cyrus's house, we noticed that his father's car was still in the driveway, so we drove around for a good 20 minutes, speaking no words, just listening to the radio of the shit that was going on.

There was going to be no argument from me about ditching school, because I knew if we had gone, another Chris PE situation would have ensued. I knew that, once again at school, the faculty was going on as if the day were a normal one, purposely ignoring and evading things because they were told to do so (well, most of them. Education).

Cyrus and me **(Correction**: Cyrus and I. Right when I was getting good at that I-and-me thing too, I mess up. Education) sat there for the rest of the day, and when morons actually came to Cyrus's house to play video games, Cyrus just gave them a blank stare and slammed the door.

The estimates were going down on the number of deaths (to a non-crappy Hollywood™ action estimate), which was a relief. More footage of the attacks was shown, and it was very hard to watch. Sometimes the news would show the second plane crashing into the tower multiple times, and it was times like those that I had to take a break from watching because it was too chilling. (Plus, the reporter had such a fake look on his face and seemed soo excited to be getting such a big opportunity at such a big event and his career would skyrocket from there on out that I felt I was going insane.)

The next day at school was a very strange one, and of course, morons, like some guys (not all) on the football team, which hadn't won a game since I had been at Independence High, looked suspiciously at anyone even closely resembling someone of Middle Eastern descent, when 90% of them weren't even from the Middle East™ (they were now going to fight the battle one mindless action after another).

Now that the news (broadcasting their non-bias news) was reporting that Osama Bin Laden™ and the Al-Qaeda Terrorist Organization™ was highly suspected of being responsible for the attacks, people dumbly gave people dirty looks and automatically suspected someone remotely looking like the pictures seen on TV of being the enemy. (But they'd pass the test, and probably, eventually, make a decent amount of money. Education.)

DISCLAIMER: I REPEAT, THERE IS NO ONE LISTENING. It was very scary to me that, when something of this nature occurred, people automatically shunned and became vigilantes for anyone who looked like the Terrorist™ photos the news was showing (seemed the news was doing a bit of terrorizing of their own). To me this was exactly what the people who made these attacks wanted. They wanted the country to become discombobulated (O'Hara would have marked me down for using this word, saying that I used my human computer's thesaurus knowledge since my work was showing no improvement above a C, which meant that I had probably cheated if I was using a word like discombobulated, especially with correct spelling, and in the right context) and lose control, and for some reason people lose consciousness (Dogma) and forget a small group of tyrants does not equate to the rest. (But of course, what did I know? I wasn't passing the tests (but I still got Cs) or planning to pass more tests after Independence. Education.)

After school I waited for Cyrus to get out of his basketball meeting, and as they were coming out, Cyrus punched one of the players in the face and just started wailing on this kid. Eventually the rest of the team got Cyrus off the kid, and when they did, he made his way to his car, and I quickly ran over and jumped in the car as he took off. Cyrus was breathing heavily, and it was the most agitated I had seen Cyrus since the first day I saw him come out of Spanish class with Señor McDonald in year 2.

"What the hell happened back there?" I asked.

"Let me catch my breath…That fucking Douche Bag was talking about the attacks, and you know what he said, he said, 'I'm not upset about the attacks. It doesn't affect me. I didn't know those people, and I don't live on the East Coast™. So I don't understand why I should feel affected about what happens over there.'"

"Who was it that said that?"

"That Douche Bag Luis."

"Which one is that?"

"He's the Metro Boy™ (my favorite superhero of all time) who shaves his whole body and talks about his shaved penis all the time and is always asking guys why they don't have tans or why they're wearing this or that clothing.

He's a real fucking moron. After he said that, I said to him, 'Yeah, what about the people who died? What about the people there right now, searching through the debris for survivors, and some of them were initially searching for survivors and are now being searched for themselves? And some of those people flew there from the West Coast™ to volunteer to help. Those people are humans, people like you and me. Just because we're on opposite coastlines doesn't mean shit. Those people were innocent, trying to get through the day, people like you, and, well, not you, but most everyone else' (Cyrus Hippie talk, Cyrus Hippie Dogma). 'Just like innocent people are unjustly bombed in the Middle East™ by us. Now the so-called leaders of both sides go 'round and 'round in their never-ending circle. I'll bet you don't think about that. You're probably thinking about if tonight's the night you need to shave your balls or if tomorrow is the night.' After I said those words, I don't know what came over me. I think it was the fact that he gave a Vampire™ smirk, and I lost control and could not take the stupidity of this guy anymore, so I just punched him, and it felt really fucking good, so I punched him again, and next thing I know, here I am driving with you."

"Well, I have to say, he got what was coming to him." (Thanks Mom, you were always right).

"Yeah, he sure fucking did, that D-Bag."

"I don't know how the hell you can stand being around those guys for as long as you have."

"You know I don't want to be on that team. I don't even like playing the game with those guys. Everyone thinks they're going to make it big, be a McDonald's All-American, because they're dumb-ass parents have filled their heads with self-glory, so every time they get the ball, they shoot no matter what. Two people on them, they shoot. We'd actually be pretty damn good if everyone wasn't soo goddamn stupid and filled with American madness, and played together. Then we might actually win a lot of games, but that won't happen with them. They're all-stars who shoot away, and when you try and tell them we'd go far as a collective group and that none of us are good enough to be All-Americans™ but are good enough to make each other good and have a really good team, it goes straight into their stupid earwax and gets stuck in it, which has stupidly, from a gradual buildup, blocked their hearing. I think everyone who gets into the game averages ten shots a game and makes one if they're lucky. But, hey, to them that one will take them to the top of the big leagues. You know I'm only on that team because if I wasn't, my parents would give me a bunch of shit, or even worse, they'd subtly be upset and never talk to me about it. So either way I'm going to have to deal with bullshit."

"Yeah, that sucks. I'm glad I'm not athletic and never was and that my parents realized that when I was young, and accepted it. It's funny, though, when you're not athletic at our age, your parents seem to give off a vibe as if you're doomed for the rest of your life because you're not good at running around with a ball and trying to put it somewhere or get somewhere with it."

"Well, of course, because they probably think that if you're not on a team now you never will be. They figure that it's good experience for when you're to work a job in some hellish place that you hate, but you have experience in teamwork, so you're well suited for the corporate world. I'll tell you what I'm going to do. I just got this really good fucking idea. Every time we play a team that has a black player, the whole team gets freaked out and frightened, as if we had already lost the game. So what I'm going to do is get Rich to try out for the team, and if he doesn't make it, I'll have the whole team nag Miles about it, and he'll have to put him on the team. That way, when we play all-white teams, they'll be scared before the game even starts. Maybe we'll get a big enough lead in the beginning to actually win a game."

"Yeah, that would be pretty damn funny, but you'll have to get Miles to start Rich for that. That would be damn funny, though, especially with Rich, because he's less athletic than me, and that's saying a lot. Rich would definitely be down for it. I think he was the only one besides me that talked to Gail when he was here. Also, you better make sure he doesn't warm up. Just have him stretch, 'cause if you make him shoot a basket, his cover will be blown."

"Well, I'm sure he'll be down for it, but I have no idea what his association with Gail has to do with it. You idiot."

"Ah. It's a complicated thing, and I would really rather you just call me an idiot than explain the whole thing to you."

"Fine with me."

Rich was another one out of 8 (so I guess there was more than 1, so there was more like 3 out of about 20. I apologize for the error. Education), except he wasn't as extreme as Gail. Rich was one funny bastard, and he really could care less about all the stupid people at Independence that were either scared of

127

him or thought that he would be fun and exciting just like some of the people they admired on TV.

Rich was always making fun of these people. He would not hold anything back, and what made him funnier than ever, and made him even more depressed, was that people thought he was just being Rich and thought he was soo entertaining, but they essentially really didn't hear a single word of what Rich was saying.

Most would never really laugh at what he said, they'd just kind of smirk and grin, give out a "pssh" sound, and shake their head while smirking, basically the way a Dead Douche Bag would laugh, aka The Real Zombies™, who really could never genuinely laugh since they had lost all sense of humor in their vainglory of making sure everyone at Independence knew them.

Rich sure could go off for a whole lunch period on all the idiots that roamed around the halls, and what he said was amazing. Rich would often talk about how he felt the most racist people were the people who believed every black person was a creature of God. Rich always said very humorously, "Man, there are bad black people, just as there are bad people everywhere. It doesn't make a goddamn difference what color you are. Few are thoughtful and genuinely try to be just, and most are mindless assholes who make one sympathize with the teenage European Existentialists™, which is a pretty damn hard thing to do. Those stupid assholes saying that are a bunch of dipshits."

One other tangent Rich would often joke about was when he would always ask, "What happened to athletes like Muhammad Ali™, Charles Barkley™, and Jordan™? There's not even one athlete anymore saying something insightful, just a bunch of fucking whores."

Any time I was around Rich and I heard him saying something like that, I would always say, "You realize that you grew up with most of these guys you talk about. And now by the age of 17 you're already talking of the good old days, like a grandpa. The good old days, when Rich was 12."

Rich would always smile and tell me to "get the hell outta here."

People would always go over to where Rich was by himself hanging out, just in case they got tired of talking of their supreme ruling and self-importance, who they had made out with or fucked, how great and genius they were for their opinion about some television show or some movie (think of those who take their Netflix™ reviews very, very seriously, for example), or who they felt like lowering and bullying so they could feel even better about themselves and never have that bad thought (the bad thought that maybe your self-serving ego isn't as important as you think), then Rich would be there making fun of them (the Independence paparazzi and their magazine buyers is what they essentially were), and then they would just say, "Oh, that Rich is such a character." (Cary Smith, The chauvinist Patriot, would like to advocate that Rich is very, very Patriotic, and he never forgets to capitalize the P in Patriotism and just liked to joke around.)

And Rich is the one who came up with BaJesus™ (short for Black Jesus™. I better give credit where credit is due, just in case BaJesus™ becomes really popular, that way Rich will get all the money from it, because I know white people like myself have a history of not giving credit where credit is due).

DISCLAIMER: I REPEAT, THERE IS NO ONE LISTENING. That night I stayed longer at Cyrus's because the President™ was giving a speech about the attacks. Quite frankly I didn't really care much about what the President™ had to say. He spoke about "The Evildoers™. (He often reminded me of some-thing I once saw on a screen. It was a British show, of course. (I just went through a British phase during these years.) There was always this character on this comedy show who gave everyone nicknames in his office and was very annoying and dumber than dirt (although I never understood how dirt was dumb), but of course, he was playing a character on a comedy show, so it was funny as hell (is hell really funny?). It was as if that nickname guy on that comedy sketch show were the President™. And pretty much anything the President said could've been trademarked instantly as a new phrase.) (**Correction**: wow, you're just ending this ( ) now? Well, at least I'm honest, and I'll say I completely forgot where the sentence was cut off when I started this ( ), and whether I had even ended ( ) this, and it took me over an hour to start writing again right after this.) He spoke about how America™ would be resilant.

He spoke often about attackin' (remember, it can't just be attackin, it must have a little ` thingy, and that there is a g after the n, and that no one talks this way, just the man who leads the country. Education) Adghanistan, which was a major hub for the Al-Qada organization™, as the President™ put it.

As I ignored the President's™ speech, I figured we would retaliate in some form, because that's just the way things worked with these so-called leaders.

I figured this by the way Cyrus's dad was reacting, even Cyrus in some way. I didn't know who scared me more: the people who were cowards enough to kill themselves and innocent people, Cyrus's dad, or even the way Cyrus reacted with Luis. No morals or thought could be mixed with fighting and warfare because it is a savage and thoughtless occurrence, so retaliation was of no doubt. (And for some reason I felt my body preparing to fight beyond my control. And it (the violence) scared the shit out of me.)

About a month went by, and sporting events were just starting up again. The President™ had thrown out the first pitch at The World Series™, and his approval rating was skyrocketing, which was understandable and expected in times like this, and people were getting back to business. American flags™ were posted all over freeways™ and on buildings. People had American flags™ all over their cars and decorated on freeway on-ramps and their lawns, and America's™ beloved NFL™ was getting back to normal. The Patriotism was running high, the pride was booming at a scary level (I was not that scared, though, thanks to my mom naming me Cary and having sex with a Smith), and people were still cautious as the holiday season came about. It was around this time when I got some weird message from a messenger boy.

Chapter 5

Chapter 4 was a little too long, dontcha think? It was just to make Brad Cruise say, "WHEEEeeeee for the history."

Chapter 6

It was a random November day when the messenger boy came to me and said, "You know Alexis really has a crush on you. Here's her number, and she says to call her tonight."

My first reaction was: "You have got to be fucking kidding me. This girl had some messenger boy come and give me her number." I felt like eating the piece of paper with her number and shitting it out the next morning, but the messenger boy had mentioned the name Alexis, and Alexis had beauty that made you believe in something else, but that was about all I knew about her.

I thought it was weird that a girl like Alexis, who was a year older than me, would do something like this. And honestly, my initial reaction was to think of her as pretty dumb, but I figured what the hell, and from what I knew, Alexis was goddessly (my human computer wants me to say godly or godlessly. And it's not because my human computer is a chauvinist, sexist pig…it just thinks I'm a fag™) gorgeous.

I figured I had nothing else to do, so I might as well give her a call. (This was about 3 years before the entire population of America had a cell phone, so that's why I called her house phone. Alexis did have a cell phone, as her mom didn't want her to not be cool, but her mom checked everything on it. Just a side note once again for the real realists really reading this right now.)

"Hi. Is Alexis there?"

"May I ask who's calling?"

"Yes, you may, this is Cary."

"OK, hold on one minute."

At this point, I was thinking to myself, "What the hell am I doing this for? I don't want to spend my time having get-to-know-you conversations, find out she's not like all the other attractive high-school girls, and then after the get-to-know-you stuff is through find out she's unbearable and a future MAL Douche Bag hypocrite looking for a future Douche Bag, hypocrite, completely-full-of-shit husband and is, in fact, like all the rest, thus, wasting all that time."

"Hi. I'm surprised you called," Alexis said.

"I'm surprised myself. I think it had a lot to do with you."

"Hehehe."

"How come you had your messenger boy come up to me and give me your number? It would've been a lot more romantic if you yourself had come up to me."

"No way! I wouldn't even know what to say, and I'd get way too nervous."

"Yeah, that's what would've been romantic and sexy" (I knew nothing about sexy or romantic, but that's the beauty of a phone conversation) "about it."

"Well, I didn't, and how come you never came up to me and said anything?"

"Well, for one, I'm an asshole. And secondly, I figured a girl like you dates guys not in high school."

"Well, I made an exception for you."

"Well, that's kind of you, so obviously you find me cute, and I likewise, or else I wouldn't have called you, but I'm a fan of face-to-face communication. It makes it more real. So I'll come to you tomorrow, and we'll talk, OK?"

"Yeah, that sounds good. So you're saying I'm boring on the phone?"

"Yes, but so am I, and so is everyone for that matter. Plus I say words like sexy and romantic on the phone. I can't see you when I'm talking to you, and I'd prefer to see your face."

"Well, you convinced me. So tomorrow we have a school date."

"At least it'll make the time go by. It'll change things up a bit."

"OK, sure. And do you realize that we're both nervous right now, because we both started our talking with 'well' a whole bunch of times? Well, see ya tomorrow."

"OK, bye."

"Bye."

"I love you." (I was very immature here, so please excuse that.) I hung up after I said that. It was mean, really, but it probably got her thinking. I just hoped she wasn't some nut who'd take it seriously and then later on down the road start to stalk me and get creepy. I figured Alexis had heard those words from guys who talked to her for the first time before, so I suspected she thought nothing of it. And I couldn't believe the joke about our saying "well" that she had made. Maybe I really meant it, who knows? I hoped I didn't, because I really didn't need that couple shit (the school day was already cheesy and completely full of shit as it was). And I remembered some quote from something I had read on my own, outside of Independence, that got me thinking how unnatural love seemed to be. It seemed like the same unnatural feeling as my magic, degree, paper-seeking, better-give-me-a-high-money-value-job education gave me. I think the quote went something like, "That death's unnatural that kills for loving."

The next day at school I left my seat on the bench at lunch for the first time since I had got up to speak to Gail. I told Cyrus all about the messenger boy, Alexis, and how I had told her I loved her. He (expectedly) told me that no relationship would ever last between me and a girl like Alexis because I do not have the patience nor the virtues to be with any girl for more than a week.

Cyrus was wrong about that. I could establish something for a long time, but that is virtually impossible to do with any girl in high school, and I guess what Cyrus said was somewhat true, because who wanted to get tied down with anyone at that age? We're living longer these days, and it's not as if I'm going to meet my dream girl at Independence, and even if I did, I felt there were soo many women out there that there had to be more than one variation of my dream girl (whatever that meant).

I made my way to where Alexis was hanging out and said, "Hello," and sat down next to her.

"So...how's your day going?" I asked.

"Oh, it's going fabulous. I mean, it's the same old same old. Nothing very interesting happened, except for you, of course..."

(I felt I was living up to my name, 'cause that dialogue sounded like something a girl would say to Cary Grant™. My mom would be proud of my love life. MAL.)

"Just sitting here, listening to my friends talk about other people who they barely know. They talk about clothes and shopping and celebrities. Good makeup products to use, the hot guys they saw at the mall. Sometimes I don't even know why I hang out with them. I never have anything to say to them because I'm finding that I really have nothing in common with them," Alexis continued.

"So why are you friends with them? You could easily just say, 'See ya later Douches.' That's what I would do."

"Well, I can't just do that that easily, and I've known these girls forever. I just sit here, though, and wonder sometimes if I'd be better off making new friends, but then I think about how all these girls are just like them. They never have anything interesting to say. They only talk about cosmetics, shopping, and other girls they want to see dead and who they barely know. And the most depressing thing is that those shitting reality shows on MTShit are almost actually real when you really get to know these girls. So I could either be a loner or be friends with any group of girls, because they're all soo similar here."

"Well…sounds like you're a coward to me, and if I were you and I felt that way, I would never be by these people, because they'll never change, and you can't change them, so I'd just leave—be a loner. You can always come sit and hang out over where me and Cyrus sit and wait for the time to pass."

"Well, I'm not a coward, you jackass, but I do feel like it sometimes when I sit here and mindlessly listen to their conversations. And I just sit there in silence and daydream of a better day, when I'm not stuck at this hellhole of a school."

"Well, me and you can agree on that at least, that this school is a hellhole and that it seems like we're stuck. You've only got about 7 months left though. I've got a year and a half. You realize we're beginning our talk with 'well' a whole bunch again?"

"Yeah, I know, and that really sucks for you but is very exciting for me. How come you never talked to me last year in physics?" Alexis asked.

"Not sure."

"I always thought it was weird too that you were in that class—a Sophomore™ in physics™, a class meant for Juniors™ and usually Seniors™. And then you never seemed to even try very hard or do much work. How'd you even get placed into that class?"

"Well, someone was being a little creepy watching me...I tested well, I think. And I'm in those classes for my mom because she's soo enthusiastic for me to go to college, but I don't think I'm a college™ type of guy."

There was a pause. (Or as the kids who are awkward because they think they're better than everyone, say, "There was an awkward silence.")

"Hey Cary? How come you never talk to me in fourth period? You sit right next to me. You seem really antisocial to me," one of Alexis's friends obnoxiously interrupted.

"Well, you see, here I am talking to this wonderful girl. And I would call that, well, socializing. You see, I'm quite social when I want to be, but, I, knowing that those are the only kinds of things you relentlessly and mindlessly think about, didn't find a bond with you. And to you, anyone who isn't agreeable to you or your wants and likes is antisocial, so when you come around, I dream of turning into a bird, flying up to the sky, and being shot down by that little, wonderful princess that is you on ground level, with Daddy's gun in your hands."

"Yeah, you're weird. I don't see what you see in this guy Alexis. You're too beautiful for him."

There was an awkward silence felt by Alexis's friend after that. For me, there was just a nice, serene quietness, and then lunch ended.

Chapter 7

It was the middle of year three of my sentence, and at this point, thoughts of dropping out, of escaping, lingered often in my mind (especially since Alexis was still trying to get lovy duby with me and make things too deep).

DISCLAIMER: I REPEAT, THERE IS NO ONE LISTENING. I knew I only had a year and a half left, but I just, no matter how much I thought about it, could not figure out why I needed a piece of paper saying I was educated. To me it was just an ego (Dogma) device, as anyone with true cleverness and smarts would know that no piece of paper could justify one had smarts and was educated. (Of course anyone who was smart and wanted respect knew the magic piece of paper was where it lied (no pun intended there, because I don't even know what a pun is. The people who helped get this book published (the people you're not allowed to sue) told me about a pun, seriously, that was just a coincidence). Of course I knew I was not smart since my human computer kept warning me and trying to stop me from writing by underlining every sentence with green and red scribbly lines and once again was telling me I was a 3rd grader…and a fag. For some odd reason I felt really good being a 3rd grader, at least when my human computer was telling it to me…and I don't know why it had such a big problem with gay people™.)

To me, being smart was only manifested in a person's actions and choices in his everyday life (like avoiding it all together), so when those weird thoughts of leaving unannounced entered my mind every day, it only made the day longer and more somber. It was during one of those thoughts at lunch when Cyrus approached me and told me, "Tonight you have to come to my basketball game, because I've had enough of the culture and the fact that this game is the only means by which my father is able to converse with me."

I had never been to any sports games at Independence because our football team was horrible. (As far as I knew the team had 0 wins my 3 years at the joint, and I'm pretty sure that was not a good thing. Usually 0 was only good for fat people on diets. Or for fat MAL kids, that way they wouldn't blame someone else for their fat child being fat and take away my Cap'n Crunch™ cereal. MAL Dogma.)

I never went to a basketball game because Cyrus always told me never to come, because he wouldn't want to put that burden on me. Really, I had never been to any school events whatsoever, because I never wanted to go to these events. DISCLAIMER: I REPEAT, THERE IS NO ONE LISTENING. To me those events were just another addition of school time because everything about the activities and sporting events were just like school. The dynamics were all alike, the only difference was you were either at the field or in the gymnasium instead of being in a classroom or out at lunch, but in any case, you were still on school grounds, and that meant additional school time, so that kept me away from them (and a million other reasons, which I won't bore you with because that would take too many disclaimer warnings).

I was very reluctant to even go to that night's game that Cyrus had so adamantly told me to go to. The only thing that brought me to that game was Cyrus's animated spirit and words informing me to go to the game that night. (To, to, to…and to again. Minus 15 points. Education.)

When I got to the game, they, of course, charged me a fee because I didn't have my student ID since every year I got my little card with my arresting photo attached to it I just tossed it in the trash because the card was only needed for school events, like the basketball game or checking out books from the library, so I had no use for the card because I read at bookstores on their comfortable couches, and I didn't want to be in debt to Independence, because I knew if I did check out a book, I would certainly lose it. (I had a fear of the

Book Bookie™ and that Book Bookie™ was my school, and that fear made me say "because" a lot^. Minus 15 points. You need to write calmly, with less "becauses." Simple, short, and easy with the commas. Education.)

So after paying 5 goddamn dollars to watch some boring high-school basketball game, I was feeling even worse, because that five dollars was never going to Independence, which obviously never used the money for the actual school. (I knew this because, during my 3 years at the joint thus far, the only infrastructure improvement that was implemented to the school was an annual repainting of the school to make it look new every year, and all of our athletic teams had uniforms from the 1980s.)

As I made my way into the gymnasium (which was rightfully darkly lit and was very cold), I was reluctant to go into the stands because the only people I saw in the stands were people like my sister and her Bimbo Trio, the football players, and parents. I figured I'd be better off standing to the side, waiting for Cyrus to do whatever it was that he was going to do and leave with him because I did not want to go home on the city bus, which always took an hour, when I only lived fifteen minutes away, and I was too tired to walk.

So I stood aside and aimlessly watched the game and the prolonged quarters tick away. It was funny to see that most of the kids in the stands were not watching the game, they were just there to gossip more, as if the school day was not long enough to get all the bullshit talk in. (And this was why I never listened to my mom when she told me to go to these things, 'cause I knew this is what happened and that they were full of shit. It was also funny that this was what they were doing when all of Cyrus's basketball buddies were building their egos (Dogma) up soo high, thinking any of these Douches were actually watching the game, specifically them.)

Cyrus was always mocking the other players on his team about this. He would always say, "Those fuckin' kids think everyone in the stands is focused on them 'cause they hear them cheer. What's great is that 90% of the people in the stands just cheer when they hear other people cheer and had no idea who or what the fuck was going on." Standing there watching, I now understood what Cyrus was talking about.

DISCLAIMER: I REPEAT, THERE IS NO ONE LISTENING. What was even funnier (at least to me, but not to Cyrus) was watching Cyrus's dad in the stands, and for that matter, a majority of the dads in the stands (and a few MAL moms). You know someone is yelling angry and violent words when you can see their spit flying from their mouths a hundred feet away. These parents were insane (always telling people like me to grow up). Cyrus had mentioned to me before that some dad from the opposing team one game had yelled a bunch of vagrant jabber at him the entire game, and afterward, Cyrus saw the man with his son and just smiled at him. I've never been to one of these events, and quite frankly, with the combination of spit-enraged parents who wished they were still in high school playing in the game and the clones, Zombies, and Martians of my school, I felt Cyrus had put me in an interminable situation, and I badly wanted him to do whatever he was going to do so we could get the hell out of Hell™.

The game seemed like it was never going to end, and finally halftime came and went, and there were only 2 quarters left. It was during the start of the third quarter, as I was still standing on the side, that I saw Alexis sitting in the stands with her Zombie™ friends. I looked over to her, and I knew she saw me because she was too slow to look away.

I had told Alexis a few weeks ago that we could not be together because of how I felt about her. How we were soo similar. How she made me feel funny. How she made me funny because I was actually liking other non-Douchey people that she liked, and I told her that all that stuff was something that would tie both of us down, and we were too young to have what we would have had. (Plus my mom always told me to find it in college. MAL Dogma.)

When I was speaking to her she just smiled at me and it gave me a stinging sensation, and she said, "Yeah, it's true. It's funny how the cycle works that way. Brings two triangles together, and yet at this point in time of the cycle, one triangle is looking for a better shape and doesn't quite yet realize that finding and connecting two triangles is a very rare thing. I understand, though. Just don't forget me through your life, and remember me in ten years when you're ready to make that triangle one. We'll get married later on in life, you'll see. You love me, and I love you, and I can see it in the way you look at me…that you get that same feeling I get from looking at you eye to eye."

I was glad Alexis understood and did not get psychotic about it (or maybe she did. Did you just read what she said about those triangles?^ I never really liked geometry myself). DISCLAIMER: I REPEAT, THERE IS NO ONE LISTENING. Although she had mentioned marriage, and that was something I had never even thought about for my future. I never understood why, if 2 lovers had something soo special, they needed to get married and show everyone they were in love, since the 2 lovers already knew what they had (or no one really ever had any of that made-up crap, and that's why marriage was soo prevalent. I figured all these couples I saw cuddling and smooching were still in their first month).

To me, marriage was just another guideline to follow. Another piece of paper telling me, this time, that I loved someone. (I guess that girl was getting to me, even though I was thinking those soo negative things about marriage. Now you know why I had to get away from her at the time.)

Since Alexis and I (or is it I and Alexis, once again I always forget what snobby people tell me when they're correcting me. So I apologize, but really, does it matter that much? Education) were on good terms, I made my way over to where she was sitting in the stands. As I made my way over to the stands I saw Alexis wave in my direction, and I looked behind me to make sure that she was not waving at somebody next to me, and she wasn't, so (I always forget where, or if I should put a comma after so, so, I will just put a comma after every so for now on, for educational purposes. It's a hit or miss. A 50/50 chance. So half the time I'd pass the test, then do a little homework and a project, and I got my C baby. Education.) I continued to make my way toward the open seat she had now created and designated for me.

"Hi Alexis. How've you been?" I asked.

"Oh, I've been the same as always, thinking about a better day outside these walls. I've never seen you at one of these games. What made you come tonight?"

"Oh, Cyrus came up to me at lunch and told me he's had enough of the culture of this game and sports in America™ and asked me to come tonight… nothing much, really. So, (50/50) I figured I'd better come, in case he needed my help."

"What's he going to do? I hope it's not too crazy."

"I'm sure it won't be. He'll probably just piss someone off and quit after the game, but really, I'm never quite sure what he'll do."

DISCLAIMER: I REPEAT, THERE IS NO ONE LISTENING. As I said that I saw Cyrus running down the court and talking to some of the kids in the crowd who were sitting on the opposite side, as if to make them recognizable as the enemy, the opponent. Cyrus had always talked about how the basketball games in the gymnasium were like a training-and-recruiting ground for the army and war. He always said how they set up the stands to designate two opposing sides. The players were on the front lines, the commander or the coach was on the side giving commands, the parents in the stands were the air bombers and the outside voices for either side, giving derogatory shouts from the stands to the referees, coaches, and sometimes even the men on the front lines themselves, and the kids in the stands were all talking politics. He always told me that if I didn't think it was true that all I needed to do was listen to an army general on TV give an analogy about the war or the fight. He always said nine out of ten times it'd be an analogy involving some sport. I always laughed at Cyrus's analogy of a high-school basketball game and could never imagine it in my head when he spoke about it, but now that I was at a game, I could see exactly what he meant, and it was eerily true. All the pieces were there. (Although I felt like Cyrus sometimes overanalyzed things a bit and this might have been one of them, but I may have just thought that because I wasn't very athletic. The only thing that truly made me feel eerie was Cyrus's dad and his buddies in the stands with their MAL wives screaming and yelling for bloody murder the whole game. They looked more like the epicenter to the problems than anything else, not the game or the players, or the kids talking politics in the stands. My name is Cary Smith, please don't forget.)

I sat there with Alexis for the rest of the game, watched Cyrus continue to yell at the opposing team's stand, and for a brief moment I looked over at Alexis and felt what I thought was one of those rare moments of absolute calmness, peace of mind, bliss (Hippie talk. Hippie Dogma). I can't really say for sure, but I knew as I looked at her for a moment, I didn't even realize I was at a training camp for battle. All was silent, and I could see nothing but her face, as if time had stopped. She was soo beautiful, and the words she had previously said to me started to run through and fill my head, and I knew then that I would never forget her and the moment. I never thought that I would have a moment of bliss on prison grounds, but that was before Alexis's beauty radiated my darkness. (Oh boy, she sure was getting to me, and I was hoping that Cyrus would hurry the hell up and do whatever it was that he was going to do, because I was saying things like her beauty radiated my darkness in my mind.)

The game was coming to an end, and Alexis's friends were talking about how they were going to run over to this Marine™ from the opposing school's team and make out with him right there. I asked the 2 geniuses which one was faster on their feet, because the guy looked like a one-woman man, and both were dumbfounded and just called me "a weird fag™." (Fag was a word that people at Independence often used in response to something confusing, or anything they didn't understand and made them feel like a fool, but they were too foolish to embrace that foolish feeling and learn something about themselves or could not generate a comeback within the hour, so they just uttered fag™.) Anytime someone ever said this as a response to something I had previously said (which seemed to be a lot), I just told them, "But I like you," and smiled and pumped my shoes. In the case of Alexis's friends, they called me "a weird fag." (I was beginning to think that O'Hara had a point with the whole vocabulary rant, but then I thought how it always was that a few idiots always give a bad name to most things.) Alexis laughed at me saying, "But I like you," so I at least knew someone whose mind was on this planet had understood what I had just said. (**Correction:** that last sentence "Alexis laughed…" I couldn't even remember what you were even talking about because you have way too many of these ( ). COME ON, ALREADY…keep it short, simple. Education. I've mentioned this before, and I'll say this one last time. Every time there's a long one of these ( ), it takes me 2 hours just to remember where I was and to start writing again (What was I writing about again?), but I hope I did an OK job in remembering where I was and you enjoy them. Really, I don't mean that condescendingly, I also get confused where I am.)

The game was just about to end, and finally it did, and Independence lost pretty badly, and suddenly I saw Cyrus start yelling at Mr. Miles. Cyrus then proceeded to not shake the hands of the opposing team. While continuing to yell at Mr. Miles, he abruptly took off his jersey and made his way to the exit, kicking a chair on his way out. I told Alexis that was most likely it and that I'd better go with him. So, (50/50) we said our good-byes, and I made my way to the parking lot. I ran toward Cyrus, and he was smiling, and we got in the car and took off.

"It sucked that we got our asses kicked. Kinda made my outburst very odd. I was hoping it'd be a close game, and a loss, so I could yell at Miles and do what I did and make it seem justifiable," Cyrus said.

"What were you trying to do, get kicked off or quit?"

"Oh, I was trying to get myself kicked off. I couldn't quit, because then I wouldn't have a valid excuse for my dad. I figured if I screamed at the opposing bench the whole game, to make it seem as if my emotions were running high and I was really into the game and we lost, I could wail on Miles for being the reason we lost and get kicked off. If that happened then my dad wouldn't say much, he'd just talk about how horrible a coach Miles was and all that bullshit. I felt really bad, though, because Miles is such a good guy. I mean, he really makes it fun every once in a while, just by him being around, so I felt bad yelling at him for no reason, except to have a validated excuse for my dad, so I don't have to hear his conventional wisdom about quitting."

"Well, it seemed to me you pulled it off…except for the fact that you lost by 30 and were on the bench laughing with someone. Plus your dad was going fuckin'" (remember there's a g to follow, it just can't be fuckin. Education) "crazy during the game. I was standing to the side, about a 100 feet away, and I could see the spit coming out of his mouth."

"Yeah, he's always like that. That's why my mom never comes to these games. She's the only one who knows I truly hate being on this team, and for the real reasons, not Miles, the real reasons being that there's 5 guys out there who sadly and truly believe in their depressing minds that they're going to be McDonald's All-Americans and get scholarships and make it big. And my dad is always ragging on Miles after every game, as if to make some excuse, and I don't even give a shit if we win or lose, because I don't even enjoy the game anymore like I used to. Truly Miles is the only positive about the basketball team. Hopefully it worked so all that bullshit can be over. It'll be funny when my dad runs out of tongue about Miles and I'm no longer in basketball, and he'll have absolutely nothing to say to me. It'll be sad and funny at the same time, but at least I won't have to listen to his mindless, Douchey condescending excuses about why the team lost," Cyrus said.

"Well, I guess we'll see tomorrow. I think I saw Agent Mulder™ in the stands with his walkie-talkie, and I'm sure he saw you running down the court screaming shit at the opposing fans. I mean anyone in that gymnasium could see your white ass running down the court, talking in the direction of the stands of the other team like a madman. It was a very fine performance, I might add," I said.

"Well thank you. I'm glad Mulder™ was there, now it will be almost certain that I'll be kicked off. You know that Douche Bag will feel a huge power trip of authority and feel this is his time to shine and put down his authority foot. Little does that Nazi™ know that he will most likely be my blessing call and be the one who orders the Miranda™ to kick me off. I was hoping someone like him would be in attendance, because Miles is too good of a guy to kick me off himself. Isn't it funny that our Miranda™ rights are read and the genesis of those rights came from a rapist, pretty fuckin' liable justice system™™ (and another trademark. Hey, gotta be safe, because you mess with the justice system™™, and you're sued for life, 'cause it's pretty hard to get justice when you mess with the justice system), wouldn't you say? Anyways, I mean Miles let Rich on the team, and Rich didn't even know how many quarters were in a basketball game."

Cyrus dropped me off at home and I immediately went to sleep. Usually when I came into the house my mom was watching the show of the night and could really care about nothing else except what was being said on the 27 inch tube. There was one time when I went into the living room during the prime-time television hours, and I went in there to tell my mom about Alexis, and how I had to cease being by her because she was the one, and I wanted to avoid the hurt and the feeling she was giving me. I came into the room and started talking to my mom when I heard my oldest brother (he was 35 and still living at home) give a big, Douchey, annoying, "Sshhhhhh." My mom said, "Tell me later," and I just laughed and went to my room and listened to some music. (And I didn't have mommy-and-daddy issues, because to have those, you have to care. Growing up, I just thought my family was a circus act and that we made money from that. We actually would have been a Reality TV™ show, but they had to get everyone's consent. I refused to ever sign the contract, so they were waiting for me to graduate high school so they could be a Reality Show and kick me out (that was going to be the pilot episode). My mom said I cost the family millions.)

I just jumped into to bed fully clothed. I didn't even bother to take my shoes off. Right before I fell asleep, for some reason the thought of Gail came to me. I started to wonder how he was, wherever he was. I wondered if there was another kid there like me who was interested in the eccentric and heard the words he had spoken to me, and if that person was in awe as I had been.

I thought it was strange that Gail came to my mind since I hadn't thought about him all year. It was even stranger to me that Gail stuck with me soo much, yet I had talked to him soo little (Hippie talk, Hippie Dogma).

DISCLAIMER: I REPEAT, THERE IS NO ONE LISTENING. The next day, once again awakened way too early for a kid in maturation, I made my way down stairs and ate Froot Loops™ and waited for Cyrus.

I didn't change from the previous day because I honestly forgot I went to sleep in my clothes. When I woke up, I thought I had changed into those clothes that morning and was just lying on my bed to rest a little more.

Cyrus was late as usual. He honked his horn, and he was honking with more animation that morning. I got in the car, and Cyrus seemed really excited. He knew he was going to get kicked off the team today, and the anticipation of the words of being off the team, officially, were taking hold of Cyrus. "This is it man. Finally the bullshit of being on that team will end. Miles will understand, he's met my dad before. I'll just give him a wink as I leave Mulder's™ office so he'll know."

That day at lunch Cyrus was MIA until the last five minutes when he embarked toward me with a melancholy look on his face, then as he got right up to my face, he smiled and laughed and grabbed my hand and started being very annoying, poking me and rubbing my head and jumping up and down. All the while saying, "Thank you, you Douche Bag Mulder™ for being at the game."

I felt happy for Cyrus and his liberation, but at the same time I felt bad for him and his situation. I felt bad for him that his dad was soo obsessive, soo demanding about him and basketball and how the sport was his only means of communication with him. Although I can't say my father and I had much communication (**Correction:** stop repressing (Dogma) your mommy-and daddy-issues. Just let it out and cry. OK, I'll just come out and say it, "I, Cary Smith, have mommy-and-daddy issues"), but I knew Cyrus would never admit that he liked the fact that his dad took an interest in him and basketball and talked to him, even if Cyrus never listened and it was all about basketball. Cyrus was used to this meaningless communication (and one last time for the paragraph with too much communication^. Minus 15 points. Education) with his father, and now he'd have none. It was sad, and I knew it would hurt him a little. He was strong, but everyone wanted a relationship with the 2 who created and brought them to Earth. (Usually having a relationship where you're pissed off at them for bringing you into this world, and where they feel like you actually owe them something, but hey, at least that keeps you from being bored.)

The next day at school, Cyrus seemed as if he had just dodged a bullet from hitting his face because the whole day he was smiling, and every time one of the players came up to him, asking why he wasn't at practice yesterday, he just smiled and said, "I'm free from you and the rest." I think the only player who did not get Cyrus's response was Luis, because he never came up to Cyrus, and Cyrus had not even looked at the guy since Luis's profound, great and monumental, and let's not forget truly genuine, remarks about all the people who died on 9/11™.

The rest of the day I watched Cyrus, and the smile did not leave once (sometimes I was a little creepy with my watching, I'll admit). I figured it wouldn't leave until he and his dad had their last Miles conversation and Cyrus pretended to listen.

After school I sat at Cyrus's house, watching people play video games and feeling my brain fry (just because I say that ^ does not mean I want these games banned, MAL, so go away) as Cyrus's smile did not disintegrate an inch. I never saw him happier than that day.

Chapter 8

The day was a beautiful spring day. It was a day that took all questions away as to why Independence High was mostly an outdoor school. It was about the only thing the founders of the school got right.

The day began like any other, waking up too goddamn early, eating Froot Loops™, putting on my Reebok Pumps™, waiting for Cyrus, arriving to class late, and beginning my day's worth of ruminations and daydreams. Then suddenly, as happened the previous year, a very loud bell noise was heard toward the end of the school day. I was in O'Hara's class at the time, and when the bell alarm sound went off, she, like me, did not seem too happy about it. It took my brain a couple of seconds to recognize this sounding alarm bell as the same sounding alarm bell that I had heard for the first time last year. The bell alarm was the new fear-implemented upgrade of the old fire-drill bell. Except now, like last year, we were to lock ourselves in a classroom while hypothetical, extraordinary, teenage mass-murdering geniuses roamed our halls. (I think that was my best sentence yet, 'cause my human computer underlined it, and now said I'd graduated 3rd grade and am ready for 4th...but weirdly, he is still calling me a fag™.)

Instinctually, without O'Hara saying anything, the whole class began to move to the corner of the class, where we were to huddle and stay clear of the door. Then O'Hara was supposed to stack the desks in front of the door because we were the kids, and we were the future (at least until we became old and complacent, just like all the other content, useless, old Douches who did everything the same), so O'Hara had to stack the desks in front of the door, just as the whole class did last year in McDonald's, except this year we were in a different situation.

To me, up to this point, O'Hara's class had been exceptional, probably the only class that I felt like doing any work whatsoever for, mainly because I needed to maintain my consecutive Cs, but all of that actual work was actually worth it, and I felt very fortunate to be in her class during the You're-Going-To-Die-And-Really-There's-Not-Much-We-Can-Do-To-Help drill because I knew she was the only one doing what she was doing.

While the very loud alarm bell was going off, I noticed O'Hara remained seated and had a very agonizing look on her face. As the class instinctually got up and made their way to the corner, O'Hara shouted, which was barely comprehendible through the Fear Bell™, "Sit back down. We're not going to practice huddling up in a corner and stacking desks, so sit back down, and once the bell is gone, we'll resume."

DISCLAIMER: I REPEAT, THERE IS NO ONE LISTENING. I started to think, finally a teacher willing to speak out against this ridiculous drill, this propaganda drill saying, "It's OK, you're at school. We practice for crazy asses who want to kill innocents. Don't be scared, we'll protect you with Fear Bells™ and teachers stacking desks. Just remain in a corner until all is safe, and make sure you tell your parents that we practiced for your safety here at school." ("MAKE SURE TO TELL YOUR PARENTS," MAL DOGMA.)

I knew that later on, either that day or the next, some kid in our class would go to Mulder's office and inform him about what Ms. O'Hara had done (the human odds were for it happening). There was always some little puppy dog in the class who was this type of person. To me, though, Ms. O'Hara was too smart not to know there would be a little Douche Bag snake in the class, so her doing what she did meant that she obviously knew she could outsmart Mulder and whoever else in Administration and continue to do what she did.

At this point I began to develop a great admiration for Ms. O'Hara, something I knew Cyrus had developed the first day of class, it just took me this long. I needed some kind of stimulus (Dogma) for my mind to react, and what she did during the drill was something I never expected to see from a teacher. I realized that she was a very, very rare breed, and I knew at that point why Cyrus today had a smile on his face from Ms. O'Hara's actions and why he had acted the way he did the first day of Ms. O'Hara's class. It wasn't a book that made me see this, it wasn't words, it wasn't hearing it from a third party, it was Ms. O'Hara's actions, her demeanor. (Of course much of her demeanor came from her vast reading.) Seeing this firsthand is what made me instantaneously and spontaneously feel a deep and truly profound respect and admiration for this very, very rare teacher (Hippie talk, Hippie Dogma).

When the bell stopped fearing and Ms. O'Hara went on about Hugo's™ love of nature and seeing God™ in every single thing on Earth™ (Ms. O'Hara had assigned *Les Miserable* for the month), some whining student in the class asked a question, which was very similar to the questions he had asked throughout the school year. The kid interrupted Ms. O'Hara and said, "What happens if this drill is real? If someone really is attacking the school as we speak? Or what if it does happen in the future and we're not prepared for it because we didn't have the necessary practice? I think this is a serious drill, and we should follow it accordingly. Something could happen at any moment, and we need to be prepared."

Ms. O'Hara laughed and just shook her head, and about 30 seconds later she said, "What if, what if. Yeah, what if something like Columbine™ did happen right this second? How could you prepare for something like that? How could you practice a prevention drill for something like that? You really think that if some stupid maniacs came onto our campus right now that any preparation would prepare you for something of that nature? What difference does it make? Whether or not we practice this fear-mongrel drill...it makes no difference. The school wants you to be scared and feel the way you do so that when we have these drills they want to keep you naïve and make you feel that by having this preparation you'll feel safer because they keep you safe. You think I'm an idiot? I lock the door all the time anyways, but there is no need to practice sitting in a corner. To tell you the truth, if some maniac really wanted to, he could bust down these doors and get in here. So, you tell me what is the point of preparing to sit in a corner, being in fear of some maniacal fool who thinks he or she is actually making a stand, and all the while thinking about the incident really occurring over and over in your brain?"

The kid responded by saying, "It prepares you." Cyrus and I laughed, and Ms. O'Hara just went on with her lecture. I knew right there who the snake puppy was going to be. The one who would scope Mulder™ out and inform him what was going on inside Ms. O'Hara's classroom.

I just despised the kid. I mean that was about all I could do. (He was the ultimate definition of what a Douche Bag is, running to someone like Mulder.) I wasn't going to kick his ass because that would solve nothing, except make me look like a big fat D-Bag myself. Confronting him about his naiveté, puppy ways would not change him, because he felt that he had justifiable logic in his preparedness and didn't even realize that he was just a little puppy dog playing into the hands of Douche Bags like Mulder, and telling him all this would not change him. He would just ignore it, say he didn't care, and go on being the despicable person he was meant to be, so I just sat there and despised him, and that soon disappeared because he was not the type of person to waste my mind on despising (well, it disappeared right after that sentence was finally over).

As the day went by, I imagined all the students huddling in their corners, desks stacked high against the door, and teachers constantly telling the students to be quiet. The lucky 30 (or maybe the 5 that were even conscious (Dogma) of what the hell was even going on, for that matter. Write out five. Minus 15 points. Education) in Ms. O'Hara's class were reading, and that seemed far worse than sitting in a corner, in the dark, in the shadow from the outside forces to most of the class, because the reading stimulated thought, and, sadly, that was an inadequacy for most in Ms. O'Hara's class.

Ms. O'Hara began to get off topic from Hugo's™ novel and began what I felt was her flaw, which was her once-a-month-rant about Feminism™, women equality, and how all men are barbarian, deceiving liars. I mean literally, she would be lecturing and then just start talking about men and women. It kinda scared me. I will say, though, I did become a Feminist™ for the duration of her tirade. (I did this mainly to prepare myself, just in case she called on me during her rant. Then I'd be prepared to say, "Yes," nod my head and say, "Yes,"

154

again, and remind her that Cary Smith was Feminist™-friendly. Maybe Cary Grant™ and his boys weren't back in the day, but Cary Smith was.)

Ms. O'Hara was saying something of this nature when a girl in the class— a girl who, I might add, was one of those girls who would raise her hand every minute and thought her opinions were unprecedented—started telling Ms. O'Hara that women seek nothing but kindness and equality with men, but it's the men who then proceed to treat women like dirt, like an object. It's the men who become the barbarians. Suddenly Cyrus jumped in, and he was very adamant, almost emotional—something I've seen in Cyrus, but not about women. It was a bit ironic that he spoke on this subject, although every day after school in the third year of my sentence, I had noticed that Cyrus no longer had his weekly Bimbo at his house, and for that matter, the number of people at his house had decreased dramatically. Really I hadn't seen Cyrus talk too much with anyone expect me, or when he spoke out in Ms. O'Hara's class.

Cyrus jumped in, saying, "First off, how can you preach equality between men and women when you call all men barbarians, blame everything on men, and say that we treat women like objects? Yeah, sure a lot do, but I guess Lisa doesn't go to the same school I go to, because while there are just a lot of men treating women like objects, there is the same amount of women treating men like objects. I don't understand how you can talk about Feminism™, which I'm all for, except for a slight name change, 'cause Feminism™ is a really annoying ism when it comes off your tongue, or you hear it, or even when you read it in print, and equality of men and women and so arrogantly say that all men are barbarians, that all men are to blame, and that all men treat women like possessions?"

Ms. O'Hara began to utter something, and Cyrus continued, "No, I'm not done, you have all the time to speak, and I'm going to finish. To say what you say, to me, only makes the inequality greater, and as I see it...something Lisa over there is unwilling to admit, because she confuses her opinion with wisdom. For every stupid male there's a stupid female, both acting in the nature that you have spoke of. It's not just males, that's complete bullshit to say that. If you so-called Feminists™ really want to make a difference, make a change, change your name to something other than Feminism™ first—that just makes me cringe saying a word like that—then I think you need to start with your fellow females themselves. And good luck on that one. And also, did I mention the suggestion of a name change? I'm mean, just look at most of these girls at this school. All they care about is what kind of high-school social stature, the beginning of social nightmares, the person has who they're standing next to. If they can, they date some hotshot guy just to gloat on fact that they are, what they're going to get at the mall today and what they're going to wear tomorrow so people will talk about it as if the story is going to get published in a magazine with a million people in its circulation. Don't get me wrong and say, 'Well, there are guys just like that,' because I know there is, I used to be on our basketball team after all, but I'm talking about starting with your fellow females, because as far as I know, females outnumber males. I just don't understand how Youism—that's Feminism's new name until a better, smoother name is implemented—always talks about equality and then bashes males as if we would all be adequate males if only it were the Roman Era™. To me, women have the beauty. Women have the power to control sex. Women have the intuition. Women are the mothers. Women carry life in their bodies, yet most of these girls at Independence will never change, you and Lisa don't realize how rare you truly are. These women will never change, never realize their stupidity. They're just products of our culture, and so are most of the males, and that's just how it is—they're all just Cash Cows™ or Cash Zombies™. And soon, when they're older, they'll be wishing they were back here in this devil's armpit, which we socially call high school, dreaming of the class reunion, and making sure they get a job that pays a six-figure wage, that way everyone can see it on their MySpace™ page, because they know people are gonna talk about it, people will know about it when the reunion comes... another social nightmare. You're forced, and Lisa is forced, to think differently, so am I, that's our American curse. We think, we see the stupidity, but the change will never come because there are just too many to change."

"Well...I'm glad you got that in, and we'll move on back to Hugo™ and my favorite character, Enjolras," Ms. O'Hara said.

I was very surprised that Ms. O'Hara did not respond to what Cyrus had said. She didn't even offer a joke as she usually did. I was in awe myself. I had never heard Cyrus talk like that before about women. He always mentioned his mom as being the only one who understood him, although he couldn't respect her completely because she was married to his dad after all. I had never heard him speak for that long, without pause, or in such a manner has he had (but

156

I definitely heard him talk a lot). Lisa, the girl who I had mentioned, seemed like she wanted to respond, but Ms. O'Hara gave her no chance and began a new topic. Ms. O'Hara usually, if not always, responded in discussions after a student had spoken, especially with Cyrus, often attempting to joke with him, and she always, and I mean always, got the last word in…but not this time, she just changed the subject.

There definitely wouldn't be much reaction from the class, because only about 7 people (1 of the 7 was just being quiet and getting really emotional in the back corner of the room and eventually just stormed out of the classroom pouting. This kid did this once a week in discussions) out of the thirty in the class were actually conscious (Dogma) and listening to what was being talked about in class and most never said anything or really had anything swirling around in their heads because Ms. O'Hara could be very intimidating, or she wasn't talking about who was getting massively bro wasted the other night or what was going to be on the test, because then all the college enthusiasts in the class got very focused (which was about half the class). It was almost as if Cyrus were talking to himself. It made me laugh pretty hard afterward, thinking of that. (He wasn't literally talking to himself, it was just a funny thought that came to me, 'cause I know how you Brad Cruise types like to think in the metaphors that make you so intellectually bright, so I figured I'd better mention that.)

I looked over at Cyrus, and he seemed dumbfounded himself that he got no sarcastic response or ridicule from Ms. O'Hara. I watched his expressions, and he seemed to change from shocked to neutral, then after some time, it seemed as if he had thought about what he said and got a melancholy look on his face, but Cyrus was not the type to keep a melancholy look for too long.

After class ended I sat with Cyrus, and we didn't talk much, really all I did was kind of observe the patterns of the majority Cyrus was talking about (boys and girls). The way they acted so obnoxious, talked loudly to garner attention, always having a self-conscious (Dogma) look on their faces, looking around thinking everyone was looking at them right at that moment as THEY SPOKE VERY LOUDLY.

I suddenly began to speak to Cyrus about the night I was at his basketball game and what Alexis's friends were talking about and what I had said to them. He started to tell to me about all the girls he would bring to his house, and how

157

none of them even realized what the hell they were doing. He began to talk about if you couldn't explain why or have a valid reason for doing something, then how could you tell yourself to do that? Cyrus just kept going on as he had in Ms. O'Hara's class, talking about how much practice it must take to make your mind not care what you're doing, not even think about what you are doing, and to pretend and lie to yourself that not making a choice is still a choice. (**Correction:** then we both began to talk, began to talk, began to talk. Minus 15 points. Repetitive. Talking, you talked. We all talked. Education.)

Cyrus figured that a majority of these girls were just followers of the true Bimbo Queen™. She was most likely very good-looking, and the followers felt that was all she needed to sway them. He felt that most of these girls must go home at night and just feel like complete shit. Cyrus very adamantly told me about how he never did anything with those girls that he brought to his house. He said that he would always get angry and tell himself he would just give into their stupidity and fuck them, but every time the time came, he just got a rush of somber and looked at the girl's eyes and felt like crying, and then he told them he was not in the mood. I had always wondered why Cyrus used to go up to his room, and when he eventually came down, the girl he had gone up with never came down with him, and never, afterward, came down (they must have jumped out of his window).

Like I knew, the next day in Ms. O'Hara's class she spoke about how she was confronted about not participating in the preparedness drill. I knew who the snake Douche Bag was, he even had a ratty look on his face and was smirking. I'm sure Ms. O'Hara did as well (not had a ratty look on her face but knew who had told Mulder), but that's who that boy was in life, so I didn't waste my energy even looking in his direction or despising him (until this sentence was over).

The snitching prompted Ms. O'Hara to start a very funny discussion. Ms. O'Hara said, "Laws are totally unnecessary and do not stop people from committing crimes. We all have within us good thoughts and very perilous and ominous thoughts, but the majority of people do not act on these perilous thoughts, and we do not act on them because of some laws. We do not act on them because we have something inside us that is unexplainable and stops us from acting on these horrible thoughts: we have a choice. Humans came together and thrived before any text or scripture of laws were created. The people that do act on them act on them, simple as that, and apparently no law stopped or scared them." Ms. O'Hara went on to give a mediocre example about how she always speeds on the highway, saying she drives what speed she feels relevant, an example she often gave.

Whenever Ms. O'Hara did mention something like this, which she usually repeated more than once, which was expected if one was lecturing every day for 9 months, a student that sat in front of me, whose name was Ryan, always turned around. This Ryan D-Bag, tool of a kid would always turn around whenever Ms. O'Hara repeated herself, and said in a very Douchey tone, "Check on that." He thought he was soo funny and witty, and everyone who sat behind him knew he was going to turn around and say, "Check on that." (He was definitely a Douche Bag all for the element of mindless wit.) I don't know what triggered inside me, if it was Ryan's Douchey tone in his voice that echoed of arrogance and mindlessness or the annoying events of the last two days, but when Ryan turned around this time and said, "Check on that," I just snapped.

"Why don't you turn around and shut your dumb mouth that makes the world much more peaceful when closed" (and that was not a question). "You're essentially doing exactly what Ms. O'Hara is doing and repeating yourself every time she does. You turn around and say, 'Check on that' every time Ms. O'Hara repeats herself, as if you were soo clever and the only one who realizes she's repeating herself. Of course you wouldn't realize your moronic 'Check on that' statement is a continuous repetition itself, which is exactly what you think you're mocking, so really you're just mocking yourself, ya unfunny D-Bag clown. And the only reason you're funny is because you don't even realize that you're basically making fun of yourself, as you repeat yourself every time O'Hara repeats herself, and say in the squirmiest voice, 'Check on that.'"

Ryan didn't respond, and he wouldn't have been able to anyways because he would need a couple minutes to think about it (at least enough time to say fag™ or to pour some water on his now fiery head that was questioned, or on his ego (Dogma)).

Ms. O'Hara told me to calm down, and quite frankly, I had no idea why I just blurted that out at Ryan, but it sure as hell felt great to tell the Douche off. I think Ms. O'Hara was surprised herself because I hadn't really ever said anything the entire year, and I suspected she could perceive that all my work was exactly the same and showed no progress whatsoever beyond a C. She couldn't kick me out of class or send me to Mulder's™ office because I was defending her. At first she almost interrupted me, but as I got going, she let me go. That guy was just such a Douche Bag (another one who fit the ultimate definition of a D-Bag), and he'd been doing that the entire year, and I just could not take his Douche-Bag, mindless ways anymore. (I guess at the time I should've been up to date with the fashion, thought about what tanning lotion to use, so I could fit right in and not have to think (and be soo pale) soo much about people like Ryan 'cause they just depressed me and hurt my head.)

I had figured he would try and confront me after class, because he seemed like a huge egomaniacal maniac (Dogma), and he did, but he didn't do anything violent. He just called me a fag™, and I said, "But I like you," pumped my shoes, and laughed.

Cyrus asked me what the hell had gotten in to me and said, "It was great that someone told check-on-that-boy to shut the hell up. I can guarantee you even the kids who sleep in class that sit behind that kid are glad you told him how stupid and annoying he was, and now he won't wake them up anymore saying, 'Check on that.' I can rest assured that Ryan will not be saying, 'Check on that,' again this year, and that is a very good thing."

I didn't feel like going to Cyrus's and playing video games or frying my brain watching people play video games after school. I felt like lying in my bed and listening to music and falling asleep and waking up on the day I was out of Independence.

Chapter 9

It was spring at Independence High, and at high schools across America™ people were getting ready for what high school was all about…where the memories of nostalgia would take place when you were 40 and looking back on your glory years.

It meant Prom™. It meant Tradition. It meant happily and lovingly finding that one to spend a glorious evening in uncomfortable suits and dresses, with high heels that gave enormous pain to all the girls wearing them. (But they looked fashionably sexy, so what the hell. Being fashionably sexy is worth a little pain and misery, it counterbalances it.)

It meant eating at a fancy restaurant in Gatsby™ clothes and pretending to be Yuppies™. (I don't even really know what a Yuppie™ is, I just like saying "Yuppie.")

It meant going to a hotel ballroom and Dry Humping™ (also known as Modern Dance), then going home and capping off a night filled of cordial and formal matters by having sweet, sweet sex on the ocean™. (Trademark? I thought I saw a cologne commercial once for Sweet, Sweet Sex on the Ocean by HalvinI'llgetyoulaidboy™.)

Unfortunately I had made a genuine and heartily promise to Alexis that I would suffer the evening with her so her parents wouldn't question her as to why she wasn't going to the Prom™ her senior year.

I felt bad for Alexis because the double standards for men and women attending galas like Prom™ were agonizingly made apparent with Alexis with her mom. (Her demoness of a mom was the only reason I said I'd go with her, so she didn't have to deal with the demoness.) I had told Alexis to make sure to bring a change of clothes that didn't make her feel like Tarzan (I tried to say Tarzan's wife, but once again my stinkin' human computer kept underling it with a red scribbly line, and telling me to put Tarzan, because it said it knew I was a fag™ and that I had a serious crush on Tarzan) in fancy attire. I told her that we'd go to dinner anywhere she wanted, go to the grand ballroom of a corporate hotel and get our picture taken so we had proof for her live-your-life-as-I-did-mother, and then we'd ditch the being at school extended gala and crash with Cyrus at his place and spend the night so her mother would think she made sweet Prom-night™ sex. (On the beach of course, all thanks to HalvinI'llgetyoulaidboy™. **Correction:** all of that^ was too lengthy, wordy. Simple, short for BaJesus's™ sake. Education.)

DISCLAIMER: I REPEAT, THERE IS NO ONE LISTENING. I was really not looking forward to going to Prom. (Trademark for any time I write Prom from here on out, 'cause I'm simply getting lazy and tired of putting that damn symbol after every Prom. I don't know why I'm soo worried, though, with a name like Cary Smith I was sure to prosper in the court of law. I guess I subconsciously (Dogma) knew that, and that's why I was getting a little lazy.) For one thing, Prom was an event built on tradition. "Do as others have done before you," should've been Prom's motto and what all the mothers were subtly telling their daughters. It was an event popularized long ago, when wearing a tuxedo and finally asking your dream girl (thanks to those damn beachy songs) if she'd go to Prom with you (unless 2 guys want the same dream girl or another girl wanted to go with that same dream girl, then you better hope that you worked out all year for Santa Claus™ and were the best boy ever), but with the true intention of wanting soo badly to have sex with your true one and knowing that she'd feel soo good after having a night Gatsby™ style. That idea was all good and nice, but times change, and with it so should the concept of Prom, yet people at Independence didn't understand that Prom was just school at night, with music and uncomfortable clothes (oh, and Dry Humping™).

Times change, and with the times changing Prom should be changed to something with the times, not some nostalgic American™ gala. (My name is Cary Smith.) If Prom were updated now, it would probably get some weird, nonsensical club name like Lash, since all Prom was was a club full of Dry Humping™, guys penises getting permanently slanted (I would've liked the dance style if it wasn't for this) from the freaking or Dry Humping™, and doing all that in Gatsby™ clothes. It was all the same, though, every year. People did the same thing over and over, year after year for Prom, and nothing new or creative was ever encouraged or implemented. (Education.)

I truly hated school events that just extended high school, and I especially despised Prom because of its traditional wisdom value, and it all made no sense whatsoever to me (**Correction:** yeah, yeah, we know you don't like extended school events, why don't you tell us again, again, again, and again, you whiny baby. Repetitive crap. Education), but I agreed to go with Alexis because I couldn't say no and be cold to her because her mother was such a typical mother of today, living in the past, wishing they were in their twenties again. Trying to date young guys, getting surgery after surgery (And isn't it funny how in our attempt to fight aging and death, the people who go through these procedures (at least for non-was-in-a-brutal-accident-or-was-an-innocent-victim-of-some-britality) are more frightening than aging and death?), wishing she could relive her Prom night and her sweet, sweet Prom sex (I'm not too sure if HalvinI'llgetyoulaidboy™ was aiding back then) every night. And I felt sorry for Alexis and knew she didn't want to go, but she also didn't want to deal with her mom's scolding and nostalgic memories if she did not go.

During Prom week, people in class were talking about who they were going with, who was planning on losing their virginity (for the 5th time), and who was going to rent a limousine. It was pretty sad if a girl waited 18 years of her life for one night called Prom to lose her virginity (especially for the 5th time).

DISCLAIMER: I REPEAT, THERE IS NO ONE LISTENING. These people, who had planned to lose their virginity on a horrible night such as Prom, would be those people who planned their whole life out now. Go to college, meet some guy by 28, get married, have kids, grow old, have grandchildren. Their whole lives would be planned ahead. They'd always be living today for the future. (And how could that possibly go wrong?) I could never plan my life and ignore feelings I had inside because I was set on my plan. Picking a night to lose your virginity, picking an age to get married, picking, setting, planning, losing all life, personality and heart…these were the thoughts that Prom night brought to my head, and it started to depress (Dogma) me heavily, but luckily I had Alexis and Cyrus with me.

On the night of Prom, Cyrus picked me up. He had no date and refused to go to school for 2 weeks so that no one could ask him to go because he didn't have the cold heart to say no (he was attractive, after all, so someone was definitely bound to ask him), so he just didn't go to school. Cyrus was only going with me and Alexis to give us a ride, and then leaving with us. And he refused to rent a tuxedo and was stubbornly set on going to Prom alone in his outfit that he wore most days and getting his picture taken alone and then leaving with us.

I walked out of my door, saying good-bye to my mom, who demanded I come right back after Alexis was with me so she could take pictures. I walked to Cyrus's car feeling like the dressed-up elephants in a circus and could barely breathe as the bow tie grasped my Adam's Apple™ like a leech. I got into the car, and there was Cyrus with his shirt, old dirty jeans, and his beat-up Nike's™, and I hated him for it and his little smirk that he gave me. Cyrus just looked at me and said, "You must really like this girl to do this for her. You should've avoided school like I did, then she couldn't have asked you."

I explained my promise I had made to Alexis upon first meeting her and about her mother's agonizing pressure of go-to-Prom-or-disgrace-me ultimatum. Then Cyrus said, "Well, at least the Young Conservatives™ are looking forward to tonight."

Cyrus pulled up to Alexis's house, and I made my elephant appearance for the circus audience. Alexis's mom was in the middle of one of her Prom™ (just a trademark in the middle as a reminder to be safe) stories when Alexis told her we were late, which we weren't, and told her mom to take the pictures so we could go.

Alexis looked like a totally different person with all the makeup her mother obviously poured unto her face. I barely recognized Alexis when I first saw her and thought she was far more beautiful without the makeup, which she never wore in the first place (at least as far as I knew).

As we left the circus, I felt weary from my performance, and I told Alexis how she was living proof that makeup does not generate beauty, and I told her how beautiful she looks naturally. She smiled and laughed, and said, "Hippie talk, Hippie Dogma," and as we made our way into Cyrus's car, I saw Cyrus waving, and I had no idea why he was waving. I heard a shrilling voice say loudly, "Who's that young man driving?"

I turned around to answer Alexis's mom, but before I could say a word, Cyrus put on a limousine driver's hat that was near his feet in his car and made his way to Alexis's mom. He informed Alexis's mom that he was a chauffeur hired by Mr. Smith. He promised her that he'd get Alexis and I around safely and to not worry because, "Your daughter is in the hands of a Chauffeur unmatched in Chauffeuring." Cyrus made sure to note that if any funny business went on in the back, he'd make sure to halt it at once. Then he asked Alexis's mom, "Unless you want your daughter doing funny business in the back? I mean, after all, after this night, life is basically over, isn't that right, Mrs. Sanjay?" Cyrus bid Alexis's mom a grand night (those were literally his words: "I bid you a grand night") and left her standing there perplexed and confused, which was surely to later morph into anger and wonder about that rude Chauffeur in the slovenly jeans and Chauffeur hat, and his manner. I thought for a brief moment that she was about to call Cyrus a fag™.

We made our way back to my place for my mom and got out of there quickly, and Cyrus scolded us and told Alexis how much of a prude her mother was and how her mother and his father should be a couple, and Alexis just nodded in agreement and told me she was sorry we had to go through this hellish Prom crap.

To be quite honest, I was just waiting for Alexis to change into herself and wipe all that makeup off her face, which she let her mom put on her to be nice, but then again, I wasn't sure if I'd be able to handle the stinging sensation of looking at her, which the makeup was blocking (The Alexis Effect Dogma). I didn't tell Alexis this or any of those types of thoughts I was having about her, but I had a feeling she knew what I was thinking as I stared out the window and saw her through the reflection of the window staring at me and talking to Cyrus about how great it was that he was going to get his picture taken alone.

(And I knew I definitely did not want be a Pastor™ then, but weirdly, my human computer was still calling me a fag™.)

I came out of my rumination as Alexis was innocently asking Cyrus about his mom not caring about Prom. Cyrus talked about how his parents were usually not home anyways, and since he was kicked off the basketball team, his parents had been going somewhere almost every weekend. Cyrus told Alexis that his parents knew he hated after-school dances and anything of its kind and that they probably didn't even know it was Prom since communication with his parents now only consisted of, "Are you eating tonight? How's school? Me and your father are leaving for the weekend, so be respectful of the house."

Alexis said she was sorry, but Cyrus was having none of it. He told Alexis that while it was sad, it was just the way his family was dysfunctional and that every family has their unique dysfunction, and that was his family's and he was willing to talk about it, which most people weren't. He also added, "Plus a lot of time spent with family isn't usually a good thing. 18 years is a long time, and being away from them is really nice." (**Correction:** Added, added. You say this over and over. Add some conversation in there, like on TV. Stop just saying he added this, said that, she said this, he said that. And spell out 18, eighteen. Minus 15 points. Education.)

DISCLAIMER: I REPEAT, THERE IS NO ONE LISTENING. "What will it be, whore?" I asked Alexis, since we were now joking about her mom subjecting her to a life as a whore, and I was her sad, gloomy middle-aged client, and Cyrus was her newly found Pimp.

"I don't know. Think this corner looks pretty good. My mom told me that if I don't want to become a whore then I'd better lose my chastity on a divine night like Prom night. I've decided to not lose my chastity divinely as my God-and-Jesus™-serving mother so fervently preached, and to lose it in the forces of Lucifer™ on this corner to my sad, lonely, womanizing client, or Chastity Slayer, next to me. Hey, Jubbee…How much did you charge this somber man to slay my holy chastity?" Alexis asked her pimp.

"Well, I told him that tonight all his sick, lonely, and confused thoughts of pedophilia were at his domain. I told him that he would be charged the Chastity-slaying rate and a miscellaneous rate for the cherry on top, so the total came out to be ten thousand dollars plus a guaranteed lifetime servitude to the devil," Jubbee/Cyrus said.

"I'm ready for dinner," I said, breaking out of character.

Alexis decided where we were to eat, and the whole meal we heard the question, "Are you going to Prom?" at least 50 times from people looking at us. So, (50/50) we ate, talked, joked some more (and also said, "Yes," 50 more times), and then made our way to get pictures taken, and then our 10 minutes of Prom would finally be over.

People stared at Cyrus as he walked in, not because he was alone, for there were many girls who went alone together (that's literally what I heard them say, "We're going alone, together"), but because he was not in a Gatsby™ outfit, although he was in his jeans and white T-shirt, with a beautiful Chauffer's hat, and he was getting his picture taken alone while holding out his arm, pretending to have his arm around someone like a mental patient. That whole Prom nonsense was worth it to see Cyrus do what he did and to see everyone stare at him and say that he was acting this way because he still had a grudge for getting kicked off the basketball team. (Of course he had a grudge, since he was such a different guy when he was on the team, right? Cyrus was no longer putting a ball in a hoop, so he was now a fag™, a weirdo with a grudge, and people at Prom just soo knew it.)

I took 2 serious pictures with Alexis for her mother and my mom, then she poured water on her face, and all the makeup that she had reapplied in Cyrus's car was smeared, and we took a picture like that (Oh, we where such horrible kids. MAL, send your kids away from wherever it was that this took place. MAL Dogma.), then the rest of the pictures were of me and Alexis ripping our attire off and changing clothes in front of everyone waiting to get their picture taken (a special request I made to the photographer to keep shooting while we changed). The night was actually turning out to be quite exciting and funny. The photographer refused to take the pictures while we were changing, but I vibrantly told him, "We paid for your services, so take the goddamn pictures, you Douchey, wannabe artist fiend."

As we were leaving and Alexis was making me sting inside again, and I now had a newfound sympathy for dressed-up circus animals, a song started playing, and the words were filtered and hardly could be understood because of the enormous boom that was heard in the song. Cyrus walked by some girls who were Dry Humping™, and suddenly the lyrics became clearer, and the Rapper™ said, "Where would a playa be witout dem sluts? My trainers, indeed, dhese sluts a playa need. You's nastie but yar God's purpose. My playa trainers, just come to me, just come to me." The girls continued to Dry Hump™, and Cyrus walked up to them, stuck his ass in the air, slapped it, and yelled, "Freak me baby." Laughing our way out, we headed to Cyrus's house, which was empty.

The Prom nocturnal gala was finally over, and it had to be just before midnight because, as I sat next to Alexis waiting for Cyrus to enter a million codes that protected and controlled every material item in his house (his dad was a bit of a paranoid tight ass), I had that feeling of a new day starting. It was strange to be awake at the dawn of a new day, and most times I was, I always had a feeling of, "Damn, I wish I was asleep right now since I have to get up soo unusually earlier for school" (at least until the minute passed and it was a new day).

I could hear Cyrus running around the house, cussing his father who was not present, but he had hoped that his bitter resentment energy would somehow travel to his father (Hippie talk, Hippie Dogma). As Cyrus was running around entering numerous codes, I looked over at Alexis, and at that moment, staring at her countenance (thanks to Ms. O'Hara's assignment of Hugo's™ *Les Miserables*, or the translation of Hugo's™ *Les Miserables,* I say countenance all the time. BRAINWASHED), I realized that 50 years from now, if Alexis and I were together (oh my god), I would still get that stinging sensation that I had gotten then by looking at her, and I could only imagine the feelings she would generate inside of me when we made love 50 years from now (The Alexis Effect, Dogma).

I finally told Alexis that she was the only girl that could generate these profound sentimental feelings of love, without having even intimately kissed, or, for that matter, even touched her skin. (Hey Ma and human computer, I guess you were right, I must really be a fag™. But really, what does it matter if another girl were thinking these things about Alexis?)

"Do you realize that I have not even touched your skin, and you're talking about marrying me whenever I come around?" I asked.

"Yes, I do. Why don't you touch my skin right now? Please don't try and kiss me, though, because a kiss that follows kiss talk is just soo Douchey, especially for the first kiss. Don't you think that asking for a kiss or talking about kissing and then a minute later kissing ensues, that it just ruins the whole idea and genuineness of kissing?"

"Yes I do, and I think it would be the same for touching your skin. Even if I touched your skin, I would be getting too close to you and starting something, that once it's begun, cannot be revamped. As I told you before, I'm not ready for what we'd have if we started it. It can't be contrived, it can't be planned, it just has to happen."

"I think you're scared of those feelings you get when you look at me, and you're even more frightened of how, if those feelings are soo strong from just looking at me, you can't even begin to contemplate how powerful the feelings will be if you touched my skin, kissed me, held my hand…if we made love. You're not sure if you have the capabilities of handling those feelings, and I understand completely, but like I said before, once you come around, I'll be waiting, because I've found the one, and so have you, but you need to develop your capacity for the feelings you'll get from me and you to me." (I had no idea what she was talking about.) "Or maybe it's that you talk about people being Douche Bags, hypocrites, not genuine, having no heart or genuine per-sonality, and on and on with you, when really, just maybe you're the one who's scared of anything having to do with love, genuineness…anything with heart. The feelings are soo powerful because you've found it, and sadly most people don't. They're always looking in the wrong places or trying too hard to find it, they fail to just let it happen, or worst of all, they force it to happen. I'll still be waiting for you, whether five years or fifty, well, maybe not that long. We'll get married and live in peace, you'll see." (My mom would've been soo proud of our 50's cinema love.)

DISCLAIMER: I REPEAT, THERE IS NO ONE LISTENING. Cyrus was still cussing his father, and he began talking about how much of a paranoid tight ass he was and how all these alarms amounted to shit, because by the time any enforcement came, the people who triggered the alarms would have done what they needed to do.

We sat there for a while, not really saying anything. Alexis was laughing at Cyrus and telling him how uptight his uptight father made him, and for some time, we just sat there together thinking our own thoughts. Our minds were swirling (yeah, so what, we had a couple drinks, thank god MAL wasn't around to ruin our experience), everyone had their own distinct thoughts, and it was extremely tranquil sitting there knowing that 3 minds became peacefully silent at the same time, without any communication. It was an understanding that needed no words, and no Douche Bag saying in the background, "Awkward silence." (Although that probably would've made me giggle a little bit.)

A little while later Cyrus broke the silence and said, "You know what's really depressing is that right now, across this country, soo many girls are losing their virginity on their desired planned night, and soo many of them will regret it later down the line. Hey Alexis, are you a virgin?" Cyrus abruptly asked.

"No, I'm not."

"Did you have a set time and night for when you lost it?"

"No."

"Do you regret losing it to the guy you lost it to?"

"Yes, I do, but I really don't think it would've been that special anyways, so better to be clumsy and awkward with a Douche."

"I'm sorry, I didn't mean to swirl bad memories in your mind. I was just curious if you were planning a big Prom nocturnal divine love fest with Smith over here."

"You can be a real Douche sometimes, Cyrus," I said.

"It's OK, and no, actually I was not. And the only reason I'm going to Prom is because I'd rather go through an hour suffering than the rest of my life listening to my mom talk about how I never went to Prom my senior year and how she knows that I deeply regretted it and how she knows that I know that the opportunity will never come again."

"I'll bet your mom and dad never go out and do anything romantic since your mom thinks life ends after high school," Cyrus said.

"Yeah, that's a wise assumption. It's pretty sad, and I don't know how my dad can put up with it. He must have really loved her when they were young and together. She must've not been soo nostalgic when he met her, because the way she is now, it's really sad, and even sadder for my father having to live with a fifty-year-old woman whose mind is in the 1970s. Where do your parents go every weekend, on a romantic getaway?"

"No, my dad usually is going on business trips and playing golf, and he makes my mom go along since she's his assistant. I don't think that's much of a romance. I don't think my parents have had sex since I was born. It's actually really sad because my mom seems to really love my dad, but he just is not human or forgets that he is, and he's gone into that abyss of a habit and now feels nothing, and if he does feel something, he shits it out every morning. All he cares about is accumulating a number so he can look at a tiny piece of paper every morning and see a big number from his bank account. It's sad when people like my dad are afraid to express what they feel in the right way, or maybe it's not sad, just pathetic, 'cause he might just really be who he perceives himself to be."

I had never heard Cyrus openly talk about how he felt about his relationship between his dad and himself and what it was really like, but Alexis had a tendency to bring out hidden fortresses in people (probably a future psychologist (modern Dogmatist)).

We sat there the whole night and on through the morning. It was basically a very long therapeutic session among three people who had no degrees in modern psychology (Dogmatism), and whenever someone talked about something, we just talked naturally since we didn't have degrees, so no one gave a textbook answer. It was a moment in life that all three of us severely needed and would never forget.

After talking all night with Cyrus and Alexis, there was no situation that could come in the future that would now make us feel distant or uncomfortable around each other. I began to fall asleep when Cyrus screamed, "Let's go to the beach since we're all now certified psychologists (Dogmatists)! Let's nurture and counsel all the poor girls and boys who lost their chastity on the beach."

Alexis had been asleep, and I came out of my daze from Cyrus shouting, and I had dozed on Alexis's shoulder, and when I woke up, and she at about the same time, my hand was holding hers, and I felt like I was going to pass out (yep, my parents and human computer were right, no doubt, I'm gay, a fag™, but I can't lie and make this moment completely idealized, because my pants were also sticking straight up near the groin region, and it wasn't because I had to pee), but Cyrus's words made me smile, and we headed out in his car and made our way to the beach. (The beach authorities allowed only Young Conservatives™ to inhabit the beach on Prom night, any other night was off limits. And it was up to the authorities to decide who was a Young Conservative™ or not and who was allowed to romanticize on the beach to complete the good ol' fashioned Prom night.)

The beach was about 40 minutes from Cyrus's house, and we got there just in time as the sun was rising and waking the inhabitants. Cyrus got out of the car, and me and Alexis followed behind him, and I looked at Alexis, and I

171

kissed her (That feeling cannot be written in words. I had wished at that moment that I could've been clumsy and awkward with Alexis.) as Cyrus went jumping around to every D-bag girl he saw next to a D-bag guy, or D-bag guy next to a D-bag guy, or a D-bag girl next to a D-bag girl, and he would repeatedly say to each one, "I'm sorry. It'll be OK. Life will go on after high school, in fact, it'll be far more superior if you can only see it. It really will get better. Don't worry. It was a mistake, but you'll get through it, and it's nothing to become seriously depressed over. It's not your fault, and I mean it's a mistake, not because you had sex, but because you just had sex with the guy, girl next to you on some old-fashioned, out-of-date, horrible, very-not-special night. Just, please, for the sake of the good of the world, do not become a future MAL. Everyone told you this night was supposed to be magical and divine. They lied, but now you're no longer callow, and you can see that it was all a big fanciful lie for people long ago who are now trying to suppress us not letting us come up with our own dance, our own tradition. I don't want Prom destroyed, but it should remain in the past, and we should be allowed to have our own gala. Don't worry, though, you'll be a better person as long as you can realize it wasn't your fault and made-up nights like these aren't as significant as we make them out to be. And that these kinds of nights really do nothing but make most people more miserable and too serious. Those are the feelings you are feeling right now as you wake up, but acknowledge them, and realize you have a choice. In fact, from this experience, I hope that you now realize that it's OK to not take these hellhole type of things and events soo seriously, as we all are together. So here's our tradition…next year you juniors should plan the last dance to be on the beach, where everyone has to come looking like they've just had too much to drink and just had sex in really, supposedly nice but weirdly uncomfortable clothes. Whether you really want to have sex or not before coming will be completely up to you. Just, please, don't call it Prom. Can't you see it right this very moment, as I can, that we're all participating in this, or am I high, or am I transforming into a Hippie™? Either way, let's you and me hold hands on the beach, and I speak especially to all of you, you beautiful ladies." Cyrus had a lot of sand thrown in his eyes that morning, and he was called fag™ around a 100 times.

Chapter 10

I meant to have ten chapters.

INTERMISSION #3

HOW TO SEEM SMART IN THE EYES OF BRAD CRUISE AND RECEIVE A GOOD GRADE WHEN WRITING AN ESSAY FOR HIS CLASS

Example Taken From Brad Cruise's King Lear Lecture

Brad Cruise's Themes/Keys For Essay: (Taken from one of Brad Cruise's classes, includes his own personal notes and lecture-note keys):

• Discuss the hasty, blind irrationality of both King Lear and Gloucester in the beginning of the play. How would the course of events for each character had changed if the two aforementioned characters used a little more reasoning and time to come to a conclusion? Or would there be any change at all?

• What are Goneril and Regan really after? Discuss the trinity of evil: Edmund, Goneril, and Regan.

• Examine Cordelia as divinity, unjustly suffering, and remaining divine, even through turmoil and cruelty.

• Discuss the ending, the "Dead March." What does it symbolize? Think of our dark times today. Who and what does Edgar symbolize? What is being alluded to with Edgar? What do his ending lines say about his character? (Hint: think of Cordelia.)

Themes/Topics One Should Thoroughly Discuss In One's Essay To Seem Smart In The Eyes Of Brad Cruise, And To Receive A Good Grade:

• Discuss the hasty, blind irrationality of both King Lear and Gloucester in the beginning of the play. How would the course of events for each character have changed if the two aforementioned characters used a little more reasoning and time to come to a conclusion? Or would there be any change at all?

• What are Goneril and Regan really after? Discuss the triangle of evil: Edmund, Goneril, and Regan.

• Examine Cordelia as divinity, unjustly suffering, and remaining divine, even through turmoil and cruelty.

• Discuss the ending, the "Dead March." What does it symbolize? Think of our dark times today. Who and what does Edgar symbolize? What is being alluded to with Edgar? What do his ending lines say about his character? (Hint: think of Cordelia.)

Another Poem From Cary Smith, Or The Other One Which He Didn't Turn In In Ms. O'Hara's Class, And This Has Been Really Long, And Took A Long Time Because It Is Very Hard To Type Fast When You're Constantly Having To Press The Shift Key Trying To Capitalize The Beginning Of Each Word

epic POEM

by

Cary Smith (A Capitalizer of the P in Patriotism)

"Does this atrocious work ever end? Greg Hawkins is no Literary Preservationist, as he claims. He is worthy of no academic title, and that title should be stripped from him for leaving in these stupid, inane intermissions. After reading this hideous poem from Cary Smith, I now grossly desire, with all of my cordial hale, to slap both in their cuckold faces until they bleed out of their noses."

—Brad Cruise

THIS

WILL

BE

AN

EPIC POEM

OF GRAND PROPORTIONS,

100 PAGES LONG,

FULLA ALLEGORICAL AND METAPHORICAL DELIGHTS

THAT ARE SURE TO MAKE THE EUROPEANS BRIGHT,

BUT

THE

GAME

IS

ON,

AND THAT IS QUITE FUN,

SO, (50/50)

WITH

GREAT ADMISSION

FOR

THE LOVE OF VIEWING THE GAME,

I

ADMIT,

ON THIS EPIC POEM...

I

MAY

HAVE...

CHEATED

A

BIT

DISCOVER WHAT'S REALLY IN THESE ( )

It has been told of Cary Smith's work here, *Four Corners or A Book That Will Tickle Your Intellectual Nipple*, that if you take every phrase and sentence in parentheses, these ( ) thingys, translate them to Greek, and then read them all backward…it is told that when one does this, they discover that they don't like The Beatles™ as much as they thought they did.

—Greg Hawkins L.P. (Or Just A Guy Who Has An Obsession With Having A Title At The End Of His Name)

4

Chapter 1

The summer went on as usual. There was plenty of sitting, television, movies, listening to music, and engaging in various activities that included getting fried, being hot, and eating a lot of food. (With all of this poop, I turned out fine (well, at least to some), so what will the MAL blame? Of course not themselves.)

Alexis took off in the middle of the night during a random summer night and only left me a note. I thought about getting a job, but I didn't care much for extra material wants, like a car or money to go out on dates, or whatever it was that a high-school teenager was supposed to do during the summer (like going to a day baseball game to make my body as tan and brown as it could get and never catching a foul ball).

DISCLAIMER: I REPEAT, THERE IS NO ONE LISTENING. A car was something that had already been a major annoyance for me, and Cyrus was there for rides, and by this summer my sister had obtained her license and was driving my mom's old car that I had once driven. My sister worked all summer at the mall and gloated about it almost all the times I heard her speaking, which was not very often, but when I did hear her speak, it consisted of talking about how much fun her job was selling clothes and greeting customers with a fake hello and, "Oh yeah, that outfit looks great on you," and talking about all the hot guys that she saw at the mall on a daily basis. I figured she was better suited for the amenities of my mom's old car because I'd rather be homeless or living on scraps than to work a job that she was working, and those were mainly the only jobs for people my age.

One of the few jobs that would even dare hire some untrustworthy high-school student was to sell clothes for 12 people sitting in a boardroom, conferring on where to put a new store and getting the designer to design new clothes, and somehow those people had the D-bagness to claim that their job actually required fifty hours a week for five days. (Minus 15 points. **Correction:** be more like Hemingway™. I never thought that I would have ever contemplated not liking Hemingway™ until I entered Independence. Luckily I had read enough Hemingway™ on my own to not let the Educators™ bother me. Education.)

So my sister was now making sales to help buy a newly acquired third house for one of the twelve board members. I figured she deserved the car, at least she could work that job. A perfect prototype for the 12 board members (she would be fine as long as she was getting free clothes every now and then).

This was it.

My final year of confinement.

The school year started at the usual time of late August, and that generally meant hot, dry weather. I've read journalistic accounts and have seen documentaries (again lots of TV) of inmates, and almost nine out of ten times, the inmate attested that the final year of confinement was, by far, the hardest. They say it was the hardest because they were soo close to being free, yet every day they still had that itch to break free and run for a path of uncertainty, for a path that might lead nowhere, but it was a path without confinement. It was a path that was free (at least until you were somewhere else, but that really wasn't the point, I guess).

I started to feel what the inmates talked about as Cyrus picked me up for day one of a hundred and eighty two. As I sat in the passenger seat of Cyrus' pig sty and looked at the power lines and the houses all lined up, looking exactly alike, only being able to distinguish one house from the other because the garages where painted different colors, or some houses kept tidy landscaping. (Is Communism™ really dead in America? Corporate Dogma.) I began to have feelings of leaving right then, not finishing high school (and I also began to wonder how many commas were in those sentences^, and why they were there, 'cause I never really paused until now. Education).

DISCLAIMER: I REPEAT, THERE IS NO ONE LISTENING. Cyrus and I had talked about leaving Independence many times, as we came to the conclusion that neither of us would go to college since it was just a process of weeding out the poor and slackers and a key component to making a good salary (Education), and we figured that we would never want to work a job that required a college degree because, for the most part, it would just be in a corporate atmosphere, and Cyrus always said he'd seen his father's employees, and that atmosphere was like high school, but instead of a 6-hour day, it would be an 8 to ten-hour day. And it was 7 hours indoors instead of 5, and there were more machines. (It was looking like we were going to be weeded out.)

We also figured that we were tired of having one excellent, genuine teacher a year and the rest being complete shit, so we ruled that out. Cyrus always talked about being a doctor, but then he always said otherwise right after saying that he wanted to, saying, "It's not worth the twelve years of school or the debt that school will incur because, when it comes down to it, most people won't respect what medical doctors have undertaken to be a philanthropist to the best of their ability. Most people want instantaneous results, perfection, and will sue you for one mistake, and then you're ruined, or you have to be soo cautious that you become frozen. Or I would be asked to not care for someone because they need to pay me and have no insurance and so I can pay my medical school bills."

Of course Cyrus and I always discussed this, but here we were at the crack of dawn in late August, making our way to finish our sentence.

So we were driving down the street, and I could now see the shopping center next to our school that always made the start of the day seem desolate and forlorn, for I always knew when I saw the McDonald's™ and Starbucks™, which were full of students getting their legal drugs for the day, that the grounds were only a few blocks away.

This morning was even more difficult because I knew that I would now only have one genuine person to talk to since Alexis had graduated and moved out of her house a few weeks later, telling no one she was leaving. I had no idea where Alexis had left to, and I didn't know if I would ever see her again, but for the first time since I was 10 years old and my dog was put to sleep, I actually had feelings of something missed.

Alexis had left me a note at my door before she left to wherever it was that she left to, and I still had not opened it. It had become my vade mecum. (Hey, I learned the word that summer, and where the hell else was I going to use it? I apologize if you had trouble pronuncing it, because I did at first.) So as Cyrus parked the car and I began to make my way to my first class, I felt it was a very good time to open Alexis's note. (And this was only day 1 and I already needed a pick-me-up. I already needed a vade mecum. I should've just gone to Starbucks™ more, now that I think of it. At least it was a legal drug.)

On the front of the note, it read: "An arcane love." I was interrupted by Cyrus screaming at me, "And I say good luck today, but not to you, to your mind."

I called him an idiot and proceeded to my first class, wondering what the hell arcane meant.

I don't know how I made it through four years at Independence High, but I do know how I made it through my last year. You finally talked to me. We had always talked before when we were in classes together, or at least I tried talking to you, and you were always soo different, especially when it comes to love. I gave you every sign whenever I was near you that I felt something that I knew I would never feel for another, yet you never realized it, it never even crossed your mind. I figured you were a prude, stuck-up or just a womanizer, but as is almost always the case, the assumptions were wrong. The way you were with me was my final year at Independence. You made me realize that it really isn't that scary and obscure to venture away from the norm, especially when the norm is not soo good. So I did it. I left. I'll probably never talk to any of those girls again in my life, although I still wish them the best and hope they don't end up like my mother, with desirous nostalgia for high school at the age of 50. I want you to know that marriage means nothing to me with you, as long as we're together. I thought about what you had told me that morning at the beach, about is what we feel lust, love, or is love just lust prolonged? I can tell you that almost every guy I've been attracted to has been a feeling of lust. Once I got to know them, I still had that same feeling that I had at the start, and soon there were no feelings at all. I can say, with you, I had the same feeling at first, but that moment when you were walking over to me at lunch and we talked about everything in so little of time, I got a feeling that

188

was not lust, it was not lust prolonged, it was love, or maybe it was neither of those words. Maybe it was something unattainable with words. Maybe I'm foolish in believing that no other can give me the same feeling you have given me, a feeling that was garnered without you even touching my skin. I always wondered why you had never tried to kiss me, you're such a fag™, wink, wink. I stopped wondering and realized you were one in a billion, you really are, and the feeling I get when I think of you almost (hehe, get it, almost) hurts soo bad I can hardly breathe. I'm sure you'll laugh when you read this and say I'm corny, and I know whenever you attempt to talk like this you just say that you're changing things up a bit and working on your Hippie Dogma speak, but I really can hardly breathe right now as I write this letter knowing that some day you'll be reading it.

"You going in, or you just going to stand out here?" I was interrupted by my American-government teacher.

"Oh…yeah, was just making my way in."

After about 30 minutes of sitting in government class and listening to the teacher give a brief description of his past and then give the outline for the course (which was usually rigorously followed, since the manual said to, Education), I began to read the letter again:

I really don't think you realize how special and rare you really are. I really hope you use your abilities to apprehend, and then stick with your thoughts and not give in so that you'll be with the crowd for good, especially when the crowd seems mental right now. I hope you realize how smart you truly are, and please do not waste your mind. You made me realize that sometimes the normal is crazy and the crazy is normal. You told me that going anywhere will never be scary as long as you don't forget that humans are humans, and while many will have more faults than others and many will seem on another planet, there will always be one who is on this planet and who doesn't make you feel like you're alone. I know you feel what I feel, but I also know you're different, don't believe in conventionalism unless it's still grounded, and you go with what you go with, you follow your heart. I hope some day you'll real-ize that you can't go at life alone, no matter how strong you are. You always say we die alone. Yeah, so what? We're living now. Everyone needs somebody, and not everybody finds what we have found. Do you imagine us forty years from now and see us feeling the same as we do now, not caring if you have let yourself go a little and I have stopped pretending my hair isn't gray? Do you imagine us never losing interest in conversation with each other? Both of us have parents that went with conventional wisdom, lived single 'til they were thirty, hurriedly got married to the first decent person they found, had kids, the kids grew up, and the love is obsolete. The conversations of only small talk and the general angst and ill will they possess. I imagine us never having this. I imagine they didn't imagine these things in the future. I imagine they didn't imagine and only planned, and to me there is a huge difference. Planning takes no imagination. In fact, I don't imagine it, I know it, you met my mom. Remember when we fell asleep on Cyrus's couch and woke up? I could've died right then and there. There was no control of my body, the feeling I had for you, the touch of your skin was soo strong. You're the only person I know who could make marriage look soo ruinous and diabolical and make the alternative seem soo genuine and true. We'll be together some day, and that some day won't be 'til we're both ready. When you come around, and if I'm not ready, then we'll be ready some other day, but I know that day will come when we consummate and make the triangle one. Let me know when you're ready to be nakedly awkward!

"OK, so we're going to watch a documentary on the founding fathers, and here is your textbook for the year," said my government teacher. Well, educational movies and a teacher using a teacher's manual...I knew this was going to be one easy C.

The movie began to run, and a monotone narrator began talking about Jefferson™ and his lisp and his fear of speaking in public, and my teacher was sadly reading his manual on the textbook, writing down lesson plans that the book suggested. I began to get bored (and realized Alexis may be trying to trap me) with a subject that had been taught to me since I could remember. (Also, after viewing that educational film, I finally knew who used those words my mom always had on her calendar. Education.)

DISCLAIMER: I REPEAT, THERE IS NO ONE LISTENING. I felt like screaming, "Yes, me love government. They do good for the people, they are not corrupt, they do not become inhuman with power, most of them just want to be exalted to the top, they're all vying for the top of the mountain. I love my country. I love the name United States™. I love the law, yes I do. I'm now an adequate member of society, and I will obey and respect the government, even if I feel wrong has occurred and I begin to malfunction. I will just ignore the thoughts with drink and not question why. Please let Robot 201,000,001 out into society as you take away the classes that give us balance and make some actually want to go to school." At the time the school had a choice between a creative class or another class like the one I was in, except with some PPP sign attached to it for the actual, human robots to earn an extra decimal point on their grade point average, or to eliminate both. The school was choosing between the PPP or elimination, and once again, I was P-P-Pretty glad it was year 4. (My name is Cary Smith, please do not think I hate America™. I'm American born, that is that. Senator McCarthy still lives on TV.) (Too much TV, but I turned out OK (to some), so hey, what'd ya say Senator and MAL?)

I began to wonder if it was a book about Jefferson™ or Confucius™ (he would have loved Prom) where I read a quote saying, "Government is a necessary evil." I couldn't remember, and the movie was now into that stage where most movies of its kind shown in school start to be repetitive and tell you only half the story (Education), so I read the rest of the letter.

I'm not going to tell you where I am, but I'm going to leave you this e-mail address, and when you find that you'll find no one else like me and that human life was not meant to be one of solitude (because, you know Cyrus is meant for other things, and he's probably not going to be around for very much longer once you guys are done with Independence), then write to me, and I'll tell you where I am. I know that you won't forget me, you seem to remember everything, but I'm still going to say don't forget me. Like you said, why do two people have to get a contract if they're in love? Why can't they just be together, fuck tax benefits and a marriage for tax benefits and being able to say we're married so we can have Douchey, contented, middle-aged married friends in order not to feel the social awkwardness, not coming from us but from those others who don't like us because we didn't do as they did (it's funny how those people at Independence who were like that and called anything they didn't understand weird or faggy, never seem to change, no matter where they are or what situation they're in). The key words in your little rant were "just be together." When you want this, write to me.

Love always,
Alexis aka Jubbee's number-1 employee.

<>

191

I knew Alexis was different, but some of the things she was saying had me saying, "Huh?" (Then I began to wonder how come short words—like how, uh, ah, eh, huh, oh, ah, aw, has, and as—are soo hard to remember eh-ow to spell. Education.)

I didn't know if I'd ever see Alexis again. I didn't know if I could ever feel the way she did about me or be able to express it as she had to me. I knew one thing, though, after I had finished the letter…I was never going to lose the letter, and it would always be my vade mecum. (And I was also confident that I may see her again, since she left me an e-mail to write her back, but I still wasn't too sure if I would write her. I felt like I could go it alone. I was also confident about this because I knew my human computer would not let me down and let me know if I was writing to her on a human level, and what grade level I would be at when writing the letter via e-mail, if and when I did. And surely if I wasn't formatting it in the so-called Educational way, I'd be in 2nd grade. Education.)

Chapter 2

I got to my final class of day one, which was right before lunch. A perk of being in the final year of your sentence, if you played your cards right (with the warden and a paper with a list of classes, Education) and got all your credits in and weren't going to an elite college, was that you didn't have to stick around for the lunch period.

Cyrus was in my final class of the day, which was good, so then I wouldn't have to wait for him at his car while he did god knows what after school. I made my way to the back of the classroom and eavesdropped on conversations going on in front of me (you don't want to know what they were, especially if you like your hair), as Cyrus had not gotten to class yet. (Well, I guess I'll tell you.) The conversations in front of me were about some Douche crap called Senioritis™ and how people were going to start missing one day of school a week in the second half of the year.

DISCLAIMER: I REPEAT, THERE IS NO ONE LISTENING. I started to smile because I thought to myself that I've had this bullshit called Senioritis™ since I was 12 years old. What was funny about those kids was that they had no idea the school would lose money for every day they missed with their Senioritis™ escapades. (Great system they had, huh? My goal was to have this be banned by many schools because it reveals the great, dumb system of how they earn money.) I wondered how much the school would lose from me missing 2 weeks before Prom (if they had actually put money back into the school while I was there, I might have felt bad) to avoid being asked because I didn't have the coolness to tell anyone no, so I figured I'd miss the 2 weeks with Cyrus and avoid the whole hellish Prom situation.

Cyrus walked in, and I acknowledged him, and as he walked over to the empty desk beside me I began to feel like I was an employee of the state, and I looked at all the students in the class, thought of all the students that made up Independence, and thought about how much money the state was making from every student at Independence who was present, and I figured it had to be quite a bit of money (I had heard that morning from Cyrus about this present=money thing, so I was a little gung ho about it, as you can tell). I wondered what the hell they did with that money they made from their free service workers, because they sure as hell were not investing any of it back into Independence, except maybe $500 (Or I should spell it out…you must, or you're stupid. Five hundred. Minus 15 points. Education.) for the annual repainting of Independence.

The teacher came into the classroom, and by the looks of it, she could have been one of the students, in fact, at first glance of her I thought she was going to make her way to the last remaining desk, but she walked right by it and took out her manual.

The teacher was a very short, red-haired woman who had the countenance (*Les Miserables*™ assignment again, and also, don't forget to insert an accent mark, since it's really hard to do on the human computer, so I'll leave it up to you) of a fourteen-year-old. As the whole class glanced her over, I looked over at Cyrus, and he gave me a funny look and said, "Is this a fucking joke? She looks like a freshman, doesn't she? She better be one damn good teacher."

"Yeah, she really does. I figured she was going to have a seat at that last empty desk."

The teacher introduced herself as Ms. Pampour (this was the last time I would respect and call her Ms…Education). She told the class that she had recently received her teaching credentials from a local prestigious university and that she substituted last year while receiving her master's, and she was then hired here at Independence (and she was soo super excited).

DISCLAIMER: I REPEAT, THERE IS NO ONE LISTENING. She was 24 years old, which gave her only 6 years more of life than most of the class, and I was thinking to myself that the state was obviously not paying teachers any of that money they made from their free laborers, because if they did, they would be able to hire far more qualified educators than a lady who was only 6 years older than most of her class, despite what pieces of paper she had obtained.

I wondered what in the hell this lady could possibly teach that we didn't already know. I mean, she really didn't have much life experience, except for what she had in college (so not very much, since she obviously had it all paid for). I wondered what relevance, what knowledge of life, this lady could teach us, because teaching (to me) wasn't just about following the curriculum and teaching by the textbook. It was also about teaching the class relevant matters in life (O'Hara Dogma), but there was no way this lady could be capable of that, and it wasn't her fault, it was just that she could really offer nothing to the class except what her lesson plan and textbook said. I guess I was now just spoiled after having Ms. O'Hara for a teacher. I just couldn't grasp how a girl just out of college became a teacher of a class full of 18-year-olds when she was only 24 years old herself. I figured this must have been how most of these teachers here started out, except for the few like O'Hara, who didn't start teaching until they were a bit older.

DISCLAIMER: I REPEAT, THERE IS NO ONE LISTENING. It was clear with this new teacher that the state could care less about their free laborers actually getting life knowledge from their teachers (Education) (And probably most of the students could care less too, and so the corrupt Administrators say then that they stop caring and take the money for themselves, but I have a feeling it was that way with the annoying few in the Administration from the beginning, they just used all the apathy as an excuse.) so long as they got the text and came to class. "Present equals money, present for the state," this must have been their secret motto. (Cyrus's truth claim was sure far from happening here, because I wrote all of that with my fingers shaking, wondering if I'd be shot soon.)

DISCLAIMER: I REPEAT, THERE IS NO ONE LISTENING. (PROBABLY WILL BE A LOT OF DISCLAIMERS FOR SOMEONE LIKE PAMPOUR, WHO OPENED THE EYES TO MANY INSANE HAPPENINGS

AND SITUATIONS. SEE BELOW ↓. AND AT THIS POINT, I WAS LESS SCARED OF MY HUMAN COMPUTER, FOR IT WAS A VERY OBIDIENT HUMAN COMPUTER. IT ONLY WENT FROM BIG TO SMALL LETTERS WHEN I TOLD IT TO. Although I do feel bad calling it an "it" since it was always trying to correct me on a human level.)

Pampour sure got the message clear about present equates money, present for the state, because as she went over her guideline for the course (which was state mandated, of course), she made it soo very clear with repeated enthusiasm that more than three unexcused absences would lower your grade one whole letter grade (Education). As she was shoving this in the class's heads, Cyrus looked over to me and said, "You have got to be kidding me" (he was saying that a lot lately). "How much of a joke is this, that this little 24-year-old who just graduated from her little college is now teaching kids she would almost be in college with? This is all a big joke, and they really got me laughing this time."

As Cyrus said this, he became very fervent and adamant, as he always did when he felt immense anger, and this was clearly a situation where he felt injustice. Cyrus was one pissed-off inmate. He abruptly, in the middle of Pampour going over her Greensheet (it was required by people who were Educators™ to call the educational outline a Greensheet) said, "What really can you teach us?"

"Excuse me?" responded Pampour.

"I mean exactly what I said. I'll give you the college explanation, I'll give you the lecture and spell it out for you. I mean, you're twenty-four years old, and almost all of this class is eighteen years old. That makes you six years older than us. Any logical person would ask themselves what in the hell could this lady teach us? I mean, she can teach us what her guide says, and what the textbook says, what her college professors said, but what can she teach us that is actually relevant and meaningful? What about life will she be able to teach through the various literature we're going to read in this class. You see teaching is not all about just reading some book and taking a test on it, or collecting a paycheck just because you needed a job since you feared people would think you're a loser if you had some other non-professional job for a little bit, especially out of college, god forbid. And what teaching is not all about, I cannot see what you can provide on that part of the equation. So I'll ask you again, what really can you teach us?"

I felt bad for the lady, but she had to be expecting those types of questions when she knew she was going to teach a room full of 18-year-olds. (Or maybe she was soo dumb and thought most were like her and wouldn't be thinking about that at all, because most weren't in the classroom after all. The only difference is that she had a mom who encouraged her to go to college because that mom was saving a bunch of money for her to go, so she didn't have to pay for it herself and be in debt, so she had motivation to really go to college. Education.)

The class actually seemed engaged and ready to hear what she had to say, but all she said was that she was going to teach us what we needed to learn in our final year. Cyrus just smiled and seemed completely dejected, and the class seemed to lose complete respect for this lady as a teacher. (But maybe she could go out with some of the girls and buy them drinks and earn their friendship, or she could just simply buy their friendship just like in her college Sorority days. Education.) Either way, this was why Cyrus and I were friends, or we were both now spoiled from having Ms. O'Hara as our teacher.

Pampour began her first lecture on the first day, which was somewhat surprising, and she pulled out her lesson plan on Existentialism™ (now the existentialists weren't soo nothingness, 'cause they could charge for their trademark^. Hopefully they start charging long after this book, the Existentialists™ I mean) since we were reading *The Stranger*™, but her lesson plan did me in. I lost it, and I instantaneously felt like walking out of that classroom and demanding to be paid from the state after three years of them getting free labor and putting none of that money back into Independence since this was now my teacher (or we must have been performing very badly on those yearly Cuckoo's Nest tests, and they didn't care who taught us).

Pampour did not have the usual teacher handbook for Existentialism™ (Why do they need to explain Existentialism™? I'm confused. Does that make me an existentialist™? Respect the Existentialist™ and capitalize the noun. Minus 15 points. Education.) and *The Stranger*™, she had something far more hilarious. She pulled out her notes from college and began writing them on the board, I kid you not. I couldn't even make up something that absurd.

DISCLAIMER: I REPEAT, THERE IS NO ONE LISTENING. The poor lady should really have been teaching kindergartners, but I guess the state was racking them in fresh, they had to be keeping that money somewhere in hiding to hire a teacher like Pampour. (Or the budget cuts were too much. "I guess you just don't understand bullshit," as my mom would often say, not in those exact words, when I would get upset about these things and tried talking to her. Although she seemed to usually just say this so she could continue watching the tube and get me outta her ears, MAL.)

She was genuinely trying (Pampour, not my mom), but she just should not have been teaching a class full of people nearly her age. Hardly anyone in the class was paying attention. Most were playing on their cell phones under their desks, and one kid said, "If Existentialism believes that the world is meaning-less, as you say, but yet we still have a choice, and many choices in our exis-tence give meaning to the world," (DISCLAIMER: I Repeat, There Is No One Listening) "then why do they have a conceptual name to derive themselves?"

A reasonable question in my mind, and Pampour said, "Great question, we'll get back to that." She continued with her second copy of her college notes, and we never got back to the question. As she wrote down the remain-ing notes, I looked over at Cyrus, and he had his hands over his face and was in complete disarray.

Cyrus didn't say anything the rest of the class period, and as the class was ending, he said out loud, "Have you read *The Stranger*™?"

"Yes, it was a very good book," Pampour said.

"So, (50/50) why don't you lecture on what you got out of the book, ask the 5 people in the class that are the only ones actually hearing this right now who got something out of the book, what they got out of the book, not what your college philosophy professor got from the book and what you had written down from that lecture, and notes about Camus™ and Sartre™ that you don't even really understand and have combined them wrongly and have confused people, BaJesus™," (also could be written out as Black Jesus, in case your memory failed you) "lady."

Cyrus didn't even wait to hear her response, and I don't think she ever gave one. I left the class and looked at Pampour's countenance and her gesticula-tions (still had those translated *Les Miserables* words in my head, so I apolo-gize if they offend you), and as I left the room, I got the impression that she had no idea that someone like Cyrus would call her out, not only about her teacher handbook/college notes but about her age, or lack thereof. She didn't seem to understand the magnitude of the situation. (Or she was an Existentialist™, or at least a college type of existentialist™, because I don't want to give them all

198

a bad name. Education. **Correction**: Existentialist, respect the Existentialist and capitalize the E.)

DISCLAIMER: I REPEAT, THERE IS NO ONE LISTENING. It seemed to me like she was a girl who graduated college, a smart girl at heart, who was unsure of herself, decided to become a teacher, and the state, wanting to keep all their present equals money to themselves, were unable to hire decent qualified Educators™, and, the state, they figured at least Pampour had a degree (Education). It wasn't nearly as bad as their failed experiment of hiring teachers without credentials during the so-called serious budget crunch, like the wannabe Spanishesque, Mr. McDonald.

As I rode home with Cyrus and got ready to embark on hours of television and video games (I still turned out fine, once again, sorry MAL, and for repeating myself to the MAL), I thought to myself that there was now only 181 days left, and after being in Pampour's class, I was sure as hell glad that my sentence was up after this year and I was getting the hell out of Independence (although she was very unintentionally funny and weirdly missable).

Chapter 3

It had to be October™, for the days seemed longer than normal, and it seemed as if the school days were invariable for during the months of October™ and March™: there were no teacher workdays, no traditional holidays, no half days because it was midweek grades, it was just nonstop, grind-it-out days (also known as The True Grit School Days™).

I certainly was not looking forward to March, but luckily Prom season started up during the end of that month. I figured I could ditch once a week like most of the kids were now doing because they had Senioritis™ and wanted to start their itis early, but like I said before, I had Senioritis for quite some time, and my absent days were on a thin threshold, and I needed to save those precious few absent days I had left for Prom season, so I was there every day in October. Plus I figured if everyone was ditching school, then maybe there'd be some reward for showing up when they weren't (but I was wrong).

DISCLAIMER: I REPEAT, THERE IS NO ONE LISTENING. It was definitely October™, because rallies were going on, and kids from previous graduation years were coming back to the school and getting ready for some football game.

All I could think about was what type of personality do those people have to have that came back to this hellhole (move on)? What type of prisoner goes back to his penitentiary? I wondered what the hell was wrong with these people, especially since most of them had just graduated recently, because I'd recognized them. They must be those people like Alexis's mom, who get this illusion at an early age that school years were your finest, and anything to follow is incomparable. (I blame all those beachy songs about school for that.)

Well, so we established it was October™ (we did, right?), and I was sitting in Pampour's class when suddenly she called everyone into a procession, and we walked out of the classroom in an orderly fashion and made our way to the auditorium for a little one on one with the school Sheriff and an ex-junkie. (Always the clichéd ex-junkie. Sometimes you just can't fight clichés, like how saying something is cliché is a cliché. Education.)

DISCLAIMER: I REPEAT, THERE IS NO ONE LISTENING. As the class walked toward the auditorium, I thought about if I were up in a helicopter right now, and it was hovering above Independence, I would see an image that looked similar to those propaganda images you see on the news of our so-called enemies all marching in a large, military procession…all waving their arms up at the same time and moving their arms back down at the same time. The procession would be far smaller, of course, and the gesticulations wouldn't be in synchronization (maybe it would look like a line of army ants invading a house, and if you saw one ant move from the pack, the helicopter would spray it with Raid™, and that would be that).

We got into the auditorium, which I had only been in a couple times. One time for Orientation, and another time for physical-education class, where I was forced to hit a white ball with my arms over a net and pretend my feet were in sand instead of on laminated hardwood flooring (and, of course, the night I watched Cyrus become a weirdo fag™).

So, (50/50 oh god, comma here, I'm not sure, I need a C, and I'm taking a risk putting it there. Those damn so's and their pauses are soo confusing) this was my fourth time in the auditorium, and like my times before, the place was dark, as if the engineers forgot to construct places for lights. It was cold, it was dusty on the floors…it literally felt like you were walking on ice, so cautionary steps were always taken, and that's why there was always a line to get into the place, because everyone was taking their sweet-ass time because they didn't want to fall and slip on their asses. (**Correction:** because, because, because you can't stop saying because. Minus 15 points. Education.)

202

It was always claustrophobic, since they always closed all four doors of the building, and every time (well, 4 times) I went in the place, there was always some authoritative-looking figure standing in the middle.

Finally, after shoe-skating my way to the bleachers, I was sitting down in the auditorium, and I waited there another 30 minutes for the remaining skaters to slide their way to the bleachers.

I thought that it must be a teacher workday, and only the free employees were not given the day off (plus the ex-junkie and the school Sheriff), because as soon as we sat down, Pampour vanished. She probably made her way to the mall to shop or went to an afternoon college Sorority Barbecue.

Cyrus sat next to me but wasn't talking much that day. He was very testy and was even more soo now that we were sitting in the cold, gloomy auditorium, and in the center of the auditorium was an overweight man with a bushy mustache in a Ranger outfit, and a very petite lady who looked like she slept way too much. (And, no, the college-minded Pampour really left, she was not the petite lady in the middle of the auditorium. I needed a little sleep myself, having to get up soo damn early every day.)

"Did you see our mind master take off right when we sat down, and notice how all the other teachers aren't here, except a few?" Cyrus finally spoke.

"Yes I did. She probably went to some college Sorority Barbecue" (I was still excited about that thought).

"She's probably eating lunch right now with the man she met in college who is soon to be her husband. She seems like the type who gets really scared right before they're going to graduate college, and she's read those crappy novels, magazines where people find their true romance in college… so she got scared, found a guy who likes callow redheads, and is now going to lunch with him while we sit here and listen to Mr. SheriffCamaro™ and his sidekick, Ms. I used to give this guy special favors but now I'm clean so the county pays me to talk about my addiction and how to bribe your local copif you have one but Ill tell you that after the show." (**Special guest corrector Brad Cruise:** I highly doubt this Cyrus character really said her name like that, you cuckold swine of a writer. This is bad. My eyes hurt after reading a name like that. The only benefit is that it probably hurts the eyes of those using portable readers more, and I detest those horrible little things more than anyone.)

DISCLAIMER: I REPEAT, THERE IS NO ONE LISTENING. (Brad Cruise had somewhat of a point on that one^, because I was a really big fan of book covers that were artfully designed, but that's the only thing I think they really take away, although I don't know if they even truly take that away, because I could only afford the basic version of them. And I hope all who are using the portable readers right now enjoyed the Etch A Sketch at the intermissions. And the Etch A Sketch may or may not have been there, because I'm not too sure how any of that stuff works. So I apologize if it was missing. Most likely it was, and this has been a pointless adage. Minus 15 points. Education.)

The now talkative I and Cyrus (or is it Cyrus and I? I still don't know. I need to put myself next to more pretentious people and become dull or put myself by wise people who tell themselves they're wise (what wise person does that?), and feel the need to correct such a tiny thing as I and Cyrus, Cyrus and I, and soon I'll get it right) sat there until finally the Sheriff started to speak very blatantly. "K" (he thought using text messaging speak would make him seem more cool in the eyes of young people) "kids, today we're going to have a little discussion on Marijuana™ and Sex™." (That's right, people who are annoyed right now (yes, we all know that you are a genius) it couldn't have been more obvious. It was a talk on Sex™ and Drugs™. Be annoyed, you sassy, knowledgeable bastards, but hey, what can I say, it's what they did, and I only write what I saw. Soo cliché. Education.) IRL. J/K! FWIW.

"This is my guest speaker for today, Ms. Craven, so please show her the same gratitude as you have shown me insofar. First off, I want to talk about the dangers of Marijuana™ and the effects it has on your brain. Driving while on Marijuana™ can be just as deadly as driving drunk. The laws are coming up to date with stricter penalties for driving while intoxicated on Marijuana. That goes for any drug, not just Marijuana™."

All I could think of was what a weird combination Marijuana™ and Sex™ was. I've already admitted that I've smoked Pot before (it's really overrated, though, so I haven't done it since. Although it seems to be good medicine for potential psychotics and really spoiled rich kids, or some would say the two go hand in hand, as it helps calm them down), and I couldn't envision anyone having the energy to have sex™ while on Marijuana™. (I thought it would be nonstop laughing sex™, and then from there, the self-conscious (Dogma) laughing would set in, and then some more laughing would ensue. Then I thought I had found my perfect lovemaking scenario, so maybe I was going to smoke pot again. Sorry MAL. J/k, J/k.)

The Sheriff went on, "What you need to know about Sex™ is that it can cause lifetime diseases, and from those lifetime diseases comes the repercussions, such as having to live with the regret or having to wake up every day, knowing you have this disease for life, and as of right now, there is no cure. Protected Sex™ is what we'll preach today. We're not here to condemn Sex™, we're only here to tell you there are serious consequences for having unprotected Sex™ with a partner, and any Sex™ with a stranger will be condemned here."

DISCLAIMER: I REPEAT, THERE IS NO ONE LISTENING. All I could think about when the Sheriff was talking was about the people who had these STDs™. I mean, most of these people who were whoring it up were only spreading it to other people who were looking to whore it up. The people who thought, "Hey, Carrie Bradshaw™ is a sophisticated woman, and she's having multiple partners, so what's the big deal?" were the type of people who had STDs™, so who really cared? (And people with severe mental issues.)

Just let those people keep spreading the sea animals to each other. (Also, I don't think television references are clever, so I apologize for that^. It just meant I watched too much television). These talks that these people gave at our school were soo useless, no one was listening, and I repeat, no one was listening because the people who had an exclusive partner and used a rubber didn't care, 'cause they knew they were fine. The people who most likely had STDs™ would not stop sleeping around because then they might get bored and then have to use their creative abilities and come up with something other than monkey sex. They'd have nothing to boast about, and they'd have no fanfaronade. (I always wondered why, whenever the dictionary gave an example sentence, that sentence was always very awkward. Well, I now no longer wondered that after using that last word, fanfaronade, in that very awkward sentence. So I apologize for using that silly word. Minus 15 points. Education.)

This little seminar on Marijuana™ and Sex™ lasted the rest of the very long day, and the ex-junkie spoke about her experiences and told her stories and the awakening she had when she choked up a white, foamy liquid substance and how she was rushed to the hospital several hours later once her junkie buddies became sober. Whenever she finished speaking, the Sheriff™ made sure we got all of the scare tactics implied in the seminar.

As the seminar was coming to a wrap the 2 veterans of life answered questions.

"Does it hurt to put a needle in your arm without a doctor's supervision?" someone asked.

"Did you have a psychedelic experience and enter a new dimension when you said you took Mushrooms and Acid at the same time?" another asked.

"Why do my pubic hairs twirl up? Do I have an STD™?" a kid asked, not joking, but he made me giggle.

All these questions were answered with the same responses by both the Sheriff and the junkie: "You should not try it. Nothing feels good about it, and I'm lucky to have survived it." (I'm not kidding either, and it was scaring the shit out of me, especially since right now as I am typing this on my human computer, it was telling me I was 8 and was trying to change words in the sentence to what it desired, what the correct, supposed human way was, and those 2 and their same robotic response scared me even more because I was feeling like my computer really was human after hearing Ranger Joe and his model junkie say those responses over and over.)

I stood up after the two were done evading the issue and asked the Sheriff how many times he had arrested the junkie. He got a quick look of disdain, and that disdain look turned to a look as if he wanted to strangle and castrate my skinny ass, but he proceeded to answer. The Sheriff said he had arrested Ms. Craven once, and that is where the two met, and that was her beginning to hit rock bottom and awaken to her infirmities. I was surprised the Sheriff answered, and my feelings^ about my computer maybe really being human after all quickly went away. The two lecturers asked if anyone else had any questions, and no one did, and then suddenly Cyrus rose and began to ask the junkie a question.

"You talk about all these experiences you've had with drugs™, the places it took you, the loss of time it created, but to me it sounds like you had some pretty good experiences, except for the foam. The way you told your stories and what was happening to your mind while on the various drugs™ really inspired me. I want to first say you should write a book on the subject, because no one has written a book about drugs™ before, and you really make your stories sound soo grand. I really was wondering about those drugs™ before and was a bit skeptical, but after your description of them, I think I'll have to try them once. Well, anyways, my question is is that you made it through all of the great experiences and the way time just seemed to slip away…through it all you did it all, probably opened your mind to a few new things, and in the end, you got a paying job out of it. So, (? 50/50) my question is, don't you think it was worth it? 'Cause I sure do."

The Sheriff's look of wanting to kill did not leave his face, and it seemed to become more profound, and they both responded with what should've been their tape-recorded answers, "You should not try it. Nothing feels good about it, and I'm lucky to have survived it." The 2 speakers said their farewells and thank yous, took their bows (not their killing weapon, although I'm sure the Sheriff wanted to use it on Cyrus's smart-ass, they were using their social weapon, The Bow™), and it took another whole hour for everyone to slide and shoe-skate their way out of the auditorium.

DISCLAIMER: I REPEAT, THERE IS NO ONE LISTENING. I thought that the Sheriff would be waiting for Cyrus and I in the parking lot and then take us to a desolate alley, plant a gun on us, shoot us, and then say we were going after him with one intention on our minds, but he never showed. (But on TV, he would have. I then knew why I watched soo much TV: 'cause that would've been a lot more interesting, but really, I really wouldn't want that to happen to me or anyone in their life.)

I figured this was why there was no days off in October™ and March™, because they had little talks like this and the teachers got their workday to grade or go to Sorority Barbecues, and the free employees of the state had to suffer through another mandate.

Before Cyrus and I drove off, we had to turn in our papers on *The Stranger*™ to Pampour's drop box, of course, since she had disappeared, and like I always did, I wrote a pretty crappy paper about nothing (or this time with Pampour it could have been a threat to get an A, since it was Pampour and she was such a college type of existentialist).

This time, though, I tried something new, as Pampour was my teacher. On the first page, I wrote about existentialism™, and then from the second page on, I wrote about how Tan Bark™ is bad for children's playgrounds because all children hate tweezers, and tweezers were required to remove the splinters that the Tan Bark™ created in children's feet. (I grew up with Tan Bark™ in the playgrounds.)

Cyrus didn't even turn in a paper. He figured that she would forget by the end of the year who had turned in what, and she would just jot down some grade.

Well, I think Cyrus may have been right about that. About a week later, as all the festivities were ending on practicing elitism and Patriotism (my name is Cary Smith) of Independence, Pampour gave the class their papers back. I received a "43/50." The paper had absolutely no marks on it expect for a 43/50 mark. I just started laughing, and Pampour asked me if I had something to enlighten the class with, and I told her to, "Trust me, you don't want me to say it."

The only problem with getting a 43/50 was that it equated to a percentage higher than the maximum grade for a C.

A couple weeks later, the class had to turn in a paper comparing our waste-20-minutes-at-the-beginning-of-class-book to a movie. The book I picked to waste 20 minutes every class reading got absolutely no word read by me, except for the title. The title of the book was *Paris Hilton™: An Idol, Such as the Likes of Helen of Troy.* I compared the book to the movie *Apocalypse Now™*, and I started writing the paper, and in a half hour, I had 4 pages of absolutely nothing. I read over what I had written before I turned it in, and I could barely comprehend anything I wrote. The paper consisted of 4 pages of incomprehensible sentences, and every third or fourth sentence I wrote, "*Pairs Hilton™* and *Apocalypse Now™*."

A week later I got my paper back, and on it was the mark of 43/50. I noticed, on the paper of the person in front of me, it read 43/50. Once again, on this paper there were no marks, except 43/50.

I asked the person in front of me if I could see his paper, and he was reluctant, so I told him that not even Hemingway™ could write a good paper on such bland topics, and he let me see his paper. I quickly skimmed through the paper, and there were absolutely no marks. I gave the paper back to him and turned to Cyrus and told him about my recent discovery of a slacker college student among us (or a college existentialist™ who misunderstood her existential™ lectures). Cyrus laughed and said he didn't turn a paper in. He told me to reprint a copy of my paper so he could turn it in to see if she would even notice.

That night in my room I reprinted my paper, then I realized I had four more hours to kill, so I went to sleep.

The next morning I gave the paper to Cyrus, and he turned it in. A week later, he got the paper back, and it read 40/50, minus 15 points for being late, with absolutely no marks on it, except the scores. Abruptly and simultaneously we began to laugh, and laugh very hard and loud. We couldn't stop laughing. It was the kind of random laughter that hurts soo bad since you can barely breathe from constantly laughing (the best kind of laughter). We didn't even hear Pampour give her usual manual, toolish statement of, "Do you have something to enlighten the class with?" It wasn't until Pampour's red hair was right in front of us, the jeans she wore every day (she was such a college student) emitted their odorous scent, and her finger pointing to leave did we hear or notice her, and boy did Cyrus and I leave the classroom still laughing. We didn't even go to Mulder's™ office, we just went home.

I gave Cyrus my previous existential™ paper on Tan Bark™ for him to turn in to Pampour, and he did. And when he got it back, he got 40/50, minus 15 points for being late.

DISCLAIMER: I REPEAT, THERE IS NO ONE LISTENING. I figured that the teachers hired a few years back that didn't even have teaching credentials were a more suitable candidate than Pampour. I mean, at least those teachers read the papers and tried to give some kind of feedback. While they still went by what the manual told them to do, they still gave an effort to read papers that were turned in.

What Pampour was was a slacker college student completely scared to venture off and experience other things in life (like maybe having to be poor for a bit (not college student poor) and work a shitty job for once in her life, since the world was full of shitty jobs, and that just might help to be a better teacher) and was now teaching a class full of high school seniors.

Cyrus and I just headed to his house, and we didn't say a word, we just both smiled. I smiled and thought it was a bit sad that there were teachers like Pampour, but then I thought it really wouldn't matter because most of the students wouldn't be interested in what was even happening or could care less as long as they passed and had good marks for their desired college. (Education.)

As Cyrus pulled into his driveway, my thoughts began to focus on the 43/50 and the percentage that came out to. This Pampour was going to ruin my consecutive C streak by her doing what she did best…nothing. (She had to have been a wannabe, college-student type of existentialist™. One will never know, though. Education.)

I figured that I would have to not turn in a couple of papers, and then my C streak would remain intact.

Chapter 4

It was cold. It was cloudy. It was gloomy outside, but none of that mattered, in fact, complacency always ran high in December™, at least for the people with another (man/woman, man/man, woman/man, woman/woman, whoever), for December™ was the month of Christmas™. This is why Independence High probably decided to fire Ms. O'Hara in December™. Although most wouldn't care anyways, because now the future generations at Independence would be clear from thought completely and could go back to writing about who they admired most and all about how they wanted to become big and powerful, just like their favorite person, or back to the lifeless essays one was forced to write because it was needed to get into a good school, and was a DD skill that was to be continued at that school, which was needed for the golden ticket of all magic papers, The College Degree™, which, in turn, was needed for a good, high-paying job, which, in turn, was needed for fear of being socially outkasted by all the Douchey scaredy-pants afraid to be themselves who were always telling people like me to grow up. (I guess my anti-gay human computer doesn't know about the amazing rap group, Outkast, since it put a red, scribbly line underneath it and tried to automatically change it to outcasted for me, said it was wrong, and told me I was a dumb dumb. Education.)

Cyrus had picked me up as usual, and as we drove to school many people had forgotten to turn off their Christmas™ lights the night before, and I had taken notice of this since the lights nearly blinded me. Usually from October™ to April™ it was always still dark when school started, and going to school and also to be blinded by Merry Christmas™ lights was just an absolute nightmare, and it made December™ even longer. I thought only those Christmas™ count-down calendars made of cardboard with a piece of chocolate inside each of the 25 days of Christmas™ could make December™ seem longer, until I started at Independence that is. (Who wasn't a bad kid in the eyes of old Saint Nick™ when it came to those countdown chocolate things…because I know I ate my chocolate way ahead. It was Christmas on the 5th of December, according to that countdown cardboard calendar every year my mom got me one of those chocolate filled things.)

We pulled into the usual spot, as far away from campus as possible. By this point in Cyrus and my veteran careers at Independence we had perfectly synchronized the time to leave for school, the place to park, and the walking distance generated from the parking space in order to arrive in class right when the first bell rang to start the day.

The day was like any other, sadly we watched the teacher come up with some new innovative way to teach the class (that his or her handbook had suggested, lazy and boring D-bags). Sat around the whole class and conversed about what we had already covered many times before, and then smiled and laughed the entire class period with Pampour. Then just as the day seemed like it could be either Monday™, Tuesday™, Wednesday™, Thursday™, or even quite possibly Friday™ (Americans love their Fridays, and so does Cary Smith), Ms. O'Hara was seen in the distance carrying a box to her car when the day was over.

Cyrus had told me to wait up a minute to see what was going on. For the 10 minutes that we held up, Ms. O'Hara had gone back to her classroom over 15 times, and every time she went in, she came out with something.

Cyrus said that he was going to see what was really going on (To see what was really going on above^. Education.) and at that point I was quite curious myself, so I shadowed Cyrus as he approached Ms. O'Hara.

"Mr. Jenkins, it's nice to see you again."

"Yeah, you too. What's going on? Are you going to another school or something?"

"No, actually…I was fired."

"You have got to be kidding me. What was their reasoning for letting you go?"

"Oh, you know, they just gave me all the vague, evading routine. They told me that an evaluation was done during one of my class sessions, and they had concluded from the report that I may be a bit too hard on the students, stress-wise that is, and that I wasn't preparing the students enough for the evaluation packet tests at the end of the year or for college (good ol' Cuckoo tests). Then they told me about all the cuts that were happening, as if I had spent all my 8,760 hours sitting on my chair lecturing and was aware of nothing else. Then they ended by saying it was a really hard decision of what teachers were to be cut back for the next semester, although I was the only teacher let go. I probably shouldn't be telling you kids this, but quite frankly, they lie to you enough as it is."

"This is a damn joke, and not a good one. How could they possibly fire a teacher like you and keep someone like Pampour?" I asked.

"Well, that's exactly it. They can hire a teacher like Ms. Pampour and pay her a low salary, and she won't complain, because she's just starting out. They can't afford to pay too many teachers with years of experience and no tenure at the school because the infrastructure budget is apparently too high, as you can see with the many renovations and expansions of schools there has been in the state, and the annual repainting of this school. Eventually Ms. Pampour will get close to her tenure, and they'll let her go and hire a new Ms. Pampour, and so on. Or knowing the way things really work, I'm sure she'll get her tenure and be here for the rest of her life."

"I don't think Pampour will even know she's up for a tenure, unless it's in her college notes," Cyrus said.

Ms. O'Hara gave us a smile after Cyrus said that and then said that she was sorry for us, and that even when she was in high school it was bad, but that was many years ago, and with time she said, "Things generally become worse, unfortunately, since people become easily contented, and it's a hard thing to teach when soo many things are set up for a teacher to do the exact opposite of teaching." (Thanks a lot MAL.) She told us to do whatever we could possible to try and alter the whole time-and-getting-worse thing, as she quoted someone saying, "Don't take a break, since the people trying to make things worse are never breaking, seek the overman in you." Ms. O'Hara gave us a farewell, and with that she was gone, and gone with her was the last remaining hope at Independence, (at least for myself). Her leaving was the twist of the knife in the leg, and I was sure glad I was getting the hell out of there. (And I was glad that I was very good at dodging knives since I had seen many action heroes dodge many knives with a variety of strategies of knife dodging.)

The next day at school Cyrus decided to go with an Eastern protest and sit in front of Ms. O'Hara's former classroom and refused to move or speak after he found out that she was the only teacher fired (but he would move to eat—he wouldn't go over the edge of not eating).

Cyrus sat there in front of that classroom and acknowledged no one, not even me. Agent Mulder™ was the temporary fill-in for Ms. O'Hara, and he had told Cyrus to get to class, but Cyrus wasn't going to budge.

I knew Cyrus was contemplating sitting in on Mulder's™ lecture, because he could only imagine what that guy would talk about, but he didn't move (except to eat). When he wasn't eating, he was sitting, staring straight ahead, and no one could distract him. By 10 o'clock that night, as the janitor was getting his suction machines ready, Cyrus was approached by the school Sheriff, who did not have his ex-Junkie, motivational speaker with him this time.

"Son, I'm going to have to ask you to get up and kindly leave the premises."

Cyrus said absolutely nothing, and the Sheriff did not take Cyrus's defiance of authority very well. The Sheriff™ must have seen way too many bad movies and felt he was superior and everyone else was subservient to him because he had a uniform on and that he was the law, because when Cyrus did not move or respond to the Sheriff's command, he acted out himself and grabbed Cyrus and hauled him to his car.

DISCLAIMER: I REPEAT, THERE IS NO ONE LISTENING. I knew Cyrus was thinking that this Sheriff™ (trademark for every Sheriff for the rest of this chapter...I'm taking the lazy way out to protect myself from getting sued on this one) had no right to take him away for doing nothing. I knew he was pissed off and felt the Sheriff should be somewhere his purpose was needed and meaningful, yet Cyrus did not say a word, for there really was no point in saying anything, which probably would have just made the Sheriff feel more egomaniacal (Dogma) and get more heated up inside. (The school's appointed Sheriff definitely was not part of The Sophisticated Sheriff's Club you see in good movies, 'cause he was obviously still feeling a grudge from Cyrus's joke in the assembly, which was sure to annoy any sassy, knowledge-able, falsely righteous bastard.)

Cyrus threw me his keys, and I followed the Sheriff's car. About an hour after the Sheriff took Cyrus into his station, I went into the station, and Cyrus came walking out, and I opened the door for him. (And in the station I noticed that not all cops were power hungry, Douche Bags, and I even had that thought before watching television and good movies with cool Sheriffs from The Sophisticated Sheriff's Club in them. Hey MAL, I guess it's not all that bad, but this Sheriff was surely not an exemplar for that deMALed argument.) Cyrus got in and had the same exact look on his face as he had the whole day.

"Take me back to the school, and then take my car to your house and drive yourself to school."

Of course I didn't have my license at that moment, but at the time, that was the last thing that entered my mind. (Plus I think the Sheriff had other, important matters to deal with, especially now that this kid was piercing his power-hungry, D-bag, self-serving self and making him all heated up inside and feeling like it was time to use his power to protect the people from Cyrus, of course. It's funny how people like the school Sheriff are always the easi-est to annoy, it must be their great sense of humor, and I'm sure they're great people to be around. Hippie Talk. Hippie Dogma.)

I didn't say anything to Cyrus after he spoke those words to me, and I took him to the school, went to my house, fell asleep and drove the car to school the next morning.

When I got to school Cyrus was sitting in front of Mulder's™ new lair, and he was sitting in the same posture, looking straight ahead. No one really cared what Cyrus was doing. Most people just called him weird, a dumb ass, a fag™, gave a scornful laugh, or didn't have much of a thought one way or the other (most people said he was just doing it because he was kicked off the basketball team and he was angry about that). A few people saluted Cyrus and told him Ms. O'Hara was the last good thing.

Cyrus's second attempt at protest did not last very long, as the Sheriff returned later that day, this time with backup (since Cyrus had clearly practiced violence in their last engagement, but he was actually a quiet, major threat).

The Sheriff once again had no right, I mean Cyrus was just simply sitting in front of a classroom in a place that was supposed to be all about being able to just simply sit in front of a classroom, then again we were in a place inside a place. We were in a place of false education. We were on the grounds of Independence. At that moment, I realized that today was Cyrus's eighteenth birthday (and that I was giving private schools a lot of solid research to give to prospective parents).

Chapter 5

I got up as usual the next morning, tired from getting up soo early, and marked the calendar with an X for the previous day that now no longer remained.

DISCLAIMER: I REPEAT, THERE IS NO ONE LISTENING. I usually slept in my clothes. I never got the whole pajama thing or sleeping in just your underwear. (I just always forgot that I always slept in my clothes when I woke up, and thought I had changed and just went back to sleep for a bit.) I had to have clothes on because my skin would always stick to my skin when I slept in my underwear, and it was already hard enough to sleep as it was in this day and age without my skin sticking to my skin.

So naturally I got up out of bed, was already dressed, and made my way downstairs to eat the American™ Breakfast of Champions…sugar mixed with a little artificial vitamins and minerals. (Which was soon to be tasty no more. Damn MAL and their obese MAL kids always ruining it for the rest of us moderate people. I figured in 20 years there'd be a little secret group from the past that I would be in. It would get together once a week and eat some sugar cereal. Each week would be a different kind of cereal that we would have to pay an insane amount of money for. Hey, at least it wouldn't be some hate group or some mass-murder hippie cult trying to stop scientists from experimenting with animals or various other things and then proceed to become exactly like those scientists by killing them, just like those Columbine™ geniuses.)

I got Cyrus's keys, since I still had his car from the other night, and made my way to his house to pick him up, or at least drop his car off and then move over to the passenger seat.

I got up to the door and rang the doorbell violently numerous times, and after doing this for a minute, no one answered. This was typical of Cyrus, so I figured his parents must not be home. So I had a field day with the doorbell, and a minute later Cyrus's dad came angrily to the door. He told me Cyrus wasn't coming to school today and to just leave the car here. I asked him if he (Cyrus or his dad) could at least give me a ride, but he said, "No," very quickly and shut the door.

I figured his dad was just upset that Cyrus had gotten arrested. Cyrus's dad was an American™ law–obeying Baby Boomer™ citizen, so naturally Cyrus's arrest on charges unknown would upset him (naturally upset at Cyrus, not the school Sheriff, of course, or the supposed educational facility that allowed one of its free employing students to be treated in such a way on supposed educational grounds).

I just made my way back home after Cyrus's dad refused me a ride. It was too late to catch the bus. My mom was gone, and to walk to school was a good 8 miles. And making a journey of that distance was only worth traveling for someone like Alexis or a rehire-Ms.-O'Hara campaign (or to bring back the tasty cereal, 'cause I don't have retarded parents who let me eat it all day long, every day, or I myself am not a dildo who eats it all day long…I enjoy it in moderation meetings).

DISCLAIMER: I REPEAT, THERE IS NO ONE LISTENING. The rest of the day I sat there in my bed doing nothing. I figured if I was going to miss school I'd might as well keep the same routine and do nothing. (Of course it wasn't really nothing or that meaningless. Respect the Existentialist™. Education.)

That nothing journey got me thinking of weird things like Mark David Chapman™, the Columbine™ Duo, and the Al-Qaeda™ attackers. My first thought was, "On with STUPIDITY. Mark David Chapman™ was just a jealous nut case unable to live his own life, and then from there proceeded

218

to admire others, literally (and he had to have been a former college-type of existentialist), but the other 2 still sat in my mind a lot lately, especially since it was my last year at the joint, which made time prolong.

I started to think how these 2 events and the people involved were very similar in nature. Both were indignant, and rightfully so. They were both mad at the world, or at America™, the power, and felt that they wanted to make a statement, a statement of their anger. A statement of their indignation. (Uh, aren't those the same words? Anger and indignation? Minus 15 points. Education.) A statement of their passionate discontent for a country unfortunately full of impassion unless something terrible happens. As I got to thinking about all of it, it seemed to me that both parties' climax resulted in exactly what they were mad about. They were mad at the bullying, the inhumanness, the arrogance, the complacency, the violence, and then they went off and did an act of exactly what they were mad about. Essentially they became what they hated in the first place. (This has been a very long paragraph and if you're brain thinks a lot, then you're probably thinking about something else right about now...you damn daydreamer. So sorry if you had to reread this paragraph because of the whole long paragraph, daydreaming thing. I tried not to do it, 'cause I do that a lot too (daydreaming, that is), so I apologize...especially since this has just made it longer. Minus 15 points. Education.)

Apparently there was some war starting up at this point called Operation something stupid, but it seemed meaningless so I didn't really remember the exact title. I only found that out because some girl was crying about her boyfriend leaving for it around that time. I was pretty sure I knew of him. He was some former football player who graduated the year before that I saw giving a crown at the Homecoming rally earlier in the year, which had to have been around October, because only a hellish event like that would occur during such a long, no-days-off month. I don't think he's with us anymore. (You already told us about October being long, and this type of rally happening in the other chapter. Minus 15 points. Education.)

These thoughts took up most of my day, and I figured it was the most thinking I had done in over 2 weeks (since I had gone to school every day for the last 2 weeks with Pampour, that damn college existential, sorority girl).

Toward what would have been the end of the school day, I made my way back to Cyrus's house. I figured he'd be there alone, since his parents were always gone after a certain hour and until a certain hour every day. I got up to his door, and again I violently rang the doorbell numerous times, and a minute later, no one answered. Forgetting the last time I had a field day on Cyrus's doorbell (which was not very long ago…OK, I lied, I remembered, but doing it again seemed more charming if I said I forgot), I began to have a field day on Cyrus's doorbell. A minute later, to my surprise, Cyrus's mom made a rare, yet serious appearance at the door. She told me Cyrus was gone. I stood there for a couple of seconds, letting my slow wit catch up, and I asked, "Where'd he go?"

"I don't know," said Cyrus's mom.

"Oh, OK. Well, tell him I came by when you see him."

"OK, sure, I'll do that," said Cyrus's mom.

With those words I made my way back home and continued my day of absolute nothingness. (Oh god, was I becoming a college type of existentialist?) I laid on my bed the rest of the day and eventually went to sleep.

The next morning it was the same routine as before. This time, though, I didn't have Cyrus's car, so I waited for him to come pick me up. He was usually late, but after an hour I figured he wasn't going to school again any time soon. I just went back to my bed and went to sleep, thinking to myself that I better get back to school soon or I was going to run out of absent days for the peak, prime asking-someone-to-Prom season.

I woke up a couple hours later and made my way back to Cyrus's house, thinking again that he'd be there alone. After having another field day with his doorbell, his mom once again came to the door to answer.

"Cyrus is not here," Cyrus's mom said.

"Where'd he go?"

"Don't know."

His mom was being really vague, or maybe it was just her nature. I wasn't sure since this was only the fourth time I had talked to or had face-to-face contact with Cyrus's mom in 3 and a half years.

"Well, did he ever come home since yesterday?" I asked.

"Not that I'm aware of."

"Did something happen to Cyrus, or are you just lying and isolating him because he got arrested?"

"Don't know what happened to him, and we can't punish him, because he's not here."

At this point Cyrus's mom's vagueness was really starting to annoy me, and she shut the door, and I went back home and eventually feel asleep.

The next morning Cyrus once again did not show up. This time I made my way to the city bus, since I had missed the school bus. I waited an hour for the bus and finally made my way to school. I was extremely late, but showing up late was better than not at all, because I needed those full absent days for the peak of Prom season. (Repeat. Repeat. Do you think I'm a dumb dumb that you need to tell me again, really? Minus 15 points. Education.)

I arrived late to Pampour's class, and the class was in groups, pretending to be proofreading each other's essays while Pampour read the recent edition of "This year's in magazine for fashion, or wait, sorry, it isn't any longer, but we will direct you to the new in magazine for fashion for these new days in fashion." Cyrus was not in class, nor did I expect him to be, but part of me (my naïve, optimistic side, which I was just glad it was still there after almost 4 years in high school) was hoping he'd be in class.

The day went by very slow, slower than usual, and I even had missed half of it. After school I made my way back to Cyrus's house, and this time his mom came to the door after my first violent attack on the doorbell. She now rhetorically told me, "Cyrus is not here, and I don't know where he is." The rest of the week slugged by, and Cyrus never showed up to pick me up, and I don't know why, but the entire week I waited every morning, hoping I would hear his horn. Never did hear it, though, and I was ready to give up going to his house after a couple more days of his robotic mom giving me the same phrase, with the same look, and she had even shut the door on me the same way.

The beginning of the next week, on my last day of waiting for Cyrus to honk his horn, I made my way to Cyrus's house after school. His mom answered again, and this time I said, "Look, I just want to talk to Cyrus for a couple of minutes."

"He's not here. I think you should come in," Cyrus's mom said.

"So where'd he go...or where has he been?"

"The night we picked him up from the police station, we took him out for his annual birthday dinner. He didn't talk much, and his father began lecturing him. He didn't look up once while his father was talking. When we got home he went straight to his room. The next morning I wondered why he hadn't gotten up, but I figured I'd let him miss school that day because he seemed so deflated since that teacher was let go. That whole night I didn't hear a single noise in his room, and the next morning, he didn't wake up again, so I got scared and went into his room. Everything was still there, everything was clean and orderly, not a single item was missing or taken, but Cyrus was missing from it. I really didn't know what to do, and I couldn't exactly call the cops to find him and force him to school since he's an adult now. You kept coming by and asking where he was, and then I started to get really worried since you didn't even know where he was. He hasn't shown for a week now, and he left no note of where he went or called to tell us where he is. His father was being the stubborn jerk that he is and said, "The kid's just looking for attention," so we didn't call the cops. It's been a week now, so I called the cops today and filed a missing person's claim. I have no idea where he is."

At this point, emotionally and naturally, Cyrus's mother began to cry. I knew Cyrus was close to his mom, but I was surprised to hear that he told her about Ms. O'Hara. I didn't have anything to say to her, so I just hugged her, and all I could think about was that I knew he was gone, and I knew I shouldn't tell his mother about our conversation about turning 18 and leaving. Cyrus was gone, and I knew he wasn't coming back.

I made my way back home and eventually fell asleep.

Chapter 6

DISCLAIMER: I REPEAT, THERE IS NO ONE LISTENING. The next morning I woke up and took the school bus. On the way to school I got an indescribable feeling in my body, it just overtook me. I couldn't remember the last time I cried, I mean really cried, and it didn't happen riding in the bus either (sorry). I think it was trying to come out, the feeling and emotion had been missing for soo long, and now, at that moment, it was trying to come out, but it just couldn't. It just sat in the middle of my body, and that was the feeling that I felt riding on the bus to school, and at that point in time I knew I would never be able to cry again. I figured this feeling was worse than actually crying, and I knew it would happen every time from now on...the tears would always just stop halfway and just lie there in my chest, dormant. (I was just glad I could still feel the tears inside me after years of being around the real Zombies™, Vampires™, Robots™ and Dead Douches™.)

Cyrus was gone and that was that. Alexis was gone. I understood completely that I was alone, and I knew that these last few months would feel like the last 3 years combined. It's hard to do time, and it was twice as hard to do it alone.

I arrived at school that day, and Pampour gave me another 43/50 on a paper, with no marks of improvements needed, and I couldn't do anything else but laugh (thank god I was still able to laugh). I got that feeling again in my body, the tears stopping halfway and releasing in my body, but then looking at that 43/50, I just couldn't stop laughing, and it was helping a lot. I figured I'd get this combination of tears stopping in my chest, and then hopefully laughter from something for a while, until I got used to going it alone in the joint.

Weeks went by, and it was as if someone kept pressing the rewind button on my life, and gradually I began to get used to not having Cyrus around, although I don't think my mind will ever gradually forget Cyrus. (I was trying to give myself good Alzheimer™ karma there (Hippie talk, Hippie Dogma), hopefully so I wouldn't get Alzheimer's™ when I got old.)

I was in Pampour's class, and I had not missed a day since the last day I missed waiting for Cyrus. Prom season was coming up, and I needed 2 weeks' worth of absent days. DISCLAIMER: I REPEAT, THERE IS NO ONE LISTENING. So, (? 50/50) suffering every day was well worth not having to suffer even more by telling some poor person a horrible excuse why I couldn't go to Prom, when I really wanted to tell them how horrible it was. I wanted to tell them that it was just an event established by rich, egomaniacal (Dogma), Douche-Baggy people who were now old and who wanted to set up an event for all of the kids to experience a grand, lavish ball, just like the rich, egomaniacal (Dogma) Douche Bags were having every weekend. They wanted all the teenies to experience that and become envious of it, become desirous of it, and then, later on in life, when you were living your simple, peaceful, mediocre life and seeing all the rich people having lavish balls and galas, you would envy and love them and worship them, and listen to their words (or try and rebel and kill them like a psychopath). You want to tell those poor people that Prom was established by very evil people who had nothing but dubious plans. Of course one couldn't tell a poor innocent soul that, not even Cyrus, or that poor people's galas were much more fun and full of life, so instead of a lame excuse, I just avoided it all together.

(DISCLAIMER FOR MYSELF AND PERSON THINKING ABOUT SUING ME RIGHT NOW: I do not actually know the man or woman who created Prom, it was just my own random thought. Thank you.)

It must have been around the end of March™, because I knew in 1 week I wouldn't be around for a couple of weeks. DISCLAIMER: I REPEAT, THERE IS NO ONE LISTENING. Pampour told us to get our waste-class-time-books-for-I-cannot-teach, and I was sitting there, and I just watched Pampour's face as she read some magazine, smiling. (Probably imagining herself in the outfit she was looking at.) I started to get that feeling again, looking at Pampour, but it wasn't because Cyrus was gone. As I was looking at Pampour, I started thinking about Ms. O'Hara, and all I could think of was, "Thank God I only had 2 months left so I could go dodge knives and the real Zombies™ somewhere else."

It seemed to be getting worse at the joint, and upon my first steps at Independence, I didn't think that possible, but looking at Pampour and thinking about Ms. O'Hara now gone, it was definitely getting worse, and that gave me that halfway feeling where tears rained down inside my body and were stuck there, but imagining Pampour imagining herself in the sexy outfit she was currently looking at, at least made me laugh for a while. (**Special guest corrector Brad Cruise:** this is the third time you mentioned this tears-stuck-in-your-chest, laughter crap. Repeat, repeat, repeat. Crap. Shakespeare never repeated something in his writing. I know that for a fact. Minus 15 points. Education.)

Halfway in between the half hour of book-waste-class-time, I saw some small, stocky man come into the classroom and approach Pampour. After a few minutes of talk the man left the room and Pampour looked down to apparently finish the article she had been reading about the outfit. A few minutes later she stood up and told the class to line up so we could make our way to the football field for an assembly. Assemblies were always the same, but one was never outside before, so I had no idea what was going on. (But one thing I was sure of was that the school Sheriff would be there, because he had not been absent from an assembly yet in my time.)

As the class walked to the football field I noticed a bunch of bodies lying on the grass, trying not to move. I saw the Sheriff in the field, but this time he was not accompanied by an ex-junkie. At this point I knew what was going on. All day I'd been wondering why the hell some kids were wearing white T-shirts that had a number written in the middle of them, and now I wondered no more as I saw all of them pretending to be dead, scattered across the field with the Sheriff standing in the middle, just like that Sheriff bear that I always saw on TV, telling kids not to do this or not to do that. Cyrus said that bear was just remnants from the quintessential American President, The Actor, and his wife's half-hearted drug initiative.

Apparently about a month previous to this profound assembly on the football field, a group of high school kids, 3 guys and 1 girl, were driving home from a party and lost control of the car and slammed into a tree head on. The

3 guys died, and the girl was now paralyzed for life. It was discovered that the male driver was still drunk from the party and that was the cause for his losing control and inability to react quickly enough to regain control. (Of course it had nothing to do with him being stupid and 3 stupid people trusting their main stupid man. MAL.)

DISCLAIMER: I REPEAT, THERE IS NO ONE LISTENING. So, (? 50/50) now Independence High was having an ingenious assembly outdoors where kids lay on the lawn with white shirts and a number, and the Sheriff got ready for his sermon on drunk driving, and this was somehow, beyond my thought processes, going to tell us something about driving drunk. I just kept thinking how sad it was that the Sheriff thought this would change anyone present. (Especially with the modern and understanding way he talked about it to all the kiddies. LMFAO.)

This assembly, I gathered, was a good metaphor for people in general. Some people were going to drive drunk, others were going to think about driving drunk while also thinking and running through their head an image of running into a car carrying a family coming back late at night from a trip, and all die except you. And you can only hope and be optimistic that people get to this point with their selves before it's too late, but for most it would be too late and they would ignore those thoughts and go driving anyways. I was pretty sure that the furthest thing from accomplishing this task ^ was having a bunch of high-school drama kids laid out across the football field and some ego (Dogma), power-tripped (Dogma) Sheriff telling everyone how bad it was (for most it would definitely be too late).

I knew this was costing some money to put together ("Everything does," as my mom always used to say about things costing money), and all I could think about was Ms. O'Hara.

As I got closer to the field, I noticed that Ryan, the check-on-that D-bag from O'Hara's class was one of the Drama-Kids-White-T-Shirt-Drunk-Driving Fatalities. He was doing such a good job of acting, lying dead on the field, and I yelled, "Hey Ryan." He got up and put his arm up in acknowledgement, not even knowing who had called his name. He even smiled instantly as he got up, as if he had trained himself to do just that any time he heard the name Ryan. And with that, he had blown his cover.

Chapter 7

Prom™ season went by and I hid inside. It felt very strange after the 2 weeks to come back to school, maybe it was because I did not leave my house once (well, I left it for 20 minutes each morning until my mom left since she was getting calls from the school after a week of me being absent, so I guess I got a little fresh air each day), but when I returned to school after that 2 weeks, my head hurt. I was more tired than I had been before. (I guess that's what self-inflicted isolation does to the human body.)

When I returned to school for the first time after my two-week Prom™ hiatus, I felt as if nothing had been missed, in fact, I felt I actually gained something educationally by missing two weeks. During the two weeks I didn't turn in a paper for Pampour's class, and by doing this, I was assured a transcript of nothing but Cs. Missing the two weeks, though, meant that I had a whole month ahead of me with no days of ditching, leaving early, or being late, and having no Senioritis™ with all the other Senioritis™-inflicted people. It was going to be one long month.

There were many people in my class missing in the last month. Most had found out they were accepted to some college, and some were just not going from their Senioritis (whatever the hell that meant).

DISCLAIMER: I REPEAT, THERE IS NO ONE LISTENING. I knew there was no way I was going to continue school, and the most absurd thing about college was that they expected you to pay for education. Pay for education. Now that was a joke, I'd rather just go to Barnes and Nobles University™ and read the same books for free. I found myself at that bookstore a lot. Most of the workers could care less if I just came into the store and read a book, came the next day and finished the book, and never purchased it. (Hey, it's pretty hard to feel bad for taking advantage of a corporation. I mean, they even played music throughout the whole store so that you'd eventually go insane and just buy the book, but I got used to the music. Sure I could've gone to a library, but it wouldn't have been as fun. And hey, if I had money, I would've purchased the books, and it's not like my mom would buy the books for me (she wouldn't believe me that I needed money for a book anyways), because buying them wouldn't result in some piece of paper, or an acceptance letter to be intellectually proud. (Most would be arrogant about it.) So I apologize.)

Also, you had to get through all the MALs hopped up on coffee, running around the store giggling to each other. I figured I'd start a group called EAMMC, which would stand for Everyone Against MAL's Morning Coffee. **Correction:** Ramble, ramble, no one cares, pointless little adage, and you just throw in parentheses all over the place, and never end them or put them inside of each other when you're not supposed to. Minus 15 points. Education.)

While I was at the bookstore reading one day in my last month, this young girl, maybe Pampour's age, had approached me.

"I'm going to have to ask you to leave sir," said the Barnes and Nobles™ lady.

"Oh, why's that?"

"'Cause you just come in here every day, and, like, read the books and never, like, purchase a book."

"No, you're wrong. I just pretend to read them."

"Come with me."

She brought me to this security place, and then she smiled at me.

"I'm just messing with you. I'm Joyce. Just wanted to introduce myself. Always see you in here."

"Oh, nice to meet you, I'm Cary."

"Cary, that's a funny name. So not Gary, right? It's Cary…I hope I didn't scare you."

"No, I wasn't too worried about it. I mean, they've got one of these mega stores every 2 blocks, so I figured get kicked out of one, go to the next."

"Ha, yeah, that's true, and, like, I would never report someone like your case. Why should I care? I get paid horrible wages, and, like, even if I did report you, it's not like if you bought the book I'd feel like I was doing some, like, proud service for the store."

"How much do you get paid?"

"About a dollar over minimum wage."

"Yeah, I don't blame you."

"Like soo many people come in here and read and never buy. Although, like, most of them buy a lot of coffee."

"Well, it was nice to meet you."

"Yeah, like, if you ever get bored when you're in here, like, come and talk to me 'cause I begin to feel dead sometimes, like, standing around watching people read."

"OK, sure. If I see your face become very sickly pale I'll make sure to come over and talk to you."

I started to develop a friendship with the Barnes and Nobles™ girl, although sometimes I felt like I was using her since I had no one to talk to, but she did approach me, and in a way she was using me too.

The more and more I went to the store I found myself not reading much anymore and talking to the Barnes and Nobles™ girl. (And to random guys coming up to me asking me if I wanted to buy a bunch of products and then sell them for a profit and join their pyramid business, and essentially be stuck with $500 worth of shampoo, energy drinks, and protein bars.)

The thoughts of either one of us using one another quickly dissolved. We often talked about making some sort of paper degree for the regulars who came in to read. We figured, in 3 years, we would just randomly go up to them and hand them the degree and say, "Congratulations, you've earned enough hours to receive your honorable Baccalaureate degree from The University of Barnes and Nobles Inc™."

DISCLAIMER FOR BARNES AND NOBLES GIRL: I REPEAT, THERE IS NO ONE LISTENING. The girl was a college graduate. She,

Joyce, had said that she was working at the store because every job offer she received told her that they would only hire applicants who were enrolled in a graduate program for the field, and she wanted nothing less than to continue her higher education. She had gone to some major, prestigious university and said she was very disappointed with how little had changed. She told me that the only difference was that the professors knew more but took that advancement way too seriously, and yet they still seemed to say soo little or were just way too pompous, but a few were excellent. She said, "I did have about five true professors, though, but that was out of fifty." She said her breaking point was when she turned in a paper to her psychology (Dogma) professor, and he told her she was the dumbest student he's ever had and told her that if she continued to write papers the way she was then he would fail her, and of course she didn't continue to write in whatever way she was writing. I asked her to show me what she had written, and she printed it out and gave it to me. It read, *"Psychologists do nothing more than explain human traits and characteristics that have been seen throughout history, and all Freud did was change their names and force his own characteristics onto his subjects' characters, and that is simply because we are human. How can you control being human? Psychologists only give these things their own made-up name, and when they do try and develop some new theory, it makes one feel not human while reading it. What are they really trying to do? Cure humans from being human? Trying to make the brains all the same, creating nothing more than robots? They tell you this and that are bad for the brain, and by doing so they only make the suffering twice as much. They say that these things can be controlled, and this is the funniest thing I've ever heard. What really have we truly explained and discovered in Psychology? 'Cause I cannot see much. Psychologists are simply modern-day priests."*

I said to her after reading it, "I think your expectations are too high. There's always going to be a ton of idiots in everything. You do have to admit this, though, because I've taken some of those pills they give out from some of the people who used to go to Cyrus's house after school who had prescriptions, and who overreact to things and see a psychologist, and they're not too bad. They're a better aid than being sprinkled with Holy Water™ by some phony priest at least." (I only did it once MAL, and it was only because of past MAL-sponsored assemblies, which inspired me to want to try some of those pills.

And I have nothing against Holy Water™, just when it involves a phony priest, and most of them, to me, seem to be false.)

She smiled and said, "That's, like, why I had to get out of college. It was making me serious, like, all the time, and then people would just get wasted every Thursday, Friday, and Saturday nights like party robots, and they weren't partying because they were celebrating or were happy, they were doing it because they were miserable. I was losing the ability to, like, really laugh and smile. Even, like, a depressed laugh was vanishing…even with their pills, but you can get those pills from a phony psychologist too" (But she had this wrong, because I got them from spoiled rich kids. And that thought made me wonder just how many pills Ms. Pampour had given out in her Sorority days, and who are we kidding, even now), "which would be the same as being sprinkled with Holy Water™ by a phony priest," she smiled after saying.

Now she was where she was at (reading Dr. Seuss™ at her work inspired that line), and she told me that it was worth it because even though the job was poop labor, she said the experiences of meeting people like myself would never happen at college or some fancy job that she could've gotten if she enrolled in a graduate program. She said, "Most of the people you meet, like, either want to get wasted and, like, talk about how they're getting nothing for their money from college, then, like, talk about how much money certain majors will be making. Or you, like, have a crappy intellectual conversation, where they talk, like, the whole time, listen to you talk for, like, a minute, criticize you, yawn, and then, like, talk some more about themselves as if they were, like, knocking you off your feet with their pretentious, lifeless wit. And, like, most of the kids that are like this all have that, like, really horrible tone to their voice. Like that soulless, droll in their tone, like they're always doing something they don't want to be doing, like they're scared."

I never saw her again after that. The next day I went in, one of her coworkers told me she went back to school. I had to laugh at that news, and the coworker looked at me funny. (And funny enough, both Joyce and her coworker had that lifeless droll in their voices Joyce weirdly talked about.)

Chapter 8

The remaining days at school were ones of isolation. There were still the people that formed the group where Cyrus and I (?) used to sit, but really in a situation like that you don't really know anyone, they're just acquaintances.

I began to abandon this group because I didn't like the feeling I got as I just sat there and said nothing, and all the people stared at me, wondering what I was doing there now that Cyrus wasn't around. I tried to make an effort for conversation, but I didn't know what the top movie of the week was, or who said what about who on last night's episode, or I couldn't quote anything from some show (even though I watched a lot of television, I didn't find it very fun to memorize the lines), or what new video game was being played or (or, or, or there were people with a whiny opinion, DISCLAIMER: I REPEAT, THERE IS NO ONE LISTENING, like me).

The only people that I found interesting were the guys who wore girls' pants, and the pants were soo tight it made them wobble around like a bunch of penguins. (These were the type of people who would read that book that Mulder™ had told me to read at the beginning of my sentence 5 times a year and were more of those Douchey people who, because they read soo much, thought they were better than most people, 'cause they read the same book every time they felt like reading, which made them soo deep and varied and full of D-bag emotions. I had just wished that they would wobble around like penguins more often in their super-tight pants, because they were a lot more likable and charming when they were doing that than when they talked to you without their skinny jeans on or when they weren't walking and talking.)

So, (50/50) I found myself going to class early and sleeping. The 15 minutes of sleep I got during the break period was a nice bonus from the serious sleep deprivation that I was under.

As the day of my release came nearer I began to realize that I might not have made it through this horrible, prolonged month if the Barnes and Nobles™ girl had never befriended me. I was there almost every day after school. It was the only thing I looked forward to. I wasn't even reading there anymore, but I didn't really need to because a conversation with a person like the Barnes and Nobles™ girl was a book in and of itself, in fact, even better… especially after she left and went back to school.

I knew at that point that I was not a person who could get through this life alone, in isolation, without anyone to talk to (and that does not include talking to myself). My mom was there, sure, but talking to her was not really talking, same with one of my brothers, who was now 37 and still living with my mom. It was just discreetness and included questions from her, basically saying I don't want to hear anything negative or real, so I'll periodically ask you questions, and I only want one answer: "Pretty good." (I think my mom was secretly part of the MAL, so she gave me 2 things. My name is Cary Smith, and my mom is part of the MAL.) I don't blame my mom. I mean it wasn't her fault that she and a whole generation had relied on extraneous sources for parenting. Television, kiddy movies, little-league coaches, grandparents, etc. (Problem was, you couldn't talk to a television. It could only talk to you, but I still enjoyed it, so please don't try and ban it and take what I just said too seriously, MAL.)

DISCLAIMER: I REPEAT, THERE IS NO ONE LISTENING. The month finally ended, and now I was gearing up for receiving my release papers…the magical paper that would declare to everybody that I was educated and had finished my schooling. (That way all the socialites didn't have to think too much, worry about anything unexpected, something out of the ordinary, and they could be quite content with knowing your credentials.)

My mom, who brought me into this world (and she never fails to remind me of that, and I remind her every time, "Don't be soo sure it's a gift, Mom"), insisted that I wear some blue, uncomfortable gown and attend the release ceremony to make the process official. So, (? 50/50) now I had to make my way back to the prison that confined me and educated me to be a prosperous member of society and officially receive a piece of paper from an official person so I'd be officially ready for the next phase, and I wasn't officially ready for it.

Chapter 9 The End or Just The Beginning, or Where I Give a Chapter a Name Again

I was done with school, yet I was not truly out until I made my way to some gibberish ceremony, where all the kids who prospered, mainly out of fear of their parents' wrath, who never missed a day and always got As, made speeches.

The day of, I felt nothing (damn you college-type of existentialists). I woke up, although when I woke up on this day, I felt well rested, since the ceremony took place in the afternoon (what a relief, I did feel something, I was not a college-type, wannabe existentialist).

The day was pretty dark and gloomy, which was very rare for an early June day. I was hoping for rain, I thought at least that would make it somewhat interesting (I wasn't a Gothic kid, though, so don't worry). I did nothing all day, and my mom told me to put my gown on so all of the family that was there could take some pictures.

They, the officials, told me I had to dress up…that it was required that I wear dress pants and a collared shirt. For one, I told my mom I didn't even know what "dress pants" meant, and secondly I was already uncomfortable in the gown and stupid hat, and a collared shirt was out of the question. I mean, what would they really do if I wasn't in the proper attire? Nothing, and I knew this (and I knew I just Douchely answered my own question), so I wasn't worried at all.

After getting the goddamn strings from my uncomfortable hat out of my mouth, I asked my mom for a ride to the ceremony. I told her I had to go earlier than her, and she was reluctant, but she said, "Well, it's your graduation day." So she gave me a ride to the school.

As I was riding to school, I wondered what I'd be doing right now if I had left, and I figured it wouldn't be as genuine as what Cyrus was probably doing. (And I was also wondering why apostrophe words were harder to pronounce than if the 2 words were separated. Like if I said, I had, instead of I'd up there^, or, would not, instead of wouldn't…see what I mean, the two separated are much easier on the tongue and jaw in sentences. **Special guest corrector Brad Cruise:** you're a swine. Don't try and speak like you have any idea or grasp of apostrophes or The English Language, what a cuckold thought that was.) I imagined that whatever I would be doing afterward, though, would be better than riding silently with my mom, having this shitty hat blow strings in my mouth, and suffering yet another day on prison grounds.

I got out of the car, and my mom told me to look for her and my brothers and sister in the stands, and to make sure to wave to them 2 times. As I walked away, I told her I would, but of course I would not. (No more apostrophes. They are just too hard on the tongue and jaw, and I apologize for all the previous ones before this. Minus 15 points. Education.) And it was not because I wanted to be an asshole but because I had imagined that my mom would think I had multiplied into 200 waving high-school kids who all had the same gown and hat on, and I did not want her to panic.

My mom dropped me off near the football field, where the ceremony was to take place, and I saw some people in blue gowns talking at the podium next to some old people looking at papers, and the stands were empty. Then I made my way to my designated classroom.

I got into the classroom and it was depressing as hell. A bunch of people were talking about how they couldn't believe how fast the time had gone, how excited they were to go to college, and how much partying they were going to do.

I sat next to this guy I knew, and I did not say much, just sat in that class-room and did what was usually required in a high-school classroom, nothing. No thought or stimulation, just state-mandated poopyness. (Of course it was something or else that sentence would not have been possible. Respect the col-lege type of existentialist with a capital E. Oh man, I'm going back and forth between something and nothing just like a college, wannabe Existentialist. Minus 15 points. Education.)

The guy I knew and sat next to asked me if I was going to the graduation party, and I said no. He told me that I should because I would end up regretting it later on in life (I still haven't). He was full of shit, and I just smiled at him and said, "No I'm (I have got no idea what the separation of I'm is. I tried to contact Brad Cruise for help on it, but he told me he would only talk to me face to face to pluck my beard and to draw swords) definitely not going."

This graduation party was on prison grounds. Why the hell would a pris-oner want to celebrate his release on prison grounds? I knew that most did not want to have the party at the actual school, but the MAL had proposed the event, in order to prevent life accidents from happening. I could not really understand why the MAL was worried. I guess they had not seen our drama kids give an outstanding performance a while back.

DISCLAIMER: I REPEAT, THERE IS NO ONE LISTENING. So, (50/50) I just sat there and knew that the only thing I would regret later on was not leaving and getting this piece of paper. I started to wonder what it would feel like to genuinely say that my time as a free employing prisoner for the state went by really fast. (And it was pretty sad that the way things were made those my thoughts on Education. Education. Sorry, just having a little fun there again. Trying to make, maybe?...another quote for private schools to use in their catalogs of why their school is really, really expensive and great and will make you feel entitled once you leave.) There was a time when I felt this, but it was soo long ago that I could only remember it vaguely. I could remember the events happening, but I could not remember the feeling. That was why I never understood photographs like the ones my mom was soo insistent on taking (I guess she needed them for entertainment during summer repeats).

I do not know why the hell they had us come soo early. Maybe they wanted us to feel locked in one last time (Hippie talk, Hippie Dogma). I was not quite sure, because all that happened was I sat in that room and listened to 20 people each tell each other how fast the time had gone and how all of it was soo much fun, and how they just never want to hear anything that says otherwise. Then some old scary-looking lady popped her head in the door and said, "Get ready to line up in the order that we rehearsed."

The last week of classes became a rehearsal for the ceremony. Everybody stood and sat in order, according to last name, and then we practiced walking to the podium and pretended to shake some old lady's hand. It didn't matter to me whether we were doing this or were in class, since both were repetitive, and I just wanted out.

So everyone got in a formally, conditioned straight line and got really excited. I noticed that everyone had some shiny, fancy black shoes on, with pants I had never noticed before, and at that point I knew what dress pants were. The girls all had on some really pretty dresses and heels that made the back of their heel red (so I figured they were the most uncomfortable).

I had on the same outfit I usually wore, with my Reebok Pumps™, and the only thing that was making me uncomfortable was the blue gown and the strings from the blue hat flying in my mouth. I figured that someone would say something to me, and that was the reasoning for sitting in the classroom, so the censors could come and check, but like I figured before I sat in the classroom, no one checked (a rare benefit of budget cuts to schools). We stood in a straight line for about 10 minutes until the old creepy lady came back and told us, "Follow behind the last person who walks by." The R's, S's and T's, followed behind the last P, just as we rehearsed (because Q was not a common last name).

I was now in a giant procession again, walking the line to my rehearsed and designated chair. The line had made its way out to the football field, and the stands were now full of old people, siblings, and the many people who didn't graduate. (For some odd reason they were in the stands. The only one missing was Cyrus.)

As the line made its way past the parents and family members, I began to think how funny it was that almost all of these families would only get together on occasions like this, usually Christmas™ and Thanksgiving™, or the others, or if someone died, and I understood this well with my family (that was why it was funny, I guess).

240

Everyone was waving, and my mom must have thought that she was in some weird dream because there was now two hundred of me's (can't fight that apostrophe, at least until I draw swords Elizabethan style with Brad Cruise and he helps me out).

Finally the procession broke off into little processions that made their ways to the chairs that were lined up. We had practiced this for 4 days, so at this point, I felt like running to my chair. Finally the S's (or this one) sat down, then I had to wait another 10 minutes for the final W's to sit down because X, Y and Z were not very common last names. The final W sat down, and then another 5 minutes went by, and finally an old lady who I had never seen before made her way to the podium.

Apparently this old lady was the principal at Independence High, or at least she introduced herself with that title. I just went along with it and assumed it was the principal. And that was the first and last time I would see the principal at Independence.

She began to talk about a whole bunch of bullshit and how everyone in this graduating class was going to be successful in life. I felt this was a good opportunity to wave to my mom, so she knew where I was in the musical chairs. So I got up and waved twice as this lady I had never seen before was talking about how "every student here, I feel, is a potential waiting to become a success." I was not sure if my mom saw me wave, I sorta hoped she did so she would no longer think that I had become 200 men and women. Suddenly, when the crazy old lady claiming to be the principal was done talking, everyone started to cheer as some girl in a black gown with fancy and mesmerizing extra ribbons made her way to the podium.

DISCLAIMER: I REPEAT, THERE IS NO ONE LISTENING. The girl claimed to be a Valedictorian™. I was not quite sure what that was, but she not soo blatantly talked about how she was going to become an elite member of society, and she was going to be able to get any job and drive a nice car (and cut you off on the road whenever she felt like it)…she had said she was going to some private college.

DISCLAIMER: I REPEAT, THERE IS NO ONE LISTENING. I thought the speeches would never end, and I sat there and listened to all these people talk about how excited they were to soon work a job, marry before 30, have kids and retire. I began to think about how much more difficult and mundane life became when you tried to plan it, but these kids seemed pretty sure of the smoothness of the planning (and I sure wished I could have had that).

Then 2 girls came up who would live the plan, but would always have affairs on the side because usually the good-looking guys were not well off, and began to give a speech together.

Each would say a word, switching back and forth. That made me laugh because they were soo arrogant up there, thinking to themselves that their speech of interchanging words was pure genius and actually thinking everyone would remember it for eternity (people just wanted to get drunk). They finally finished, and everybody cheered (mainly because their interchanging, tortuous speech was finally over), even I cheered. I thought at least they made me feel something other than melancholy.

The principal came back to the podium and said, "It's nice to see most of you for the first time. Now congratulations and tip your strings to the other side, and the class of lalala you are commenced." My strings were stuck in my mouth from a gust of wind just as we stood up, so I couldn't tip it to the other side. Everyone began to cheer and threw their blue, and a few black, hats in the air.

DISCLAIMER: I REPEAT, THERE IS NO ONE LISTENING. I looked around and knew that I was released. My time had been served. I thought at this moment that I would feel absolute and complete happiness and fulfillment, but I felt the same. Maybe I had been changing all along and I was just expecting the change to come at some sudden, instant, moment like this one. It was more I felt the same, that nothingness, and it felt OK. (At least that's what I was going to tell the bastard that was nothingness. It was a lot more fun that way than to be a college, wannabe existentialist.)

It was a feeling that I couldn't worry about the Douche Bags willing to douche their way through life, and I had simply been overreacting <(not really). But I knew also (**Correction:** try, "But I also knew") that I wouldn't stop quietly making the Douches sweat.

I couldn't even imagine, nor want to imagine, what the Douches of this world would possibly do without that sweating, and so, luckily, the feeling wasn't nothing…I was pretty sure I was there participating in it (**Correction:** Minus 15 points for saying you were not going to have any more apostrophes and then using a whole bunch of them. There are just too many apostrophes to fight, sorry, and now I prefer them more as my energy (Hippie talk, Hippie Dogma) about them quickly went away, and I became lazy about them. Education.), and I could then gladly say I was not a college type of Existentialist™, or now I could tell myself I understood what some of them were saying, and that it was people like Pampour who needed some label like Existentialism™ to help you through your misunderstanding.

(Not really, though, I mean people like Pampour needed that label, I'm talking about what those so-called modern, or postmodern, or postmodern-modern, or after all the post moderns, or here in the now, past the modern and post-moderns modern, or the after it all post, and past moderns, modern philosophers were saying and understanding it. You really couldn't know what they were saying unless you were part of their club. And in order to be in that club, you needed the following step in your life. What you need to do for the step is, you need to jam your head soo far up your own ass and reach that point of ultimate self-love and seriousness, where there is no return to bring it about in life. Once you jam your head up your ass far enough for that point to be reached, then you see inside there is the club, and as you move your head around [as that is all that appears in the "Up-Your-Ass-Philosophy-Club," the Philosophers Heads], you see all the other club members are there, and it's one giant circle of heads, specifically Philosophers Heads. Then once there [up your ass], you are now capable to understand what they're saying, and now you are ready to write your own up-your-ass essay that will be passed around to the other members of the "Up-Your-Ass-Club," or as it is more acceptably and politically correctly known, "The Philosopher's Heads Club." [Since there are nothing but heads, the heads simply think constantly, and the writing is done for them automatically, through their thinking heads.] And since you know there is no return and possibility to bring about your philosophy in life, you will have no choice but to write more and more up-your-ass essays according to your new understanding of what one of your other up-your-ass members had thought and was automatically written for him/her. And I knew about this up-your-ass club because several weeks before Cyrus had disappeared, he had been talking about an up-your-ass meeting that he had been to. [Plus I've been there once too. I can't deny that.] Really though, I mean if you could just get through the music that the stores played and read on your own, you might find a very pleasant surprise.)

(Where are we in the story? Sorry. ^ That was for extra credit.^)

DISCLAIMER: I REPEAT, THERE IS NO ONE LISTENING. I threw my gown off to the ground of the Earth, and when I finally got the strings out of my mouth, I threw the hat to the ground as well, and then I whipped my little red, shinning slippers in the air and tapped them together, then I pumped them.

Everybody's family members were coming down to congratulate them and tell them where to meet for dinner. After I threw my uncomfortableness on the ground I began to make my way through the crowd. I got to the end of the crowd and just kept walking out, not looking back, and thinking maybe it could have been different. I stopped wondering that for good and I was now a good distance away from the crowd, and I knew that I would just keep walking.

DISCLAIMER: I REPEAT, THERE IS NO ONE LISTENING. I did not look back...wait, maybe I did, no, I guess I didn't, I might have, though. To be honest, I don't really remember, but I do remember it wasn't that dramatic, so then I might have thought that I knew I would never come back. (Hey, leave my memories alone. They were fighting with what I really thought and what the Douches had tried to train and program me to think and remember, which (the training), was exactly how they unfortunately felt about most people...to train as they're little doggy, and I'm kidding, I did not look back.)

So, (50/50) then I continued on, and I thought if this was some supposed dream, then I was ready to wake up...wait that line was pretty cliché (cliché to say cliche. Education). I lied again. (Not about the part about being awake, 'cause at the time the real Zombies™ and DDs with their DD parents were asleep enough to make my eyes feel wide open. GODDAMN NOTHINGNESS. EXISTENTIAL BACK AND FORTH AGAIN. OOOOHHHH THE AMBIGUITY. GODDAMN eXISTENTIALISTS AND MY READING OF THEIR WORKS, AND HEARING PAMPOUR'S COLLEGE LECTURE NOTES ON EXISTENTIALISM.)

Really though (I will stop being soo silly), I did not look back because I knew exactly where I was going...I had written an e-mail a couple days before graduation...I was going to go be nakedly awkward. (50,000 words+! Thank nothingness, I made it to novel status. I'm pretty sure there's over 50,000 words+. I just wanted to say that. So I apologize.)

I hope I get a good grade on this, but no more than a C.

*Also, P.S. I promise this was not intended to be some epic, sperm-quest type of novel, and that my passive egg (Alexis) was waiting for me, so if you read it that way, I think you're trying too hard and have severe mental issues, sorry. I'd call it more of a hand-in-hand type of deal.

No, just kidding…my sperm is victorious in my epic sperm-quest story… farewell.

*Play the Simon and Garfunkel song "America" or the Led Zeppelin song, "Ramble On" here…or how about any song you'd like, but make sure to pick a song. It'd be a good ending to my story to play a song right after it has ended (make sure The Book is closed), instead of written words, because music, to me, is the best art we have, and don't ever let the MAL try and take it away because they need something to blame other than themselves (play song after ↓). I think I'm the first non-literary-not-worthy writer to have suggested to close The Book and play a song, although, probably not, because I certainly have not read as much as the Bard, Sir Brad Cruise, to know if I'm the first non-literary-world-not-worthy writer (what a blessing, seriously) to have suggested that.

*Also, P.S.S. Don't forget to calculate the total amount of times I may be sued from the Intermission.

*Bonus suggested tracks to play: David Bowie's "Kooks," Jimi Hendrix's "May This Be Love," or Bob Dylan's "Simple Twist of Fate."

P.S.S.S. (I don't think you are supposed to do a P.S. in this (Education, so goes the tale of people who cannot explain truly why you cannot). So, (50/50) P.S.S.S.S. THIS IS A DISCLAIMER FOR EVERYTHING CYRUS SAID IN CASE HE IS STILL ALIVE. P.S.S.S.S.S.S. YOU NOW MUST WRITE A REALLY BORING AND LIFELESS ESSAY EXPLAINING IF YOU (BUT NO YOUS PLEASE IN YOUR PAPERS) BELIEVE CYRUS IS DEAD OR NOT. IT MUST BE NEAT AND ORDERLY SO THE INTRODUCTION WRITERS CAN QUICKLY SCAM THORUGH IT SO THEY CAN WRITE MORE REALLY BAD AND BORING INTRODUCTIONS. (EDUCATION.) REMEMBER THERE IS NO RIGHT OR WRONG ANSWER, BUT IF YOU

DISAGREE, THEN YOU WILL BE MARKED DOWN. P.S. EDUCATION THIS WAY OR YOU'RE STUPID. (EDUCATION.) ONCE AGAIN MY HUMAN COMPUTER HAS SAID I WAS 8 YEARS OLD, A FAG, AND HAS UNDERLINED EVERYTHING IN THIS PASSAGE WITH GREEN AND RED SCRIBBLY LINES, AND I SAY, "THANK FUCKING GOD" (Education).

    *Also, I don't really remember what I've just written, now that it's over. And I hope you don't get too crazy about all the previous stuff. I hope you had fun and enjoyed my story, and please don't read it more than 4 times, 'cause you might start to scare me. Unless you're unfortunate and are being forced to read it over and over again to memorize all of my wisdom by some very unwise person(s). Well, if that's the case, then let's always remember, every time you get to this line, that that person forcing you to read this over and over is poop on a stick. Mindless scum on a city light poll, empty and void of any life and what it really means to be human (meaning fighting our hypocritical, low and natural human ways), and hopefully you will be blessed with fortune soon in this life, or for the next life, because love is strong, especially for people in your situation.

*Play song here.

"I should be closed if you're playing the song or the song you picked,"
—The Book

ABOUT THE AUTHOR

Cary Smith is a pain in the ass vagabond. No one knows where he is, and he always has his agent tell us he's dead. I may be an annoyed publisher, but when you deal with Cary Smith, you deal with an asshole. And the only time I use this vulgar language is when I think of Cary Smith. Cary Smith's residence is unknown, and who knows if any thing he says about his past is true. He sent us a note after we finally accepted his book, reluctantly I might add, and if he did not email us every day, and sit outside of our office every day, we never would have accepted his book, because, really, we were just trying to get a gnat out of our face. Anyways, since there's nothing else to put about the author except this probably fake picture, with his probably fake dog (see back cover), here's how the note read:

For the about the author sleeve. One, Cary Smith, noble man and owner of a Golden Retriever, is currently working on an index to supplement Four Corners or A Book That Will Tickle Your Intellectual Nipple. Cary Smith is currently working on the index with the Golden Retriever of Professing, one Sir Brad Cruise. The index is entitled: The Some's, Them's and They's of Four Corners or A Book That Will Tickle Your Intellectual Nipple.

Also, Cary Smith would like to say he is not part of any New Age Movement or cult. When someone first said to Cary Smith that he was New Age, Cary Smith had no idea what that person was talking about, in fact, Cary Smith thought that person just meant he was part of the new generation, that he was young and part of the new era. Only later did he find out that New Age was a whole religion and philosophy, and apparently as Cary Smith denies his New Ageism, this makes him New Age. Cary Smith would like to be a part of no New Age cult, and is currently a part of no New Age religion or philosophy...because he's way too damn old school.

www.ingramcontent.com/pod-product-compliance
Lightning Source LLC
Chambersburg PA
CBHW021955170626
46808CB00001B/168